Kill or Bee Killed

Also available by Jennie Marts

The Bee Keeping Mysteries
Take the Honey and Run

The Page Turners
What to Do About Wednesday
A Halloween Hookup
A Cowboy for Christmas
Tangled Up in Tuesday
Just Another Maniac Monday
Easy Like Sunday Mourning
Another Saturday Night and I Ain't Got No Body

Hearts of Montana
Stolen Away
Hidden Away
Tucked Away

Bannister Brothers
Skirting the Ice
Worth the Shot
Icing on the Date

Cotton Creek
Catching the Cowgirl
Hooked on Love
Romancing the Ranger

Cowboys of Creedence
Wish Upon a Cowboy
It Started with a Cowboy
You Had Me at Cowboy
Caught Up in a Cowboy

Creedence Horse Rescue
A Cowboy Country Christmas
Every Bit a Cowboy
Never Enough Cowboy
How to Cowboy
When a Cowboy Loves a Woman
A Cowboy State of Mind

Hallmark Publishing
Cowboy Ever After
Rescuing Harmony Ranch

Lassiter Ranch
Save the Date for a Cowboy
Love at First Cowboy
Overdue for a Cowboy

Kill or Bee Killed

A BEE KEEPING MYSTERY

Jennie Marts

CROOKED
LANE

NEW YORK

Published in the United States by Crooked Lane Books, an imprint of The Quick Brown Fox & Company LLC.

Crooked Lane Books and its logo are trademarks of The Quick Brown Fox & Company LLC.

Library of Congress Catalog-in-Publication data available upon request.

ISBN (hardcover): 978-1-63910-658-5
ISBN (ebook): 978-1-63910-659-2

Cover design by Ben Perini

Printed in the United States.

www.crookedlanebooks.com

Crooked Lane Books
34 West 27th St., 10th Floor
New York, NY 10001

First Edition: June 2024

10 9 8 7 6 5 4 3 2 1

This book is dedicated to

Pamela Ruth Muth,

my forever friend.

Thank you, Pam, for almost thirty
years of friendship,

for supporting my dreams,

and for always believing in me.

Chapter One

B ailey Briggs wrinkled her nose at the scent of stale beer and cheap perfume, barely masked by the lavender air freshener in the bar's restroom. "I told you this was a bad idea," she whisper-yelled as she hoisted her best friend up toward the small window that sat two-thirds of the way up the wall.

"This was *your* idea," Evie whisper-yelled back before she poked her head out the window.

In truth, Bailey couldn't remember which of them had had the grand idea to sneak into the biker bar and nonchalantly ask a few questions about money laundering and gunrunning. Taco Tuesday at Evie's had started out with a few margaritas and a spirited discussion about the latest mystery Bailey was writing. The book was due to her editor in less than a month, but Bailey was struggling with a scene she was working on that involved a motorcycle gang. Tequila on the brain might have encouraged the original poor decision to come to the bar, then another round when they arrived, as they'd tried to fit in, had been what had landed them in their current predicament.

Bailey watched as Evie shimmied her body through the window. She made it look easy as her feet followed and she disappeared.

Evie made everything look easy. Evie Delgado Espinoza had been Bailey's best friend since they were eight years old, and this wasn't the first scrape they'd found themselves in during their twenty-four-year friendship. Or the first time they'd snuck out a bathroom window in the middle of the night after breaking in somewhere they shouldn't have.

Evie's face appeared in the small frame of the window as she waved Bailey forward. "Hurry up. And don't worry—there are some crates out here to stand on so you won't fall to the ground."

Small consolation, but Bailey would take the win, considering how much trouble they were in. She contemplated the tiny window as she climbed not so gracefully onto the counter and reached for the sill. Someone had conveniently spray-painted the bar's name, Hog Wild, in hot pink on the wall below the window, presumably to remind patrons where they were, in case they were too drunk to remember. Other things were scribbled on the wall, mostly insults and crude suggestions aimed at another person, and a few "for a good time, call" numbers as well as several "x loves y" proclamations.

The writer in Bailey had to give credit to a few of the more elaborate poems—it took skill to find things to rhyme with bodily functions—but she couldn't understand why someone would want to declare their love for someone on this disgusting restroom wall. And seriously, who brought a can of hot-pink spray paint to a bar with them?

"Come on," Evie hissed. "We have to get out of here before those biker chicks realize we're gone."

The two women, Hornet and Karma, had mistakenly thought she and Evie were flirting with their men. Not that Skeeter and Buzz weren't fine, upstanding . . . um . . . biker menfolk, but they'd just been having a conversation. Bailey had been asking them about what life was like as a biker, and must have appeared too interested in their responses. She *had* been excited by some of their stories, but more for research purposes than any kind of romantic interest. Neither of the men was really Bailey's or Evie's type. Although trying to explain that to their girlfriends was what had prompted the promise of a beat-down and thus Bailey and Evie running toward the bathroom to formulate an escape plan.

Squeezing through the bathroom window and running for their lives had been the best plan they'd come up with, but not for the first time that night, Bailey was doubting the soundness of their decision-making skills.

Especially now, as Bailey stuck her head and arms through the window and commenced to wiggle herself through. With one hand on the sill and the other pressing against the outer brick wall of the bar, she squirmed forward. She grimaced as her hand landed in something sticky, then let out a cry of frustration as her hips jammed in the window frame.

"What's wrong?" Evie was holding her arms out like she was a baseball catcher on home plate, ready to grab Bailey as she popped through the window.

But she *wasn't* popping through. Instead, she was lodged in the window frame. She let out a frustrated groan. "I'm stuck."

"What do you mean you're stuck?"

"I mean I'm stuck. I can't fit through the window."

"Sure you can. You got this."

Bailey glared at her friend, now certain it had been Evie's wise idea to come to the bar in the first place. Yes, margaritas had been involved, but she was still blaming Evie for this harebrained scheme. "I appreciate your belief in me, and your pep talk, but neither one of them are my making my butt any smaller."

Evie was five nine and had curves for days, and she'd wiggled through the window, so Bailey had been confident that she'd fit. She was a few inches shorter and would describe herself as curvy as well, but apparently being back home on Honeybuzz Mountain Ranch and eating her grandmother's home-cooked meals and biscuits slathered with honey—okay, eating pretty much *everything* slathered with, dipped in, or drizzled with honey— must've added a few pounds. Because she was good and stuck.

And she could now add "no self-control" to the list of humiliating things about this moment. Not that the list needed any more items—it was long enough. She pushed against the windowsill and kicked her feet against the wall. "Ugh. I'm just like Winnie the Pooh," she whined. "I ate too much honey, and now I'm stuck, just like he was in the door of Rabbit's house."

Evie barked out a laugh, then covered her mouth, trying to stifle the giggles. "I'm sorry. It's not you, I promise. I just had the image of Rabbit trying to shove Pooh out the hole. And I was thinking that it's good that you're not Pooh, because he wasn't wearing any pants."

Her eyes widened, and she pressed her lips together to hold in another laugh at the same moment that Bailey remembered that, in their slightly tipsy strategy to fit in at the bar, they'd decked themselves out in all denim and leather. They'd raided Evie's closet, and Bailey's friend had convinced her to wear a denim miniskirt, a black leather jacket, a pair of tall black boots, and a black Metallica T-shirt they'd found in Evie's brother's room.

The only thing of her own Bailey was wearing was a pair of hot-pink and white polka-dotted underwear—which now, thanks to the stupid miniskirt, would be on display to anyone who walked into the women's restroom.

"It's fine," Evie said, obviously thinking the same thing. "Just wiggle," she instructed, doing a frenzied hip-wiggling dance, as if Bailey didn't understand the movement.

"I *am* wiggling." Bailey scooted forward again and heard a clink against the window frame. "Oh, shoot. It's the glass," she said. "That stupid signature margarita glass. It's in my jacket pocket."

"Well, take it out."

Bailey waved her hands at her friend. "I can't. My hands are out here, and the glass is in there. And if I force myself forward, it might break. And I can't ease back in because my feet are already dangling in the air. And even if I could, there's not enough room around my hips to get my hand back in or to pull the glass through." She hated the whine in her voice, but a small wave of relief washed through her as she realized at least she wasn't stuck because of too much honey.

"Is okay," Evie said, slurring just a little as she clumsily climbed down from the rickety pile of crates. "I'm coming around to help."

"No! You can't go back in there. Hornet and Karma are inside waiting to girl-fight us." Bailey waved her hand toward the parking lot. "Just go. Save yourself."

"No way." Evie shook her head, and her high ponytail of thick, gorgeous, dark hair swung from side to side. "I'm not leaving you. I'll just sneak back in, get the glass out of your pocket, and then either pull you back in or shove you the rest of the way through."

Bailey groaned again as she weighed their options. They could go with Evie's plan. Although when Bailey tried to imagine her voluptuous friend, "sneaking" through the bar in her short black miniskirt, red cropped Moto jacket, and thigh-high, spike-heeled boots that made her stand over six feet tall, it already felt problematic. But the alternative was hanging out in the window—she groaned again, thinking about how much of her was *actually* hanging out in the women's restroom—as a sitting duck waiting for the two biker babes to come in and pummel her.

"Fine," she said, waving Evie on. "But hurry."

Evie took off and snuck around the side of the building.

Bailey looked around the grungy dark alley they'd planned to escape into and suddenly wondered if facing Hornet and Karma wouldn't be preferable to what could be lurking in the shadows of the dumpster among piles of trash, empty boxes, and discarded bar furniture.

Fear crept into her chest like a cloud moving in front of the sun. Suddenly every shadow and dark corner held something menacing. Was that a rat? She smelled cigarette smoke and sucked in a terrified breath that someone with nefarious intentions was about to walk into the alley and find her there.

She let out a yelp as a hand grabbed her leg.

Evie had just disappeared around the side of the building. There was no way she could've made it all the way back through the building and into the bathroom.

So, who had a hold of her leg?

Chapter Two

B ailey kicked out and heard an exhaled oath as her bootheel connected with something solid. Then two large hands clamped onto both of her legs and began to pull her back into the bathroom.

It had to be the biker babes. They'd found her. This was how she was going to die—beaten to death in a borrowed miniskirt and Metallica T-shirt, and left under a not-so-original graffitied poem claiming, *Here I sit, all brokenhearted* . . .

No. She refused to go out this way. She tried to kick, to fight, but the hands holding her legs had a solid grip as they hauled her back through the window and wrapped an arm around her waist to catch her before she fell to the ground.

She grabbed the sides of the window frame and tried to pull herself back through, which in hindsight was a stupid plan, since she already knew she wasn't going to fit.

"Help!" she yelled out the window, trying to kick and buck against her assailant.

"Stop fighting me," a voice said against her ear. A deep voice and one that did *not* belong to either Hornet or Karma. This was a man's voice. And his grip on her waist tightened as he spoke again. "Bailey, stop. It's me."

The fight drained out of her, and she sagged against the hard, muscled chest of the man behind her. Because she recognized that voice—had known it since she was a girl. And that same voice had been filling her dreams lately.

She turned and threw her arms around his waist as she buried her face in his chest. He smelled like cologne and leather and laundry starch, and she wanted to inhale him. "Oh, Sawyer. Thank goodness you're here."

But her relief turned to apprehension when she noticed the stiffness of his posture, and she pulled back and saw the annoyed scowl on his face. She realized too late the laundry-starch scent meant he was wearing his sheriff's uniform shirt. And if he was in uniform, that could only mean he was here in an "official capacity."

"What are you doing here?" She took a step back and tried to tug down her miniskirt. In retrospect, none of the women in the bar had been dressed like her or Evie. Most of them wore jeans and cute tops.

"Forget about me. What are *you* doing here? And why are you dressed like that?" He scowled down at her faded T-shirt. "You don't even like Metallica."

He would know. Sawyer Dunn knew her almost as well as she knew herself. Or he *had*. Back when they were kids. They'd practically grown up together, and she'd been in love with him since they were twelve years old. They'd been friends since the fifth grade, but somewhere around fifteen or sixteen, they'd become something more. Sawyer had been her first kiss, her first real love, her first *everything*. And she'd thought they'd be together forever. Until the night they'd stolen a tractor, and he'd gotten shipped off to his uncle's place in Montana.

Then she hadn't seen him again for almost thirteen years—not until she and her twelve-year-old daughter, Daisy, had come home to Humble Hills a few months ago and found out that not only was Sawyer back in town, but the former bad boy and love of her life was now the sheriff.

In the few months since she'd been home, they'd discovered a dead body, held hands four times, and almost kissed twice. They'd tried to go out to dinner three times now, but every time something had gotten in the way. Twice it had been a sheriff-duty call for him, and once it had been a sick-daughter, mom-duty call for her. But right now, the look on his face didn't indicate that he was thinking about their missed dates.

"That's a great point," Bailey said, trying not to slur her words. "I do not, in fact, like Metallica. So, I think I'll just head on home and change out of this shirt." She tried to sneak around Sawyer, thinking she'd take her chances with the biker babes over the scowling sheriff.

"Not so fast," he said, reaching for her arm. "You haven't told me what you're doing here."

The bathroom door flew open, and Evie burst in. "We gotta get outta here. Sawyer's truck is outside . . ." She pulled upright. "Oh. Hi, Sawyer. I didn't see you there. Err . . . ya havin' a good night?" Her words slurred the slightest bit as she tried to casually lean her hand on the bathroom counter. But her palm missed the edge, and she stumbled sideways for a second before righting herself, then crossing her arms over her chest. "We were actually *just* leaving. But we'd love to catch up soon."

She reached for Bailey's free arm and tugged her forward. But Sawyer still had a hold of her other arm, and he pulled her back.

9

"Bailey was just getting ready to tell me what brought her out to this fine establishment on a Tuesday evening," Sawyer said.

"Oh, it's a funny story," Evie said, pulling Bailey toward her again. "We'll have to tell you about it sometime. But right now, we really need to go." She looked at Bailey and tilted her head toward the door. "Like, right now."

"Yeah, we'll tell you all about it," Bailey said, moving toward Evie. "Soon."

Both women yelped in unison as the door of the bathroom flew open again. Then they both pressed back into Sawyer as a very tall, very broad, bearded man wearing black jeans, black boots, and a black leather vest stepped into the room. His thick, shoulder-length hair was that gorgeous shiny blue-black color, and his dark beard was cropped close to his face. He wasn't wearing a shirt under the leather vest, and tattoos covered his thick, muscular arms. He was crazy good-looking, but in a scary Jason Momoa way. His face wore a scowl as his narrowed eyes landed on Evie and Bailey, who were now both behind Sawyer, using the sheriff's body as a shield.

"Everybody okay?" the man asked, his deep voice as rich as dark chocolate mixed with fine whiskey.

"Yeah, we're good," Sawyer said, reaching out to shake his hand. "Thanks for calling me, Spike."

"*You* called Sawyer?" Bailey asked, now recognizing the man as the bartender who had served them their margaritas.

Spike nodded. "You two aren't our normal clientele. And I got a little worried about what Hornet and Karma had planned for you. Figured it was easier to have the sheriff come pick you up." He smiled shyly at Evie, and his face transformed from scary grizzly to sweet teddy bear. She had that effect on most men. "I'm

Mike, by the way. But all my friends call me Spike." He held up his arm to show several leather bracelets with metal spikes circling his wrist.

"Thanks, Spike," Evie said, smiling in return as she eased out from behind Sawyer. "We appreciate the help. I'm sure Karma and Hornet are very sweet women . . ."

Spike laughed as he shook his head, and his hair swung in a shiny curtain against his shoulders. "No, they're not. And they have it in for you two, so I suggest you get out of here quick. You can go out through the back door of the storeroom while I try to distract them with a couple of free beers."

"That would be great," Evie told him, resting a hand on his arm. "You would be our hero." She shot a glance at Sawyer. "No offense, Sawyer. We appreciate you too."

"None taken," Sawyer said in a wry tone as he passed Spike a twenty-dollar bill. "The ladies' drinks are on me."

Spike huffed out a laugh. "Those two are no ladies. But I appreciate the cash." He nodded down the hallway. "Now you'd better git."

Bailey and Evie didn't have to be told twice. Checking to make sure the hall was empty, they hurried toward the storeroom and out the door. The air in the back alley smelled like beer and barbecue sauce, but Bailey was just happy to be out of the bar.

"I didn't see either of your cars in the parking lot," Sawyer said as they walked around the side of the building.

Bailey shook her head. "We didn't drive. Since we'd been drinking, we took a Tuber."

Sawyer arched an eyebrow. "Last I checked, this town was too small for an Uber service."

"Not *Uber—Tuber*. You know Larry Tuber's Bait & Tackle shop on the edge of town? Old Larry decided he was tired of his teenagers sitting around watching television all the time, so he hires them out to drive people when they need rides. You just call the bait shop, and a Tuber will come pick you up. For fifteen dollars, they'll take you anywhere in town." She pulled out her cell phone. "Let me just give 'em a quick call, and we can put this whole crazy night behind us."

"Don't bother," Sawyer said, nodding toward his truck. "I'll give you a ride to the ranch and drop Evie off on my way back to the station."

Bailey wasn't sure if listening to the lecture he'd surely be giving them on the drive would be worth saving the fifteen dollars, but she was cheap, so she followed him toward his truck, and she and Evie climbed into the back seat of the king cab.

"Ouch," Bailey yelped. Something had stabbed her in the leg as she scooted toward her friend.

"Sorry," Evie said, holding up her hand to show Bailey the black leather, spike-studded bracelet snapped to her wrist. "Spike gave it to me. Along with his number."

"His number? What about Griff?" Bailey asked, referring to Griffin Yates, the private investigator as well as one of her best friends, whom Evie had been seeing.

"What about him? I'm still totally into him. Just because I took Spike's number doesn't mean I'm going to call him." Evie shrugged. "What was I supposed to do? Say '*No, thank you*' to the sweet, scary guy who just saved our tipsy tushes?"

"Good point."

* * *

The drive to Bailey's grandmother's ranch took less than ten minutes. The drive to pretty much anywhere in Humble Hills took less than ten minutes. The town was only a few miles off the highway and nestled against the gorgeous backdrop of the Rocky Mountains. The population was less than fifteen hundred, but Bailey had often wondered if they might have included a few dogs or horses in that count.

The great thing about living in a small town was that you knew everyone. But the bad thing about living in a small town was that they all knew you. Bailey had grown up there—she and her mother had moved in with her grandmother after her father left them. Then, when Bailey was ten years old, her mother had walked away from her too. Granny Bee and her sisters, Marigold and Aster, had raised her, and she was glad to be back on the ranch, having those same women help to raise her daughter, Daisy.

She loved the old, rambling two-story farmhouse with its wide wraparound porch. The house itself was big, having been added onto over the years so that it had numerous bedrooms and lots of bookshelves and reading nooks. It always felt like home to her, with its cheery yellow and white paint and the porch swing and rockers forming a cozy circle on the porch. During the summer months, cattle grazed in the green pastures, and neat rows of bee boxes sat among a colorful flower-filled meadow. The house was nestled against the mountain range, vying for attention with the huge white barn, the Honeybuzz Mountain logo emblazoned on its front. The building next to the barn held Granny's workshop, Busy Bee, where she processed and packaged her honey and had a small storefront that sold bee-inspired products and crafts from local artisans.

"What's going on out here?" Sawyer asked as he pulled up to the ranch house.

All the lights in the house were on, and several cars were parked in the driveway. Bailey recognized the cars as belonging to the women in Granny Bee's book club, affectionately called The Hive. Her great-aunt Marigold's car was there, and wherever Marigold was, Aster was sure to be with her. She also recognized the blue minivan that belonged to Evie's abuela, Rosa Delgado. There were several blue minivans in Humble Hills, but this one had "Spill the Beans," the name of Rosa and Evie's coffee shop and bakery, written on its side.

"I don't know," Bailey said, leaning forward against the seat. "I hope they're not here because they're worried about us." She was out of the truck before Sawyer had even turned off the engine. And Evie was right on her heels as she raced up the porch steps and into the house.

From the foyer, polished hardwood floors led to a spacious, sunny yellow kitchen on the left, loaded with lots of kitschy bee decorations, and a large living area to the right. Chintz-covered sofas and wingback chairs in pale pink and green florals sat clustered in a conversation circle, with a coffee table in the middle holding a silver tea service.

A long counter divided the kitchen from the dining room area, which held the same antique oak dining table Granny Bee's father had made from trees felled in the forested areas around the ranch.

The women of The Hive—Rosa, Marigold, Aster, and Bailey's daughter, Daisy—all sat around that table, which was strewn with folders and loose papers. Bailey and Daisy's golden retriever, Cooper, lay sprawled under Daisy's chair, his head resting on the girl's feet.

Granny Bee held court at the end of the table, her long silvery-blond hair braided into two plaits. Even though her name made her sound older, she was only in her late sixties and looked younger in her ankle-length jeans, white tennies, and a yellow T-shirt with a cute bumblebee and the words *Bee Whisperer* printed on it. She looked up as Bailey and Evie rushed in. Her eyes narrowed as her gaze traveled over their outfits. "Where have you two been? And why are you dressed like that?"

"I just picked them up from Hog Wild," Sawyer explained as he sauntered in behind them. He'd taken his cowboy hat off as they'd walked in, and he smoothed his chestnut-brown hair. Bailey and Evie had filled him in on their covert mission during the drive to the ranch. "They were doing research for Bailey's new book."

Bailey's aunt Marigold cocked one eyebrow as her gaze also traveled up and down their outfits. "Doing research on what? Prostitution? Because you're dressed like a couple of—"

"Don't even say it," Evie interrupted as she held her hand up to the eldest Briggs sister. "We're supposed to be dressed like cool biker chicks."

"You don't look like any of the biker chicks we know," Aunt Aster chimed in matter-of-factly.

Bailey planted a hand on her hip. "Oh yeah? Do you *know* a lot of biker chicks?"

"Sure we do," Aster replied with a casual shrug. "And if you had any questions about them, you should've just asked us. We have lunch at Hog Wild every other Tuesday. Their barbecued ribs are to die for."

Bailey blinked and her shoulders slumped forward, as if the indignation had deflated from them like air out of an old balloon. Her great-aunts never ceased to surprise her. "I'm sure I'm going to regret asking this—but why are you noshing on Hog Wild's barbecued ribs every other Tuesday?"

"Oh, we play bridge with the owner's grandmother. Then we all go over and have lunch at Spike's place. That's her grandson—Spike Larsen. His real name is Mike, but all his friends call him Spike."

Yes, they were familiar with Spike. Although Bailey hadn't realized the burly bartender was the owner of the bar.

"He's a big guy," Aster continued, "and he looks scary at first, but once you get to know him, he's a real sweetheart."

Marigold huffed. "You're just saying that because you thought he was flirting with you the last time we were there."

Aster fluffed up her short bob of silvery curls and batted her eyelashes at her sister. "He was. Didn't you hear the way he offered me *extra* barbecue sauce?"

Spike, the ominous biker bartender somehow seemed a little less menacing now that Bailey knew he'd been flirting with her sixty-something-year-old great-aunt. Even if it was just about barbecue sauce. She'd liked the guy when he was helping them escape from getting beaten up by the biker babes, but she liked him even more now. Maybe she'd bake him some cookies as a thank-you. Then pick his brain about biker gangs and gunrunning.

Granny Bee smacked the table with her palm, making them all jump. "Who cares about bikers and barbecue when we have real problems. The annual Bee Festival that *our* family is sponsoring is in jeopardy. It's supposed to start this Friday, but we may have to call the whole thing off."

Chapter Three

B ailey heaved a small sigh of relief. The members of her and
Evie's families had apparently not been concerned about
their whereabouts. There was a different kind of crisis at play.
Probably best not to bring up the two biker women who'd wanted
to punch their lights out.

"What's going on with the festival?" she asked, dropping into
an empty seat and reaching for a honey cookie from the plate in
the center of the table.

Now that she knew the souvenir glass was to blame for the
window issue, she could have a cookie without guilt.

"What's going on," her grandmother repeated with her normal theatrical flair, "is that our beloved Bee Festival is in peril.
And if we don't figure out a solution quick, we may have to call
the whole thing off."

Marigold let out an exasperated sigh. She was the oldest, and
tallest, of the sisters, having just passed seventy on her last birthday. Her straight shoulder-length hair had gone completely white,
and she wore it in a sensible chignon at the nape of her neck.
"Now, Bee, let's not exaggerate. I don't think the *entire festival* is

in jeopardy just because we don't have enough contestants in the Miss Honeybuzz Pageant."

"Well, shhhh-ugar nuggets. Is that the big crisis?" Evie asked, sinking down into the chair next to Bailey. She'd been working on trying not to swear so much. "The pageant?"

"It's more than just a pageant," Granny Bee huffed. "It's a prestigious title. I held it myself back in the early sixties. And it's the cornerstone event of the whole festival. And now, thanks to Bud Heppner, who pulled both his girls out of the contest so they could help with their family's harvest, we only have four contestants. According to the bylaws, we need at least seven to hold the pageant."

"Doesn't seem like a problem to me," Sawyer said, brushing Bailey's shoulder as he reached around her to snatch a cookie off the plate. He pointed the cookie at Evie and Bailey. "Looks like you have two extra contestants sitting right here. They're both beauties, and they could use 'finding trouble' or 'climbing out windows' as their talent in the competition."

Bailey shook her head, trying not to be distracted by the heat of Sawyer's arm as it touched hers or the fact that he'd just called her a beauty. Ignoring the warmth creeping up her neck, she scoffed at the idea. "No way. I'm not pageant material. And Evie can't because she'll be too busy. She has enough on her plate with the Bee Festival Bake-Off." Bailey let out a giggle as she leaned toward Evie. "See what I did there? On her *plate*? Because of the Bake-Off?"

Apparently, the margaritas hadn't completely worn off, because even if no one else thought Bailey was hilarious, she did.

"Yeah, we get it," Sawyer said, offering her the slightest wry grin. "And that bad pun is proof you shouldn't choose 'stand-up comedy' as your talent."

"Not *entering* anything is my talent. Which is why I will *not* be entering the pageant at all. Besides the fact that Granny's put me in charge of, like, six different events, so I'll be running around all weekend, I'm way too old and have too many stretch marks to be competing against a bunch of twenty-somethings." She'd just turned thirty that year, but having a twelve-year-old daughter made her feel like she was in a completely different age category from the contestants in their late teens and early twenties.

Sawyer frowned. "You're not that old." He wisely kept silent about the stretch marks. "And is there an age limit on who can enter the pageant?"

"No, there's not," Aster said as a wicked gleam lit her eyes. "Which means *we* could do it." She pointed from herself to her older sister.

Marigold raised an eyebrow. "Who is this *we* you're talking about? You got a mouse in your pocket?"

"No. I mean *we* as in you and me. We could enter the pageant. The grand prize is a vacation package for two to Hawaii. If either one of us wins, we could take the other."

"Maybe we need to recheck that medication the doctor gave you last week," Marigold said.

"Why? It was just a vitamin supplement and some extra calcium."

"Because you sound delusional. I love that you think we could even *enter* a beauty pageant, and then that you somehow imagine we have a snowball's chance in heck to actually win the grand prize."

Aster huffed and lifted her chin. "I don't see why not. You've turned plenty of heads in your day, and we both have numerous talents. You play the piano, and I used to twirl baton. I may be getting older, but I've still got sparkling wit and great legs."

Marigold stared at her sister. "Humph. First of all, I hate to break it to you, but you're not *getting* older; you *are* old. And despite your sparkling wit and great gams, if you start twirling that old baton around our house, I'm moving out."

The two sisters lived in a huge Victorian, called Lavender Manor, located in the upscale part of downtown. Built in the early 1900s, it had been their family's house in town. It had always been painted in variegated shades of purple, their mother's favorite color, and thanks to the sisters' green thumbs and impeccable weeding skills, the lush gardens surrounding the home were full of purple-colored flowers and thick lavender bushes that had originally been planted for their father's bees.

Aster waved a dismissive hand at her sister. "We'll talk about it when we get home. But it would be a great way to get to meet Rex Rafferty."

Securing the celebrity host for the Bee Festival had been the coup of the season. The handsome, dark-haired newscaster lived in California and appeared daily on a morning news show called *Wake Up With Rex and Rachel.*

Bailey licked the sugar from the corner of her lips. "I'm still not sure how we managed to get Rex Rafferty to host and film *our* Bake-Off for a feature on his show. I mean he's a huge star, and we are a pretty tiny town."

"Now don't go knocking our small town. Or the Bee Festival. It's been around for sixty years," Granny proclaimed. "It's got notoriety."

"What surprised me was how little we had to pay him to do it," Aster said. "We made a lowball offer just to start the negotiations, and he took it. Said something about always wanting to see the mountains of Colorado."

"He may have taken a small compensation, but he had ridiculous demands in his contract." Marigold held up her fingers as she ticked off his requests. "He wants his own lavish trailer with a *private* bathroom, a cool-mist humidifier, Wi-Fi, *two* bottles of some expensive Scotch, *freshly* sliced lemon wedges, a professional-grade steamer, and four gallons of water *per day*. And not just any water—some fancy stuff, that we don't even carry in town. We have to go to Denver tomorrow to get it."

"Oh, and we forgot to tell you," Granny Bee said, waving toward Bailey. "He also wants a signed copy of your newest book."

"*My* newest book?" Bailey asked. "Why?"

Granny shrugged. "Who knows. He must be a fan."

"He sounds like a diva," Evie said.

"You haven't even heard the best one," Aster said, then nudged her sister's shoulder. "You forgot to tell them about the M&M's."

"Oh mercy. How could I forget the M&M's?" Marigold gave an exaggerated head slap. "This man wants *four* of those big two-pound bags of peanut M&M's."

"Wow. That seems like a lot of candy," Sawyer said. "But that seems like a tame request compared to freshly sliced lemons and expensive Scotch."

Marigold raised one eyebrow. "That's because I haven't told you the rest of the request. He wants four bags of peanut M&M's—with all the red ones removed."

Daisy wrinkled her nose. "What's wrong with the red ones? Don't they all taste the same?"

"Of course they do." Granny Bee huffed out an annoyed breath. "He said something about not eating anything with red dye number three, which isn't even used in M&M's."

Aster laughed. "And he also said the color red makes him angry. Which kind of makes me want to sneak some red throw pillows into his *lavish* trailer."

"Where did you even find a lavish trailer for him?" Sawyer asked. "I didn't think the fairgrounds had the budget for that."

"It doesn't," Aster told him. "Helen Dobbs is loaning us her fancy motor home for him to use. Apparently, she's a big fan."

This time Marigold huffed. "And now she's also getting her name *and* her real estate company listed as a sponsor of the festival."

"Are you nervous?" Daisy asked Evie. "Having to compete in front of and cook for someone so famous?"

Evie shook her head. "Not really. He may be on television and have weird taste in posh water and M&M's, but he's still just a man. Like Granny says, he puts his pants on one leg at a time, just like the rest of us." She looked toward Granny Bee, the fondness for the woman shining in her smile. "Besides, I don't know if I'll even get on the show."

The town had voted for their favorite restaurants and chefs to compete the month before, and the contestants had been narrowed down to the top five. Rosa and Evie's coffee shop and bakery, Spill the Beans, with Evie as the chef, had been selected as one of the contestants. The show would start on Friday, the first day of the festival, with the top three contestants being announced. Then they would immediately start baking.

"Of course you'll be chosen, mi vida," Rosa assured her with an affectionate pat on her granddaughter's knee. "You are a star."

Evie held up crossed fingers. "I think I will. People love our bakery. And with *our* recipes"—she pointed toward her abuela, then to Bee—"and Granny Bee's signature honeys, I think we have a solid chance to win the whole thing. But I've still got to make it into the top three then impress the heck out of the judges."

* * *

Friday morning broke sunny and clear. It was a perfect summer day in the Colorado mountains. The Bee Festival was off to a great start, and the fairgrounds were teeming with people.

The Briggs family had hosted a street breakfast that morning to kick off the festival, and they'd enlisted the help of Sawyer, Rosa, Evie's brother Mateo, and Lyle Ambrose, the ranch manager and Granny Bee's sweetheart.

It was good they had so much help, because it felt to Bailey like the whole town had shown up. They'd flipped at least a thousand pancakes, scrambled dozens of eggs, and made numerous pots of coffee. The delicious scents of sausage and maple syrup permeated the air.

The celebrity host, Rex Rafferty, had even made an appearance, his cameraman in tow. But the most Bailey had seen of him had been to say a quick hello as she passed him and his cameraman each a plate of pancakes. Rex apparently hadn't done his homework on the town, as he'd dismissed Bailey and her family, who were some of the town's founders *and* the hosts of the festival, as if they were the hired help. She didn't care how he treated her, but her grandmother and aunts deserved some recognition.

From her first impression, she wasn't super dazzled by the man. He was handsome, with his dark hair and whitened teeth, but he also seemed arrogant and dismissive. She'd noticed he didn't even take one bite of the food, just walked by the picnic tables set up in the street, accepting the adoration of the crowd, and then dumped his untouched plate in the trash. The cameraman had wolfed his food down in a few bites, like he was used to eating on the run, then called out his thanks before hurrying after Rex.

The Bee Festival Bake-Off was scheduled to begin at two, and all the contestants were to be in attendance. Rex would announce the three winning restaurants, and then the chefs from each one would come onto the stage, set up with three working kitchen stations, and immediately begin baking their first recipe.

The event would last all three days of the festival. The first day the contestants would make a breakfast dish; the second, an entrée; and the third, a decadent dessert. They could make whatever they wanted—the only stipulation being that they had to use honey in some form in all their recipes.

It was more of a *Cook*-Off than a *Bake*-Off since they were cooking main dishes as well, but Granny Bee liked alliteration and thought Bee Festival Bake-Off sounded better. And they all knew not to argue with Gran when it came to the Bee Festival.

Evie had missed the street breakfast, instead choosing to spend the morning preparing for the chance that she would get chosen. Bailey was supposed to meet her by Edwards Hall, the building that would house the Bake-Off, thirty minutes before the event started.

"Wow, you look amazing," Bailey told her friend as she and Daisy walked up to meet her.

Evie wore a pair of dark denim jeans with the cuffs folded up at the ankles and a hot pink V-neck T-shirt with "Spill the Beans" emblazoned on the front in glittery rose-gold letters. Her curly hair had been straightened and was pulled back into a sleek ponytail. She stood over six feet tall in a pair of strappy gold four-inch spike heels.

"Thanks." Evie gave her a hug, then stepped back with a wince. "My feet are already killing me."

Bailey looked down at her shoes. "Then why are you wearing those stupid heels?"

Evie shook her head and made a low growling sound in her throat. "Because they're my highest ones. And because Rex Rafferty told me not to."

"What?"

"Well, not Rex himself. But he had his assistant tell me that he doesn't like the women on the set to be taller than him, so he didn't want me to wear anything over a one-inch heel. Can you believe that? The arrogance of this guy."

"Yes," Bailey told her. "I can believe some Hollywood big shot would be vain enough to not want a woman taller than him. But I can't believe you showed up in four-inch stilettos just to annoy the guy. I mean, first of all, he *is* the host, and his comments can probably sway the judges, so you should at least start out trying to play nice. And secondly, if you think your feet hurt *now*, wait until you're running around the bake-off kitchen, trying to cook."

"I know. And you're right, dang it. The guy is just so pompous. He rubs me the wrong way. And he's a total flirt, but in more of a smarmy way than a charming way."

"That's weird," Bailey said. "He seems so nice on television, but so far, I haven't been real impressed with the guy either." She pointed at the heels. "But I know you can't wear those. You need to be at your best if you're going to win this thing, and you won't even be able to focus if you're thinking about how bad your feet are hurting."

"I know. But I don't have time to run home and change." Evie leaned down and winced again as she pulled at the thin strap cutting across her ankle.

Bailey stared down at their choices. She was wearing a pair of midcalf Roper cowboy boots, and Daisy had on the pair of faded blue Converse sneakers she'd been wearing all summer. "Okay, everybody take off your shoes."

Chapter Four

Bailey barked out orders as she pointed to the shoes piling up in the middle of the three women. "Daisy, you put on my boots. Evie, you take the blue Chucks. And I'll put on the heels."

Thankfully, because Bailey's daughter was tall, they were all within a half size of one another. Evie's feet would be a little squished in the sneakers, but she'd be way better off than in the heels.

"You can't even walk in these," Evie said, passing Bailey the sandals.

"I won't have to. I'll mostly be sitting," Bailey said, sliding her feet into the heels and buckling the straps. In preparation for the festival, they'd all three gotten pedicures the week before, so with her glossy, watermelon-pink toenails, her feet looked amazing in the sandals. If only she were wearing something other than a pair of khaki shorts and a yellow Bee Festival T-shirt. She looked like she was trying to mimic Daisy Duke.

"Ahh." Evie sighed with relief as she tied the sneakers. Then she pulled Bailey and Daisy into a squishy group hug. "Thanks for this. Really."

"Well, aren't you just fancy?" Granny Bee said, walking up to them and peering down at Bailey's footwear. "Are you thinking about entering the pageant after all?"

"Not a chance," Bailey answered. Before she had an opportunity to explain about the shoe swap, Rex Rafferty himself came out from behind one of the side stage curtains and strode toward them.

"We need the contestants backstage for a briefing," he told Evie, as he slid a possessive arm around her waist and gave her a squeeze. "But don't worry, hon, you're going to do great."

"Thanks," she said, forcing a smile at Rex, then shooting an "I told you so" glance at Bailey.

"We haven't met yet," Granny said, sticking her hand out, which forced Rex to let go of Evie to shake it. "I'm Blossom Briggs, but everyone around here calls me Granny Bee."

"Rex Rafferty," he said, as if they didn't already know who he was. "Is the 'B' short for Blossom, then?"

Granny shrugged. "Sometimes. Depends on who's using it."

"It's mostly because she's a beekeeper," Daisy piped in. "This festival is named after *her* bees. And I'm Daisy, by the way."

"Well, not *my* bees, but my father's," Granny corrected.

"How interesting," Rex said, with a bored expression that didn't make it seem like he was interested at all. Although the way his eyes kept roaming over Evie's body established just how interested he was in *her*.

Evie was right. The guy *was* creepy.

She knew her grandmother and The Hive were imagining that Rex would be this charming handsome movie star who would sweep the town off their feet, but Bailey just wasn't seeing the appeal.

Sure, he was good-looking: tan and fit—built in a way that suggested daily workouts or a personal trainer. She guessed he was in his early thirties, but no wrinkles creased his skin. His dark hair was expertly cut, and his clothes were obviously tailored. The crisp white cuffs of his shirt were just visible below the sleeves of his tailored navy-blue suit. The ladies on the fair board had all been swayed by his charm. They found him almost as handsome as he found himself.

She'd heard throughout the morning that he'd been making the rounds around town. He'd been spotted coming out of the hardware store downtown, grabbing a slice at Harv's House of Pizza, and buying ice cream for some kids at the Tastee Freez.

Just then, a young woman who looked to be in her midtwenties came hurrying up to Rex. She was pretty, with large brown eyes, long dark eyelashes, and a perfect complexion. Her thick, wavy black hair was pulled into a messy bun on top of her head, and a set of white AirPods were tucked inside her ears. A large tote bag was slung over one of her shoulders, and she wore jeans, a black T-shirt and running shoes. Her voice was soft, but her tone was firm. "Twenty minutes until go time. I'll need to get you miked up in ten."

He waved a dismissive hand toward her. "This bossy young woman is my assistant, Sibia Kumar."

The woman dipped her head at them. "Nice to meet you. You have a beautiful town."

"It's nice to meet you too." Granny Bee's voice was warm and kind. "And we like it. I hope you get a chance to see some of the sights while you're here. We have some great hiking trails with amazing views of the mountains."

"I don't pay her to take hikes," Rex said.

"The studio actually pays me, but you know I'm always happy to take care of you," she said, smiling sweetly at Rex as she handed him a white takeout cup. "I have your hot tea with lemon for your throat."

He grabbed the cup, took one sip then grimaced and shoved it back into her hand. "It's barely even hot."

"Oh, sorry," she muttered, taking a step back. "I'll get you a new one. I brought you some water too." She pulled from the tote bag a bottle of the fancy water Marigold had told them about, and held it out to him.

He grudgingly took the water. "This will have to do. For now. But I need that hot tea to prep my throat before I go on."

"I know. Of course. Sorry about that. I'll go get you a fresh cup now." Sibia dipped her head again, this time so low that her chin almost touched her chest, before scurrying back toward his trailer like a mouse scampering into its hole.

Bailey couldn't quite figure her out. She seemed to be organized and in charge, yet also humble, and seemingly doted on Rex. Like maybe she was good at her job but still a little awestruck by the star, although Bailey couldn't see why.

Rex shook his head with a frown. "Hard to find good help these days."

Granny Bee narrowed her eyes, and Bailey could tell they felt the same way about this nimrod. "She seems wonderful to me."

"Sure, maybe by Podunkville, Colorado, standards, but not for Hollywood's. I've already been taking applications for someone new. Hopefully Sibia can find me a replacement who's better than her."

He was having his assistant hire her own replacement? *What a tool.*

Bailey tried not to cringe as Rex put his hand in the center of Evie's back. "We'd better get backstage," he told her, leaning forward to speak closer. "There's just a few things we need to go over."

"Yeah, sure," Evie said, turning back to give Bailey another one of those "do you believe this guy?" looks before hurrying up the steps and out of his reach.

"We'll go save some seats in the front," Bailey called to her, thinking it was weird that her friend was the only contestant that Rex had come out to personally guide backstage.

"Save a couple for my abuela and my brother too," Evie called back.

"Already planning on it."

Bailey gestured for Daisy and Granny Bee to go ahead of her. Mainly because she didn't want them to see her hobbling along in Evie's high heels. She'd been doing okay while she was just standing still, but now that she was trying to walk, she felt like a little girl playing dress-up in her mother's shoes. But her current main objective was just trying not to trip or turn her ankle.

They found some great seats in the front row and staked out their spots. Bailey checked her watch. They still had fifteen minutes before the program started, and she'd just remembered that she had a pair of sneakers in her car from the Zumba class she and Evie had gone to the week before.

Her car was parked in the field behind Edwards Hall. She had plenty of time to run out there and back. Or she *should* have plenty of time. If only she weren't wearing four-inch heels with a tiny strap that was digging into her ankle so that she could barely walk, let alone run.

She looked at her watch again. She could do this.

"I have another pair of shoes in the car," she told Daisy. "I'm going to run out to change. Be right back. Don't let anyone take my seat."

Her phone rang as she was hobbling from the building, and she almost tripped over her own feet as she tried to pull it from her pocket. "Hey, Griff. Where are you?" she asked after checking the display and tapping the screen to answer.

"I'm about five minutes away," he said. "Just coming up to Evie's house. Have they started yet?"

"No, you still have time. But since you're near Evie's place, would you consider making a quick stop that will make you look like a total hero in her eyes?"

"How do you know I'm not already a total hero in her eyes?"

He had a point.

"Okay. Then even *more* of a hero."

"I'm just teasing. Sure, what do you need me to do?"

She quickly told him about the shoes, then hung up and resumed her hobbling. She was managing all right while she was on the concrete, but then she reached the dirt field where her car was parked. She stepped into the dirt, and her heel sunk, throwing her off kilter. She stumbled forward with the other foot, her arms pinwheeling. Her ankles wobbled as the other heel sank, and she completely lost her balance and pitched forward into the field.

Chapter Five

The ground came flying toward Bailey. Then a pair of strong arms caught her before she face-planted into the dirt.

"Whoa there, I got you," a familiar voice said, and she looked up into the handsome face of Sawyer Dunn.

She clung to his arms, her breath heaving and her shins burning from trying to walk in the stupid shoes. "What are you doing here?"

"I was called out to check on some vandalism at one of the vendor's booths."

She shook her head. "Sorry, that came out too harsh. I'm really glad you're here, but you just seem to always show up right as I'm making a fool of myself."

He was grinning down at her as he held her snug against his chest. "Just doing my job, ma'am."

Ugh. She wanted to whack him in the arm, but she was afraid if she let go of him, she'd fall over. "Don't *ma'am* me. I'm not your grandma."

"Yes, ma'am. I mean yes, Bailey." He was teasing her. But she didn't mind that much.

In fact, she could easily have just hung out in the circle of his arms the rest of the day. Except the clock was ticking, and she had to get back inside. Still clutching his arms, she tried to take another step to the car, but her ankles failed her again, and her knees buckled.

Sawyer held her up as he let out a frustrated sigh. "What is going on, woman? Why are you wearing those crazy heels? Are you practicing walking in them because your aunts talked you into entering the pageant after all?"

"Heck no. And why does everyone keep asking me that? These shoes are Evie's."

"Okay. Well, that explains . . . pretty much nothing. Why are you wearing Evie's shoes?"

"It's a long story. But I'll tell you all about it if you help me get to my car." She pointed across the field to where her blue compact SUV sat. "I'd take these blasted things off and go barefoot if there weren't so many stickers and probably broken glass and who knows what else in this field." She tried to take another hobbling step forward while hanging onto his arm.

"Okay, stop," he said, stepping in front of her. "You keep going like that, you're going to break your ankle. Or worse." He bent down and pointed to his back. "Get on. I'll give you a ride."

Bailey huffed out a sardonic laugh. "Not a chance in heck, buster. I'd rather risk the broken glass." There was *no way* she was letting him piggyback her.

"Oh, come on. We used to do this all the time."

"Yeah, back when I was a skinny sixteen-year-old, and you were a strapping seventeen-year-old who worked on a farm."

He turned to look at her, one eyebrow raised. "First off, you're still . . ."

She raised an eyebrow back, daring him to say it.

"Well," he sputtered. "I still work on the farm. And I'm still 'strapping' enough to carry you across this field. Now get on my back or you're going to miss seeing your best friend being selected as a contestant in the bake-off."

Ugh. That sealed it.

"Fine," she huffed. He bent down again, and she hoisted herself onto his back and wrapped her arms around his neck.

"Now you can't ever doubt my muscles again. And also, who says *strapping* anymore anyway?" he asked as he strode toward the car. "Where are we? Elizabethan England?"

"Me. I say *strapping*. I can't help it. I'm a writer, and I like clever words." She tried not to think about his strapping muscles, or his broad shoulders that she was currently pressed against, or the amazing way his neck smelled. Instead, she focused on telling him about the shoe swap as they made their way across the field. When they got close enough, she let go of his neck, to pull the key fob from her pocket, and hit the button to open the hatchback.

He turned around and deposited her into the back of the car. She let go of him, and he turned back and lifted up her foot, cradling her heel in his palms.

She sucked in a breath, the embarrassment of the piggyback ride forgotten as his thumb skimmed lightly over her ankle. He gently undid the buckle and eased the shoe off, grazing his fingers over the angry red marks the straps had left.

Oh, she was in trouble here. She had never gotten over Sawyer—he had always been the one true love of her life. For years, she'd tried to push him out of her mind, but she'd never really stopped dreaming about him or wishing they'd had another chance to get it right, even though she'd gone over a decade without seeing or hearing from him. But now that they were back in the same town, she couldn't stop thinking about him. She felt like that same sixteen-year-old girl who became heady just being around him. For heaven's sake, the man was barely touching her ankle, and it was practically sending her into a swoon.

He rubbed his thumb over the shiny pink gloss of her toenail polish. "You know I've always been partial to hot pink." His lips curved into a roguish grin as his gaze rose to meet hers. "Especially hot pink with polka dots."

Oh. My. Gosh.

* * *

Bailey's cheeks were still burning as she hurried back into the bake-off building.

In the front row sat Evie's brother, Mateo, and then Rosa, Evie, Daisy, and Granny Bee. They had saved seats on either side of Daisy for her and Griffin, and Bailey slid into the empty one next to Evie.

"Where'd you go?" her friend asked. "And did you run there? Why are you all red and out of breath?"

Because apparently the other night, she had flashed her hot-pink polka-dotted unmentionables to the boy—make that *man*, an extremely *hunky* man—she'd been in love with for over half her life. "I ran out to my car. My sneakers were still in there from our Zumba class." She passed her friend the gold heels, leaving out the rest.

Sawyer had kept that flirty grin on his face as she'd jerked on her socks and tennies and relocked the car. He might still be smiling. She couldn't be sure because she'd mumbled a quick, "Thanks for the lift" and run off as soon as the locks clicked.

He'd hollered back, "Anytime," and she'd heard the amusement in his tone.

Soo embarrassing.

A large purple tote bag sat at Evie's feet. Bailey could see her friend's makeup bag, a flat iron, and a bottle of water as Evie pulled it open and tossed the sandals inside. Then Evie's face melted into a gooey smile as she looked at something behind Bailey.

Evie Delgado did not *do* gooey smiles. Or she hadn't. Until she'd met Bailey's grouchy PI friend, Griffin Yates.

Bailey turned to see Griff smiling back at her friend. He held up the pair of rose-gold running shoes she'd instructed him to grab from Evie's house on his way here. He'd even tucked a pair of socks into one of them.

"Oh my gosh, wow, thank you," Evie gushed as he passed her the shoes. "How did you know?"

He nodded to Bailey. "A little bird told me you might need these."

This was the part where her friend would normally offer her an appreciative smile, maybe even a quick hug. But Evie only had eyes for Griff.

She wasn't the only one. Half the women in the room had turned their heads to watch the tall, dark-haired man walk into the room. He was self-conscious of the slight limp he had from a bullet he'd taken to the leg when he'd been a cop, but he still carried himself with the composure earned from years on the force: back straight, eyes watchful, in full command of the room. Evie had described him as a young Hugh Jackman, like Wolverine without the claws, and it was a fitting description. Yet, even with his handsome looks and seriously broad shoulders, he also knew how to blend into a room or disappear into the shadows of a street. That skill is what made him a good cop and a great PI.

Bailey had met him years ago when a friend had introduced them, thinking Griff could help her with some research for the book she'd been working on. He'd been just as grouchy and gruff and standoffish back then, but they'd hit it off and been friends ever since. *Only* friends—been there, tried it once, hadn't worked out.

None of the dates she'd gone on ever seemed to work out. Apparently, she was still stuck on the tractor-stealing guy she'd fallen in love with as a teenager.

Evie clutched the shoes to her chest. "Thank goodness the door was unlocked."

Griff scoffed out a sardonic laugh. "Like that lock would have stopped me." He nodded to the stage. "You're gonna do great."

Evie's eyes cast to the ground, and holy crazy wonders never ceased—was her bestie actually blushing? "I don't even know if I'll get selected."

Griff gave her a hard nod—and a wink! What was happening? Who was this man? Griffin Yates was *not* a winker. "You will."

Bailey's great-aunts came rushing through the door and slipped into the two empty seats she and Evie had saved behind them.

Marigold pressed a hand to her chest as she tried to catch her breath. "What'd we miss?"

"Nothing," Bailey told her. "It hasn't started yet. You just made it."

Aster put a hand on Evie's shoulder. "You're going to be amazing."

Evie squeezed Aster's hand as the atmosphere in the big hall changed. It went quiet for a second, then burst into animated murmurs. The room crackled with excitement as Rex Rafferty strolled onto the stage. He walked with an air of cool conceited confidence, flashing his bleach-whitened teeth at the crowd.

Armed with a healthy budget and the knowledge that the stage was going to be filmed for a television show, the festival committee had gone all out with their decorations. The stage had been decked out in full Bee Festival style. Everything was either black, yellow, white, or gold and carried either a bee or a honey motif. There were three cooking stations, each with a shiny new black KitchenAid mixer and light yellow cannisters that looked like honeycombs with bees for a handle. The towels had cute bees embroidered on them, and the cushioned mats in front of the stations were black, with cute bees buzzing around yellow and white daisies. Even the soap dispensers next to the portable sinks were shaped like small honeycombs and filled with yellow antibacterial soap.

The set was adorable, but functional too. A long counter ran behind the contestants, and they would each have access to a microwave and a refrigerator with a freezer. Each station was also equipped with measuring cups and spoons, baking pans, and mixing bowls.

The crew from California included Gregory London, a set designer/stage manager, and he'd been working closely with the women on the festival committee. Charming and gregarious, he had the women wrapped around his little finger, and they'd all been working together to create an amazing look. A large screen sat high above the back of the stage so the audience could see what the cameraman was filming. Obviously, the actual show would look a little different after editing, but it gave them a good sense of how it would appear on TV.

Rex walked through the kitchen stations and out to the edge of the stage. "Hello, Humble Hills! Are you excited to be here today?" he called into the crowd. After a lackluster response of a few *hellos*, he tried again, raising his voice. "I *said*, are you *excited* to be here today?"

This time the crowd cheered and whooped, and Rex bowed his head demurely, as if the cheering had spontaneously broken out for him. The cameraman, who Bailey had learned was named Toby Patel, would probably edit out the part where Rex had solicited the cheers.

Rex did a little introduction, mostly about himself, but he also included some of the talking points about the Bee Festival that Marigold had written and printed out for him. Bailey was pleased that he introduced Granny and her sisters, and everyone clapped and cheered when the three women stood up.

"The town of Humble Hills may be small, the kind of place where most directions begin with *'Turn left or right at the Longhorn Steakhouse'* or *'It's the road before or after the stone cabin on highway 24,'* but the selection of restaurants and great eats around here is still amazing." Rex paused and let a loud cheer go up from the crowd. "You know what I'm talking about. You haven't lived until you've had a piece of Heavenly Hershey pie at the Roadside Diner or a slice of Toni-Roni at Harv's House of Pizza." More cheering.

Bailey had to agree. The Toni-Roni was amazing. It was a specialty pizza with two kinds of pepperoni, crispy bacon, and extra cheese, and had been named for Harv's mother, Toni, because it was her favorite. It was on the menu as "Mama's Favorite," but it was nicknamed the Toni-Roni.

"With that being said," Rex continued, "I know it had to have been hard to narrow down the Bake-Off finalists to five restaurants, and then to only three chefs who will get to participate in the final round." He walked behind one of the kitchen stations and pulled out three rolled-up bundles and set them on the counter in front of him. Each one had a gold envelope tucked into it.

Rex took the first envelope, then shook out the bundle to reveal a black and yellow apron with the words "Bee Festival Bake-Off Finalist" in glittery gold letters across the front. "Now, what you've all been waiting for . . . the first contestant in the Bee Festival Bake-Off is . . ." He draped the apron over his arm like a wine sommelier, then opened the envelope and drew out a black and yellow card. "Charlotte Shine from the Sunshine Café. Come on up!"

Applause erupted as a woman flew out of her seat like she'd been ejected from an airplane, and started jumping up and down and yelling, "I did it! I won! I won!"

"Well, you haven't won yet, honey. You still have to do the baking competition." Rex rolled his eyes, and the tone of his voice sounded the slightest bit annoyed. He waved her forward. "And you can't do it from down there, so come on up."

Bailey frowned, confused by his attitude. The guy had agreed to come here, and all of his absurd demands had been met. He was getting the VIP treatment, and he was the star of the show. Why was he suddenly acting irritated?

"Yes, I'm coming!" Charlotte raced up to the stage and practically tackled Rex in a hug.

"All right. Take it easy there. I'm not one of the judges." He patted his perfectly coiffed hair as he laughed good-naturedly and winked at the audience. "I haven't had that kind of greeting since my neighbor's dog ran into my yard and started humping my leg."

41

Geez. Why did everything that came out of his mouth sound condescending? He seemed so lovable and sweet on the morning show, but now he just came off like a pompous jerk. There seemed to be quite a difference between his television personality and the real Rex Rafferty.

Charlotte, however, didn't seem to notice or care. She practically ripped the apron from Rex's hands and yanked it over her head. She couldn't stop grinning as she took her place behind the kitchen station Rex motioned to.

Charlotte was married to Ben Shine, and they'd opened the Sunshine Café almost twenty years ago, right after they'd gotten married. They had two daughters, and both had grown up helping around the café, busing tables and filling salt and pepper shakers. Charlotte's personality was as sunny as her name, and she had a knack for remembering names and greeting her customers with a smile.

Charlotte had gone all out with the theme of the festival. She was wearing a shirtwaist dress made of black material covered with honeybees buzzing around little white and yellow daisies. The fabric almost matched the pattern on the kitchen floor mats, which was both kind of neat and kind of awkward. She had on yellow ankle socks with black sneakers, and her hair was pulled back from her face with a black headband that had a bee attached to it with a little spring, so it looked like it was buzzing above her head.

She was of medium height and medium build, with medium-length brown hair—everything about her was medium. *Except* for her pie-baking skills. Those were *gigantic*. She was outstanding in the art of flaky crusts, marshmallowy cloud meringue, crisp apple filling, and tart lemon curd. The food at their café was good, but Charlotte's pies were legendary.

Rex clapped his hands, drawing the crowd's attention back to him. He held up another envelope. "Our second contestant is . . ." He drew out the pause as he tore open the envelope and pulled the card from inside. "Michael Larsen with Hog Wild."

Bailey's and Evie's jaws dropped at the same time as they turned to look at each other.

The tall man stood and waved at the folks cheering for him as he sauntered to the stage. He'd pulled his long dark hair into a ponytail and wore all black, from his boots to his jeans, to his Hog Wild T-shirt.

"It's Spike," he told Rex as he accepted the second apron.

"I'm sorry?" Rex shrank back from the man towering over him. It was funny that he'd been worrying about Evie wearing heels when Spike stood well over six feet tall and had a good six inches on him.

"Spike. My name. I go by Spike." He pointed to the spiked dog collar around his neck and the bracelet around his wrist that matched the one he'd given Evie.

"Okay, then. Good to meet ya, Spike." The expression on Rex's face was a mix of terror and awe as he pointed to the station on the other side of the stage from Charlotte, leaving the middle kitchen station for the final contestant.

Spike pulled the apron over his head and tied it around his waist, then smiled and waved at the whoops and catcalls from the audience.

Rex turned back to the crowd and held up the final envelope.

Evie grabbed Bailey's hand and squeezed it in a death grip.

"All of the restaurants were amazing, but we only have one spot left, and that spot goes to . . ." He ripped the envelope open with a flourish, and an odd smile crossed his face as he read the name. It was only there for a second before he lifted his chin and called out, "Evie Delgado Espinoza with the Spill the Beans Coffee Shop and Bakery."

Bailey and Evie shot out of their seats and jumped up and down, hugging each other. Then Evie hurried toward the stage, pausing only for a second as Griff reached out and squeezed her hand as she passed. She had changed into her own tennis shoes and left Daisy's Converse All Stars under her chair, and Bailey was so thankful she wasn't tottering toward Rex in those silly gold heels.

As she reached for her apron, Rex opened his arms and drew Evie into a hug. She was normally the first to pass out affection and hugs, but Bailey noticed the stiffness in her posture as she gave Rex a quick squeeze, then pulled away and focused on pulling her apron over her head and hurrying toward her kitchen station.

Spike offered Evie a small wave and a warm smile, but Charlotte's attention stayed fixed on Rex, the anticipation emanating off her like heat from the sun.

Rex smiled at each contestant before turning back to the audience. "Our contestants are ready to go, and the ingredients they requested have already been placed at their stations. Now they have one hour to create a honey-inspired breakfast dish. So, without further ado, let the Bee Festival Bake-Off begin!"

Chapter Six

The next hour flew by in a flurry of mixing and measuring, and the contestants rushing between the refrigerators, microwaves, and their kitchen stations. Toby filmed it all as Rex wandered about, talking to each contestant.

He stopped at Evie's station and leaned over her shoulder. "Hey, *honey*, tell us about your honey-inspired breakfast dish."

Evie did her best to smile for the camera while inching away from Rex. She picked up a serrated bread knife and casually waved it around as she explained her dish, and Rex backed up as it came precariously close to his face. "I'm making honey-ricotta-stuffed French toast with honey-vanilla baked pears on the side."

"Wow. That sounds delicious."

"I'm also serving Iced honey lattes to drink."

"Those sound good too. Really rich and creamy. Tell us more about your recipe."

Ugh. Bailey grimaced. The way Rex practically purred out the words *rich and creamy* as his gaze traveled over Evie was super creepy. Luckily, Toby had the camera trained on the fresh loaf of French bread sitting next to a bowl of beaten eggs.

"The key is to slice the toast really thick. That makes stuffing it easier. And really, the stuffing is the best part," Evie told him, holding up first a slice of French bread and then a small mixing bowl for the camera as she explained what was inside. "The mixture of ricotta cheese, lemon, and honey gives it a sweet and savory taste that's to die for. After grilling the toast, I'll sprinkle it with powdered sugar and a few tart berries, then drizzle it with the honey base from the baked pears. The judges are going to love it." She flashed a smile toward the judges' table.

For the Bake-Off, the festival committee had chosen three judges who, they claimed, had great taste and were upstanding citizens of the community. Bailey was pretty sure they were just the only people who'd agreed to do it.

The first judge was Lon Bracken, Humble Hills' new mayor. The last mayor had died the month before, from a bee allergy. In truth, he'd been murdered by a jar of Granny Bee's Honey I'm Home hot spiced honey—and right after she'd threatened to kill him. Which had made Granny Bee the prime suspect. Thankfully, Bailey, Evie, and the rest of The Hive—with a little help from Griffin and Sawyer—had banded together to solve the case and keep Granny out of the slammer.

Bailey and Sawyer had been the ones to find the mayor's body, and that crime scene had been where she'd met Dr. Leon Foster, the county medical examiner, and the festival's choice for the second Bake-Off judge. With his wild hair that made him look like a cross between Einstein and Doc Brown from *Back to the Future*, and his penchant for bad coroner jokes, Bailey had liked the ME from the start. When he'd offered to help her with her research for her next book and told her to come on down to the morgue and they'd crack open a cold one, she knew they'd end up as friends.

The third judge was Iris Dunlap, and she was probably the most qualified for the job. She wrote a weekly food column for the *Humble Hills Herald*, where she reviewed restaurants and shared recipes and cooking tips. Iris appeared to be in her mid-forties, with a stylish curly bob of salt and pepper hair. She was known for wrapping her ample figure in colorful floral print dresses and for her glitzy jewelry and fun, hearty laughter.

Rex moved on to Spike's kitchen. Unlike at Evie's station where he had practically been on top of her, at Spike's station he maintained several feet of distance between the bartender and himself. He peered down at the neatly arranged ingredients and freshly wiped counters. "Tell us about your recipe, Spike."

"I'm making honey-cinnamon scones with a warm honey glaze, paired with honey-cinnamon roasted pineapple spears." Spike gestured to a plate of perfectly cut and arranged pineapple skewers.

Wow.

"Who would have thought *he'd* go with scones?" Bailey whispered to her daughter.

"Impressive," Daisy whispered back. "And it all sounds amazing."

"I wish we could taste everything too," Marigold said in her normal voice from behind them. "This is making me hungry."

"Shh," several of the audience members whispered in their direction. Applause was okay, but they'd been told to keep audience comments to a minimum.

Bailey turned and shot a "would you behave yourself" glare at her great-aunt.

"What?" Marigold said with a shrug, which gained her another "Shush."

Bailey turned back to the stage, where Rex had sauntered over to Charlotte and asked about her dish.

The kitchen station in front of her was a disaster of spilled cream, cracked eggshells, an empty vanilla container, all under a fine dusting of flour. Egg yolk dripped from the side of the counter, and Charlotte had more flour on one of her forearms and across her cheek.

Her voice had ratcheted up a notch, and she spoke with the same frenzy with which she was currently whipping together ingredients. "I'm making a breakfast honey bread with whipped pecan-praline honey butter and honey-roasted peaches on the side. The bread takes a full thirty minutes in the oven so as much as I'd like to . . ." She paused for a moment to look adoringly at Rex. Bailey swore she might have let out a swoony sigh before she returned to her harried whisking of honey, milk, and eggs into her dry ingredients. "I'm sorry, Rex, but I really don't have time for chitchat."

Rex pulled his head back, his expression a little stunned—he probably wasn't used to anyone *not* wanting to chat him up—but he tried to cover his reaction with a laugh. "You heard the lady. She doesn't have time to chat."

Charlotte blew a wispy section of bangs that had escaped from her headband off her forehead and shot a perturbed glare in Evie's direction. "I didn't know we were allowed to add a *drink* to our recipe."

Rex shrugged. "The rules state you can add embellishments and/or accompaniments as long as you finish them in the allotted time."

Bailey drew her feet back as Rex's assistant, Sibia, slipped past her and grabbed Evie's purple tote bag. Evie had told them that each contestant was allowed to bring one bag with essentials they might want or need backstage. There was a list of approved items they were allowed to bring. And a few things they weren't—like alcohol, firearms, or their own personal knives. The assistant already had a small black duffel and a pink tote bag over her shoulder that Bailey assumed belonged to Spike and Charlotte, respectively.

Bailey's attention was drawn back to the stage as one of Charlotte's mixing bowls flew off the counter and crashed to the floor. Thankfully, she had already poured the contents into a pan, but there was still enough left in the bowl to fling yellow batter across the stage and send Gregory scurrying forward with a towel.

The rest of the time flew by without any other major mishaps, with the audience oohing and aahing in the appropriate places— thanks to Gregory's stage-side direction—as the judges took bites and tastes from the perfect plates set in front of them.

Spike stood next to Evie, but Charlotte kept a healthy few feet between herself and her fellow contestants as they waited for the judges' scores for this first round.

"Everything was delicious," Iris Dunlap said, standing and clasping her hands to her chest. "I've been to each of your restaurants and know that you all are outstanding chefs, but I have to admit, I was surprised by both the delicate and robust flavors of your dishes. The ricotta stuffing in the French toast was so rich and creamy, I practically moaned out loud, and the combination of peanuts with the honey-drizzled roasted peaches was so outstanding, I almost cried. And that warm honey-cinnamon glaze on those scones tasted like I'd died and gone to heaven." She looked at each chef as she complimented their dishes. "But alas, we can only have one winner for our first day. And that winner is

. . ." Her face broke into a warm smile as she turned to the winner. "Evie Espinoza with her honey-ricotta-stuffed French toast, honey-vanilla baked pears, and honey lattes."

Charlotte's face crumpled, and her shoulders sank as she took a step back toward her station. But Spike offered Evie a hearty clap on the back, coupled with a sincere "Congratulations."

While they'd been waiting for the judges, Gregory and the festival committee had swept in behind them and cleared away all the dirty dishes and ingredients from their stations, wiped the counters down, and restored them to their previously perfect appearance.

"You did it." Bailey threw her arms around her friend a few minutes later, when she'd descended from the stage.

"I can't believe it," Evie said, still looking a little dazed.

Rosa pulled her granddaughter in for a hug. "I never doubted it, mi vida. You couldn't miss with that stuffed French toast. I think we need to add it to our menu."

"I agree," Griff said, stepping up to stand next to Evie. "Watching all that made me hungry. Anyone ready to grab a bite to eat? My treat."

"Sounds good, but we have to pass," Bailey said, pointing from herself to Daisy. "Granny's holding us to a tight schedule, and we need to be at the next event in ten minutes." She squeezed Evie's shoulder. "I'm so proud of you. You were amazing. You all have fun, and we'll catch up with you later."

Bailey and Daisy spent the next few hours racing between festival activities, running from the quilting bee competition where groups competed to see how quickly they could complete an entire quilt, to the pageant hall to set up chairs. The pageant was being held in Norris Hall and officially started the next morning, but Granny wanted everything in place and ready to go the night before. Because she'd wrangled so many volunteers for the festival, however, most of the work had been done by the time they arrived.

The Hive had been experimenting with making charcuterie boards, and they'd created a gorgeous one the night before to present to the television crew. Bailey and Daisy's last task of the afternoon was to take it out to them after their first day of filming.

The lavish motor home brought in for Rex had been parked facing the corner of Edwards Hall, where the Bake-Off was being filmed. Using one side of the building and the motor home's awning for shade, the festival committee had set up a sort of communal area for the film crew to hang out in, complete with folding chairs, a picnic table, and a propane fire pit.

This is where Bailey and Daisy found Gregory sunning himself and Toby cleaning his camera when they arrived and deposited The Hive's immaculate charcuterie creation on the center of the picnic table, next to a gallon-sized Ziploc bag of all red M&M's.

Gregory perched on the side of the table and nabbed an olive from the tray. "Gorgeous spread, ladies. Did you do this yourselves?"

"Not a chance," Bailey answered. "This is courtesy of Granny Bee's book club, The Hive."

He stacked a square of white cheddar cheese onto a Triscuit. "I love it. The board *and* the book club's moniker."

"I like your socks," Daisy told him.

"Oh thanks." Gregory grinned broadly as he pulled up the ankle-length purple socks to give Daisy a better look. "They have pugs on them. Aren't they adorable? We have a pug at home— well, he's a mix between a chihuahua and a pug—so my husband calls him a *chug*. His name is Simon, and he's just the cutest. But he's also a weird little thing. We buy him all these charming stuffed animal toys, and I swear he gets this wicked gleam in his eyes as he absolutely *murders* them. He tears their stuffing out, chews up their eyes. It's a little barbaric. But he's so cute, we just go out and buy him more toys to assassinate."

Daisy giggled. "I have a golden retriever. His name is Cooper, and he's weird too. He loves to eat snow, and when we go on walks, he tries to bring back the biggest stick he can find, even if it's like a giant dead branch that fell off a tree."

Toby chuckled as he carefully placed his camera parts back into their bag. "I like this dog."

"He'll like you too," Daisy told him. "He likes everybody."

Bailey stole a chocolate-covered almond from the tray. "Where's everyone else?"

"Imani went back to the hotel to grab a nap," Toby said as he picked up a cracker and studied the cheese choices. Bailey hadn't yet met Imani Lewis, the crew's makeup artist, but Evie had told her she was magic with an eyeliner pencil. "And Sibia is running around here somewhere."

"Probably doing some inane task that Rex put her up to," Gregory said. "Like color-coding his sock drawer or polishing his one newscasting trophy he was awarded at a local station in some diddly-squat nowhere town he worked in after college." He winced as he looked at Bailey. "No offense to *this* town."

Bailey shrugged. "None taken. But I do feel bad for Sibia. She does seem to work awfully hard for that man."

Toby huffed. "*Too* hard. And with no reward to show for it."

"Oh, she got a reward for it," Gregory said, waggling his eyebrows at Bailey. "If you know what I mean."

Yes. She knew what he meant.

"That's enough," Toby said, a scowl darkening his normally relaxed features. "We don't know if anything ever happened between them. But we all know he doesn't really care about her."

Gregory tsked. "Don't tell *her* that. I think the poor thing is smitten."

"She's *not* smitten," Toby said, a little too loudly. "She just takes her job seriously."

"And her job is to keep Rex happy." Gregory quirked a knowing eyebrow at Bailey. Geez, the guy's eyebrows were sending more messages than Instagram.

The scowl remained on Toby's face as he focused his attention on folding a piece of salami onto a Ritz cracker. "Sibia is way too smart and too beautiful and kind for a jerk like Rex," he muttered.

Obviously, Sibia wasn't the only one who was smitten.

"You guys, look what I have," the woman in question called as she came around the corner of the motor home, her arms filled with stacks of folded brown furry material.

Toby jumped up to help her.

Yep. Smitten all right.

"What are those?" Gregory wrinkled his nose as he looked down at the stack Toby deposited on the table.

"They're bear suits for the Bear Run tomorrow night," Sibia told him, grabbing one and shaking it out. She held it up in front of her, and it looked like a bear onesie. It zipped up the front and had a big, tawny-colored, oval-shaped belly and a hood adorned with a black snout, brown eyes, and cute furry ears. "Everyone who's running or walking in the Bear Run will be wearing one. Aren't they so cute? I'm going to wear mine for pajamas when this is over."

"Good for you," Gregory said. "But why do you have *five* of these teddy bear union suits?"

"Because I told Granny Bee that we'd *all* participate." She tossed a medium suit to Gregory and an extra-large to the tall cameraman. "You don't have to run. You can walk the whole course. You just have to show up in the suit."

Gregory held the onesie up in front of him. "You mean *you* have to show up in the suit."

"Oh, come on. It'll be fun," she said.

"It really *is* fun," Bailey assured them. "I think close to two hundred participants signed up this year. And it's always a hoot. People go all out dressing up their bear suits. Last year there was a whole group of *Star Wars*–themed bears. And we've had people do the cast of *Harry Potter* in bears too. People get really imaginative." She hoped she was appealing to Gregory's creative side. It would be fun to have the television crew participate, especially if they decided to film some of it or use shots on the show. Gran would love that.

"I'll do it," Toby told Sibia. "Especially if it helps you out."

"Fi-n-ne," Gregory said, drawing the word out in an exaggerated sigh. "I'll wear the suit. But I'm not running."

"You can walk with us," Daisy told him. "We're bringing Cooper, and we already made him his own bear suit. It's adorable."

Bailey loved that Daisy was excited about the Bear Run. The move to Humble Hills and the ranch with Granny Bee had been good for both of them. She'd been writing more, taking advantage of the late nights after the rest of the house had gone to bed, and Daisy had flourished spending time with Granny and Lyle, the ranch manager. Granny had been teaching her about the bees and how to extract their honey, *and* already had Daisy working in the Busy Bee shop and helping with the online orders. She'd gone horseback riding, and Lyle had even let her drive the tractor. Her freckled nose was pink from the sun, and her arms and legs were tanned.

Bailey looked and felt better too. She wasn't as tan as her daughter, but she was taking daily walks around the pastures and spending way more time outside than she had in the city. Which was good because she needed the extra exercise, being around her grandmother's cooking.

She was pulled from her thoughts about fried chicken and honey-butter biscuits by a petite woman, who waved as she came around the corner of the motor home and headed toward them.

"Hi there, I'm Jane Johnson, a reporter with the *Humble Hills Herald*." She wore khaki pants and a beige polo shirt, and had a tan leather messenger bag slung over her shoulder. Her brown hair was plaited into a braid that hung down her back, and oversized, square black glasses sat on her nose. She held up a pen and a well-worn steno pad. "I hate to bother you all, but I'm wondering if I could talk to Rex or any of the contestants. I'd like to get a quote for the paper."

Before any of them could answer, a loud crash sounded from inside the motor home. They all turned to see the door fly open. It hit the side of the camper with a loud bang as Evie stomped down the stairs.

"You bitch!" a male voice yelled from inside. "You're gonna pay for this!"

Evie was dressed the same as she had been earlier, but now the front of her shirt was untucked and her hair was pulled partially free from her ponytail. Her mouth was set in a tight line, and her eyes flashed fire as she headed toward Bailey.

"And you can forget any chance you have of winning this contest!" Rex appeared in the doorway of the motor home. The front of his shirt was covered in a wet brown stain, and his cheek bore a red tint, as if he'd just been slapped. And judging from the pissed-off glare in Evie's narrowed eyes, Bailey imagined she'd been the one to do it.

His eyes widened as he caught sight of the group of people assembled in front of the motor home. Maybe he guessed Jane was a reporter because his demeanor changed as he smoothed his hair back and pasted on a camera-worthy smile. "I'm just kidding. Obviously. Miss Delgado and I were just foolin' around."

"You wish," Evie hissed, not quite under her breath.

Bailey and Daisy formed ranks around Evie, stepping up to stand on either side of her. Not that Evie needed their protection—with the steel-hard glare on her face, she looked like she could take down a grizzly bear.

Rex's breath was still coming too fast, and he was obviously flustered, but it was impressive how quickly he was pulling it together and pouring on the charm. "That was obviously a joke about the contest." That was the second time he'd used the word *obviously*, although it was *obvious* to all of them neither he nor Evie were joking around. He offered Evie a friendly wave. "See you tomorrow, Miss Espinoza. Looking forward to your next culinary creation." Then he grabbed for the handle of the camper door and yanked it shut behind him.

"Are you okay?" Bailey asked her friend, wrapping an arm around her waist.

"I'm fine," Evie said, brushing her bangs off her forehead and pushing her shoulders back. "But if that little maggot ever lays a hand on me again, I'll kill the mother-trucker."

Out of the corner of her eye, Bailey caught Jane, the reporter, furiously scribbling on her steno pad.

It looked like she'd just gotten her quote.

Chapter Seven

Bailey watched in horror as a spray of crumbled white queso fresca cheese went flying off a spatula and landed across Evie's cheek and in her hair like flakes of cheesy snow.

It was Saturday afternoon, and this wasn't the first mishap of the two-hour cooking show. Unfortunately, the majority of the mishaps had been happening to Evie, and not all of them seemed accidental.

Toby tried to lower the camera, but Rex yelled, "Keep rolling. This is the kind of action that happens during a cooking show. Our audience will *eat it up*." He laughed at his own pun.

But this was not the kind of action that happened in *every* cooking show. This was the kind of action that happened when the host walks by and "accidentally" knocks into the contestant as she is slicing a plantain, hurling her cutting board and the freshly sliced fruit to the floor. Or when the host "accidentally" whacks the spatula sitting in the bowl of queso and sends crumbled cheese flying.

It was taking everything Bailey had not to run up on the stage and "accidentally" give Rex a fat lip. From the thin line of Griff's lips and the tense set of his shoulders, she could tell the PI sitting next to her felt the same way. And she didn't know what all the Spanish words that Rosa kept muttering meant, but she was fairly certain Evie's abuela was putting a curse on Rex's testicles that involved hot fire ants and the sting of a thousand hornets.

Gregory came hurrying out with a handful of paper towels. He handed one to Evie, who used it to wipe the cheese from her face while he cleaned the mess on the floor. Imani, the makeup artist, was right on his heels, and she skillfully picked clumps of cheese from Evie's hair then gave her cheeks a quick swish with a brush dipped in highlighter.

Bailey had finally met the makeup artist that morning when she'd dropped off some fresh pastries to the television crew. Imani had been backstage setting up a space to do the contestants' hair and makeup and had gratefully accepted a cheese Danish.

"I heard what happened with Evie and Rex last night," Imani told her after swallowing her first bite. She was a curvy Black woman who looked to be in her early to mid-forties, with a wide smile and streaks of rich burgundy in her curly black hair that she wore in a chic chin-length bob. She had on khaki shorts, bright red high-top sneakers, a red tank top, and a billowy white dress shirt that she'd left unbuttoned and tied in a knot at her waist. Her sleeves were rolled up, and she wore a fanny pack filled with an assortment of makeup supplies, from tubes of foundation to various brushes, sticking up from its many pockets. Her pack looked like a MacGyver Beauty Kit. "It didn't surprise me," Imani said. "But I feel bad that I didn't get a chance to warn her ahead of time. The rest of us know not to get stuck in a room alone with him."

Her statement had shocked Bailey. "If you all know that, why don't you do something about it?"

Imani had quirked an eyebrow. "Who says we're not?" She took another bite of pastry, and then Gregory strode backstage with a flurry of set issues, and Bailey scooted out of there before he put her to work. She had enough on her list from Granny already.

Now the back doors of the hall opened, and Bailey turned to see her great-aunts stride in and head toward the empty seats Bailey had saved behind them. They were decked out in full-length formal gowns and looked like geriatric princesses who'd escaped from a theme park. Both wore purple—Aster in soft lavender and Marigold in a deep shade of royal plum—and both had sparkling tiaras pinned into their silver hair. Aster wore silver heels adorned with purple and white rhinestones while her older sister, the more practical of the two, wore a pair of black ballet flats.

At the final hour, Aster *had* talked her sister into entering the pageant, and in an act of desperation for the event to continue, Granny Bee had let them.

"What'd we miss?" Aster asked as they slid into their seats with a swish of taffeta and chiffon.

Marigold's eyes widened as she sat down next to her sister. "Oh my stars, what happened to Evie's hair?"

"Estúpido," Rosa muttered. "He's trying to make her look like a fool."

Bailey lowered her voice to a whisper. "It seems like Rex is trying to sabotage Evie's recipe."

Marigold drew her head back, then pinned Rex with an evil-eyed glare that would make even the heartiest plant wither on the vine.

"Also, you all look amazing," Bailey told her aunts, trying to distract them before Marigold charged onto the stage and gut-punched the host.

Aster's shoulders went back, and she pressed her lips together in a modest but pleased smile. "Thank you. We didn't want to miss anything, so we didn't take the time to change."

"You look so pretty," Daisy told them. "Did you have the formal gown event this morning?"

"Oh no, that's tonight," Aster informed them. "This morning was just the question-and-answer session. Everyone else was dressed in casual wear, but we thought going formal might give us an edge."

It gave them an edge of something, all right.

Griff was sitting next to Bailey, and he gave her shoulder a nudge. She turned back around to see Spike passing Evie one of his cutting boards. The large man gave Rex a glare that rivaled her aunt Marigold's.

Evie offered him a smile of thanks, then brushed off the queso incident like the true star she was.

"Tell us about your recipe," Rex asked Charlotte as he stepped closer to her and peered into her mixing bowl. It seemed his attention had transferred from Evie to Charlotte, but the diner owner was lapping it up like a kitten with a saucer of cream.

Her station, and her apron, were covered in cornflake crumbs and white flour. She even had a dab of it on her forehead. She wore another dress today, this one a soft pink color with large roses on the fabric. She had switched to pink sneakers and had a fresh pink headband, but it still had a springy bumble bee attached to it, so it looked like it was bouncy-buzzing around her hair. She must have bought the little bees by the dozen, because she had placed a couple of the springy things on the corner of both Evie's and Spike's kitchen stations at the start of the show, with a wish for good luck and a reminder to "Bee Exceptional."

"Thanks for asking, Rex," Charlotte said with a big smile. "Today I'm making crispy hot honey chicken with honey butter smashed potatoes. And I'll be featuring a deliciously refreshing sage honey pineapple blended mocktail." She flashed a haughty smirk at her neighboring contestant, but Evie was focused on her own recipes as she sliced up a new bowlful of plantains.

"Sounds wonderful," Rex said, sidling closer to Evie's station. "How do you plan to top that, Miss Espinoza?"

Bailey knew her friend well enough to recognize the flash of fire in her eyes when she looked at Rex. *Take it easy. Don't blow this. You're going to be on television.* She sent those psychic-friend brainwaves to Evie and was relieved to see her take a deep, calming breath and plaster a smile on her face. But the smile was directed at the camera, not Rex.

Evie ignored the host and spoke directly into the camera. "I'm celebrating my cultural heritage with recipes passed down from my abuela. My honey garlic mojo chicken is simple to prepare but bursts with the Puerto Rican flavors of garlic and citrus. Then I'm pairing it with orange-honey plantains." She tipped her mixing bowl toward Toby so he could get a better shot. "I'm marinating my sliced platano maduros, also called plantains, in a mixture of orange juice, brown sugar, honey, cinnamon, a pinch of salt, and a small amount of vanilla bean *paste*, not extract. Next, I'll fry them in butter until the edges get nice and crisped. Then I'll drizzle them with Granny Bee's Honey Bee Good sweet clover honey and some Mexican table crema, and top them with some of the crumbled queso fresca that didn't end up on the floor or in my hair." She laughed as if the whole cheese mess had been an inconsequential silly mishap.

That's my girl.

Bailey could tell from the way the audience was leaning forward and chuckling with her that Evie had won them over. And she'd had her friend's plantains and knew they were just as delicious as Evie described. She also noted how Evie had gotten in a little plug for Granny's honey. It had been Granny's biggest seller at Busy Bee, the small store her grandmother ran from the ranch, until last month, when it was surpassed by her Honey, I'm Home hot spiced honey, which had been used as the murder weapon in the unfortunate former mayor's demise. The notoriety of the murder had been fantastic for Granny's sales, but maybe not so great for the mayor.

As the contestants started baking and frying their ingredients, the building filled with tantalizing scents of citrus and garlic and fried chicken. Not to be outdone, Spike had chosen to make the honey-barbecue wings that were so popular at his restaurant, but had upped their wow factor by wrapping them each in a slice of honey-pepper bacon before baking. His side dish was jalapeno cheddar popovers drizzled in warm honey butter.

It was fun to watch the three finalists mix and pour and race from one area of the stage to another as they prepared their recipes. The audience didn't seem to need much direction or goading from Gregory today—they all seemed enthralled with the fast-paced drama unfolding on the stage. Their gasps of delight and spontaneous applause all seemed genuine as they cheered and rooted for the contestants.

When it came time for the judging, Spike and Evie stood together as they had the day before, each giving the other nods of respect and encouragement as they awaited the results. Charlotte again stood a few feet away as she clasped her hands to her chest. Her apron was a total mess of splattered grease and sticky honey, but her hair was, surprisingly, still perfectly coiffed.

After groans of gastric appreciation, exclamations of appetizing awe, and much whispered deliberation, the judges came to a decision.

"This was a tough one," Lon Bracken, the new mayor, said as he wiped a stray dab of barbecue sauce from his chin. "Everything was amazing. You are all remarkable chefs, and today's fare was exceptional. You made our decision quite difficult, and I'll admit, we debated this one quite a bit. But we all know, we have to choose the one that stood out the most, and today that was . . . Spike Larsen's honey-barbecue wings. That honey-pepper bacon was the thing that took them over the edge."

Evie's shoulders slumped the slightest bit, but she kept a smile on her face as she gave Spike a congratulatory pat on the shoulder. Charlotte's face was crestfallen, and she bit her lip as if to keep from crying. Unlike the day before, when she'd stomped away, her steps were heavy as she plodded off the stage to where her husband waited with a hug.

This Bake-Off thing was tough. Bailey liked Charlotte, and the recipes Charlotte had chosen for today had sounded, and smelled, amazing. Bailey sure didn't envy the judges.

* * *

Later that night, Bailey and Daisy arrived back at the fairgrounds along with hundreds of other people—all of them decked out in brown bear suits. They'd planned the event to start later, to give the evening air a chance to cool off so they weren't all sweltering in their furry onesies.

Daisy had Cooper on a leash—he looked adorable in his bear costume and the fluffy ears they'd tied around his head. But he wasn't the only dog there. Dogs and kids, and even a pet pig, were in attendance, all dressed like bears.

They wove their way through wagons and strollers and so many bears, to get to the front of Edwards Hall, where they'd planned to meet everyone in their group. Evie, Griff, and Rosa were already there, all decked out in their bear outfits, although Griff wasn't wearing the hood with the bear ears.

"You guys look amazing," Bailey told them as she gave an extra nod to Griff. "I never would have believed you'd show up in a suit."

The PI shrugged and emitted a small growl. "What can I say? I'm a joiner."

Bailey barked out a laugh. "Yes, I'm sure that's it." She cast a quick glance at her friend, who looked gorgeous, even with her hair twisted into two knobby buns on either side of her head.

Granny Bee and her sisters came walking toward them, and Bailey had to hold in another burst of laughter. Granny held a shiny gold honey pot, and she wore a glittery black and gold tutu and a snug yellow T-shirt over the top of her bear suit that read "She Works Hard for the Honey." Which was funny enough, but Aster and Marigold were wearing shimmery tea-length formal gowns over their bear suits and sparkly tiaras hooked to their hoods. Both of them had wide sashes draped over their shoulders that read "Future Bee Festival Queen."

"Wow, you all look great," Bailey told them, admiring the pink shimmer of Aster's gown.

Her great-aunt flashed a wide smile. "You know, we have closets full of these formal gowns. We're having the best time getting them out and finding excuses to wear them."

Marigold frowned and fussed with her dress. "I can't believe the things your aunt talks me into."

"Your shirt is cute, but I hope you don't have to go to the bathroom," Bailey told her grandmother.

"Me too," Granny said. "I wasn't thinking about that when I squeezed into it. Lyle had to help me get it on over the suit. But now I'm stuck until later, because there's no way I can get this shirt off by myself."

The television crew came around the corner then. Sibia must have convinced them to participate, because they were all dressed in bear suits.

"You made it," Bailey said.

Gregory offered her a sigh. "Just *bearly*." The edges of his lips curved up at his dorky pun, so Bailey figured he was having at least a *little* fun with it.

Toby wore a colorful Hawaiian shirt unbuttoned over his bear suit. "We figured as long as we had to do it, we might as well get in the spirit of the thing." His gaze shifted to Sibia, who wore a lei of teal flowers around her neck.

Imani wore a matching lei, but her flowers were a dark cranberry-pink shade similar to that of her hair. Rex had walked up with them but had been stopped by a local asking for his autograph.

Bailey turned to ask Daisy a question, but her daughter's attention was focused elsewhere. She was standing on her tiptoes and peering around Bailey as if she were looking for someone.

Daisy's face broke into a broad smile. Bailey turned her head to see who had earned such a grin and was shocked to see a tall man walking toward them. Cowboy boots stuck out of the bottom of his bear suit, his hood was down, and he wore a brown felt cowboy hat.

"You made it," Daisy said, her smile growing even wider.

Bailey blinked at the handsome sheriff. "Sawyer, is that you? I can't believe you're here. *And* wearing a bear suit."

He shook his head as he reached to give Cooper's neck a scratch. "I can't really believe it either. But your daughter invited me to walk with her, and I couldn't say no."

Daisy invited Sawyer? Why?

Bailey stared at her daughter laughing with Sawyer and swallowed back the emotion suddenly clogging her throat. She'd skillfully evaded her daughter's questions about her father for so long that Daisy had given up asking about him and had just accepted her mother's assertion that her dad wasn't ever going to be part of their lives. It was easier than trying to explain the truth, and they'd both accepted that it was just the two of them. But now, seeing her daughter look so happy made Bailey wonder if she shouldn't have tried harder to give Daisy at least a father figure.

Her chest tightened as she looked at them with what felt like possibility. Or maybe hope. She wasn't sure. It had been so long since she'd dared to dream of either.

A muscular arm wrapped around her waist and pulled her against him.

"Hey, Bailes, I made it," Mateo said, dropping a kiss on the top of her head. He wore his bear suit like a fighter pilot wears a flight jumpsuit, with the top part off and the arms tied around his waist. The fabric of the white T-shirt he wore underneath clung to his broad shoulders and sizable biceps. "My last customer was a talker, and I was worried I'd be late."

Evie's brother owned a garage and auto-repair shop in town, and his lean body showed the evidence of rotating hundreds of tires and hauling around engine parts. He had thick black hair; brown eyes the color of dark chocolate; and a flirty, easy smile that was hard to resist. Bailey would know. He'd charmed her into dating him for several months after Sawyer had left her behind.

While Evie introduced her brother to the television crew, Bailey glanced from him to Sawyer, to her beautiful daughter.

Yeah, those thoughts were going to have to wait for another day. She pushed them down, *way down*, just like she'd been doing for the last thirteen years. She must really like sand because she'd kept her head buried in it for years.

"Bear runners, take your places," a voice boomed over the loudspeakers.

Someone screamed, and Bailey, whipping her head around and bracing for danger, reached for Daisy.

Then she gasped and covered her daughter's eyes as two muscular twenty-something men ran by wearing nothing but sneakers and red G-string thongs.

The men laughed as an elderly volunteer chased after them, yelling, "It's not that kind of *bare* race."

Chapter Eight

Bailey caught a grin tugging at Sawyer's lips as Daisy pushed her mom's hands away. The streakers had run around the corner of the building, the festival volunteer in hot pursuit, and Bailey planted a hand on her hip and faced the sheriff. "Aren't you going to go after them?"

He shrugged, his grin widening. "Seems like an honest mistake."

She tried to hold it back but couldn't keep a laugh from escaping. He laughed with her as they fell into step next to each other, with the hundreds of other bears crowding in toward the starting line. The route was clearly marked, winding through the fairgrounds, then looping around the livestock barns and rodeo arena; making another loop around the carnival area, then back through the fairground buildings; and ending in the neighboring park, where homemade ice cream would be served.

The more competitive runners were pushing through the crowd, jockeying for a better position closer to the starting line.

"Watch it," Sawyer told one as they jostled into Bailey. He looked down at her. "Do you want me to cuff that bear so you have a better spot to start?"

She laughed again. "Not hardly. It doesn't matter where I start. As far as I know, everyone in our group is planning to walk the course. Besides," she said, nudging his shoulder and offering him a coy grin, "he *bear*ly touched me."

He cringed at her bad joke. "That was bad. Downright em*bear*assing."

Bailey's chuckle turned into a full-on laugh as her daughter rolled her eyes at them. "Now we've done it. We're em*bear*assing Daisy."

"You guys need to stop," Daisy told them. Then the smallest grin curved her lips. "You're un*bear*able."

The three of them cracked up together as they squeezed in behind their group. Bailey loved hearing her daughter laugh and, as she'd done a hundred times over the last month, sent up a silent prayer of thanks that confirmed that this move back home to Honeybuzz Mountain Ranch had been the best thing for them both.

She hadn't been sure at first. But they'd had no choice. Their landlord had decided to sell the house they'd been renting, so it was either move them back home to Granny Bee or live out of their car. And her car wasn't big enough for *her* to live in, let alone her daughter and a hundred-pound golden retriever.

"Let's get a picture," Evie said, holding up her phone and drawing Bailey out of her thoughts. "Selfie time. Smoosh in behind me."

Their group smashed together, all trying to fit into the frame.

Gregory patted the pockets of his bear suit as he took a step back. "Dang it. I don't have my phone. I must have left it backstage. I'll be right back." He slipped out of the crowd and jogged toward Edwards Hall.

Bailey had just a second to lean in close to her daughter before Evie clicked a shot.

Then a voice came over the loudspeaker again. "All right, bears—take your places. Everyone get your *bear*ings." The emcee chuckled at his own joke. "Sorry about that, folks—you'll have to *bear* with me. I'm just so excited to start this race. On your marks. *Teddy?* Set! Go!"

The starting gunshot sounded. This *was* the mountains of Colorado, so of course they used a real shotgun instead of a small race pistol.

Then a sea of bears took off, some sprinting, some jogging, most walking at a brisk pace. There were families pulling wagons and pushing strollers, some holding kids and some holding dogs. But everywhere around them was the hearty sound of laughter.

It's a good night. Bailey had just a second to form the thought before she was dragged into the ocean of bear suits weaving its way through the fairgrounds.

The Bear Run itself lasted about an hour, and by the time it was finished, their party had split off into smaller groups.

Bailey, Sawyer, Daisy, and Cooper had stuck close to one another, but Granny Bee, Lyle, and the aunts had dropped off somewhere near the benches outside the grandstands. They'd lost Evie's family near the restrooms by the livestock barn, and Bailey had no idea where the film crew was.

The plan was to meet up by the picnic tables in the park after the run. They headed for the ice-cream line, and each had a bowl of vanilla drizzled with chocolate and caramel by the time the rest of the group caught up with them.

"I was planning to invite everyone out to the farm to keep the party going," Granny Bee told them. "But I'm about dead on my feet, and I have another big day ahead of me tomorrow."

"Me too," Evie said, leaning against Griff. "The final segment of the Bake-Off is scheduled for tomorrow morning, so I need to go home and make sure I'm all prepped for my recipe. It's the dessert round, and I'm trying something new, so I want to make sure I'm prepared."

Rosa nodded. "And you don't want bags under your eyes, mi Ángel, so you need to get your beauty sleep."

Griff leaned close to Evie's ear, and Bailey heard him say, "You're already beautiful."

Aww. Her heart swelled for them. They both deserved to be with someone good, and they were two of the best people she knew.

* * *

The next morning, Griff and Rosa were already in their seats when Bailey and Daisy came rushing into Edwards Hall. They'd been running late all morning. Bailey had bolted out of bed before six, when she'd heard the telltale sound of her dog retching and tried to get him out of the house before he threw up. Or at least off the carpet. *No such luck.* And her morning had gone downhill from there.

She hadn't been able to find the shirt she'd been planning to wear, they were out of milk for their cereal, Daisy had overslept, and neither of them had counted on Granny Bee needing them to help her load and then unload a bunch of stuff for her Myth or Murderers program she was leading that afternoon on killer bees.

There was a palpable tension in the air, and Bailey could see Toby, Gregory, and Sibia in a heated conversation at the side of the stage. Daisy took the seat next to Rosa as Bailey hurried over to the television crew. "Everything okay over here? You all look stressed.

Anything I can do to help?" Yes, she was being a little nosy—her curiosity always did get the best of her—but she was also on the festival committee, and Granny would've wanted her to offer.

"Not unless you know where to find Rex," Toby said with a scowl.

"What do you mean? The Bake-Off is scheduled to start in a few minutes. Isn't he here?"

"Nope."

"Is he in his trailer?" Bailey could imagine the celebrity doing a little extra primping.

Sibia shook her head. "No. I've checked twice. And either he woke up early and made his bed, or he never slept in it last night."

Gregory huffed. "He probably found some local groupie to spend the night with. Someone he could get to show him what an adoring fan she is. It wouldn't be the first time that's happened."

Sibia's brow wrinkled in concern. "Yeah, that's what I'm worried about."

Bailey couldn't tell if the concern was more about Rex being late or about him spending time with another woman. Or maybe it was about him having an adoring fan like the one in Stephen King's book *Misery*—the kind that might have Rex chained to a bed and locked away somewhere.

Toby's scowl deepened. "That guy doesn't think about anybody but himself."

Bailey checked her watch. They had four minutes before the official start time of the Bake-Off. "What's your backup plan?"

"We don't have one," Gregory said.

"Well, we'd better come up with one quick," Bailey told them. "All we really need is someone who can step in and host, right?" Her gaze traveled from Gregory to Sibia, to Toby.

"Don't look at me," Gregory said, pressing a hand to his chest. "I am strictly a behind-the-scenes kind of guy."

Toby shook his head. "Don't look at me either. I'm the only one who can run the camera." He turned his gaze to Sibia. "You could do it. You've been waiting for an opportunity to get in front of the camera. And Rex isn't here to send you on a coffee run or out to pick up his dry cleaning. This could be your chance to show the studio your talent."

"You have experience newscasting?" Bailey asked Sibia.

"Yeah," Toby answered for her. "She's amazing."

Bailey wasn't sure if he was talking about her newscasting skills or just her in general. With the way he was smiling at her, it could be either. Or both.

Sibia chewed her lip, then looked down at her black T-shirt, jeans, and sneakers and shook her head. "I can't. I'm barely even wearing mascara."

"*Yes*, you can," Imani said coming out from behind the stage curtain. "You're a natural beauty, so all I need is three minutes and I can have your hair and makeup ready." She shrugged out of the cropped blue blazer she was wearing and held it out to Sibia. "You can wear this, and I have some jewelry you can use too. And Toby will make sure no one sees your feet."

Sibia's brown eyes were huge as she looked up at Toby. He gave her an encouraging nod. "You got this."

She nodded back, taking the blazer. "Okay. I'll do it."

Imani pulled back the curtain, and the two of them rushed backstage. Gregory hurried after them.

Bailey looked up at Toby. "Do you really think she can pull it off?" She prayed, for Evie's sake, that the show wasn't ruined or that the studio wouldn't choose to dump it without Rex at the helm. *What a jerk.* She still couldn't believe the guy hadn't even shown up.

"Of course she can," Toby scoffed. "She has a degree in journalism and had four years of newscasting experience at a small station before she moved to California."

Bailey gawked at him. "Then why is she working as Rex's personal assistant?"

"Because Rex is a grade A prime A-hole."

"Tell me something I don't know," she muttered.

"Sibia applied for a newscaster position. But Rex's latest assistant had quit the day she was hired, and he talked Sib into"—he crooked two fingers in air quotes and raised his voice to a near perfect imitation of Rex's—"*helping him out* for a few days. A week tops."

Bailey winced, knowing what was coming next.

"Yeah," he confirmed. "That was over a year ago."

"A *year*?" Bailey hadn't been expecting that. "Why doesn't she quit or apply somewhere else?"

"Because Rex keeps dangling the carrot of giving her a newscaster spot '*any day now.*'" The cameraman wasn't doing a great job of disguising the bitterness in his voice.

"At least that's the carrot he's dangling. From what I've heard, he uses *other* means, like the casting couch, to offer the women on his staff a chance to get what they want." Okay, Bailey hadn't heard it exactly like that. She might have been fishing a little to see if what Imani had suggested was true.

Toby took the bait and leveled her with a steely stare. "I've heard the rumors, but Sibia's too smart to fall for that nonsense. And if I ever found out that he *really* did something to Sib or tried to get *her* to do something to *him*, I'd kill the bastard."

Bailey's blood chilled at the menace in the otherwise sweet and easygoing cameraman's voice. Then she saw his gaze soften as his eye caught something behind her. She turned to see Sibia coming out from backstage.

Her hair has been released from its elastic band and lay in soft curls on her shoulders. She wore Imani's blazer and a long silver necklace that matched her small hoop earrings. The makeup artist had worked her magic, enhancing Sibia's brown eyes with the barest touch of smoky shadow and giving her skin a perfect healthy glow. She looked gorgeous.

And Toby was right. After a few shaky sentences, Sibia's gaze sought his, and with another encouraging nod from him, her shoulders relaxed, and she closed her eyes just long enough to draw in a deep breath. Then she opened them again, and a grin spread across her face as she welcomed the audience and introduced the contestants.

Evie looked amazing too, in a short-sleeved, flowy floral top; ankle-length white jeans; and low-top pink sneakers. Her hair was pulled up in a ponytail, and she looked ready to tackle her recipe.

Spike had on his usual black jeans, but today he wore a fresh black Hog Wild T-shirt and running shoes instead of his motorcycle boots.

Surprisingly, Charlotte seemed even a bit more disheveled today than normal. She had on another cute dress, this one light blue with pale yellow daisies on it. But it didn't seem as starchily crisp as her previous ones had. Her hair wasn't as perfectly coiffed either, and she was missing her cute headband with the springy bee. Instead, it looked like her hair had been pulled back into a hurried ponytail, and small strands were already escaping the elastic band.

After the introductions, the show was off and running, and Sibia had the audience eating out of the palm of her hand. "I might not be the best baker myself," she told the crowd with a wink, "but I hope to *rise* to the occasion and just go with the *dough* today."

Bailey chuckled. Sibia was doing great. Maybe the reason Rex hadn't put her in front of the camera was because he was threatened by the competition. Bailey's laughter died as she caught the concerned look on Evie's face. She nudged Griff.

He leaned toward her and whispered, "Yeah, I know. Something's wrong. She's been frowning at her mixing bowl for the last few minutes."

Evie had been creaming butter and sugar together, and she stuck her finger into the mixture then dabbed a bit on her tongue. Her lips puckered as if she'd just sucked on a lime; then her eyes narrowed as she glanced from Charlotte to Spike.

Sibia was standing in Charlotte's kitchen space, listening intently as Charlotte explained her recipe. "I'm making a salted honey cheesecake with mini baklava tarts in the shape of honeycombs on the side."

"Wow. You're really going all out," Sibia said. "Not making just one amazing recipe, but two."

"Go big or go home," Charlotte muttered as she knocked over a bottle of vanilla in her haste to crush the ginger snap cookies for her crust. She seemed different today, more anxious maybe, or just scattered. Her elbow knocked the empty cream cheese wrapper to the floor, and she didn't seem to even notice.

Sibia grabbed the bottle of vanilla and righted it. "I'll admit, I've never heard of salted honey."

"It's similar to salted caramel. The salt in the honey boosts the flavor and gives it a beautiful golden color and a caramel-like taste and appearance."

Bailey was listening to Charlotte but watching the puzzled look on her friend's face. Evie licked the tip of her finger, dipped it into her sugar canister, touched the granules to her tongue, then made the same grimace as before.

"Sugar and butter should've been sweet, but Evie's face looks like she just tasted roadkill," Bailey whispered to Griff.

In a move that probably fooled everyone but Bailey and Griffin, who'd been watching her for the last few minutes, Evie *accidentally* knocked her bowl *and* the canister of sugar to the floor. The metal mixing bowl hit the stage with a clang, and creamed butter splattered across the floor.

Sibia whipped her head around and reached out a hand, as if trying to save the fallen bowl.

"Oh no," Evie cried in an Oscar-worthy display of dismay. "It's all ruined. I'll have to start over. Do we have more sugar in the back?"

"You can use some of mine," Spike said, passing her his honeycomb-shaped canister. "I only need a few more tablespoons, so I'm happy to share."

"Thanks, Spike," Evie said, reaching for a clean mixing bowl and fresh measuring cup.

"That was weird," Bailey whispered.

Griff scowled as he nodded. "Yeah, it was. There was obviously something wrong with her sugar. But the way she looked at her fellow contestants makes me wonder if she suspected one of them of messing with it."

"That's what I thought too."

"Shh." Aunt Marigold shushed them from her seat behind them.

The sugar incident had cost Evie valuable time, and she was going to have to stay focused and hustle to catch up to the other contestants.

Gregory hurried out and whisked away the mess on the floor as Toby kept the camera on Sibia. Avoiding the sugary mess, she crossed to Spike's kitchen area and asked him about his dessert.

"I'm making the most incredibly moist and delicious vanilla honey cupcakes you've ever tried. And I'll be piping a honey and cinnamon cream cheese frosting on top of them, so they'll look like little honeycombs." He held up a clear jar full of tiny yellow candied bumblebees. "Then I'll decorate the honeycombs with these little sugar bees."

Bailey smiled. She couldn't help loving the fact that the big tough biker dude was piping frosting on cupcakes, to create honeycombs, and then adding adorable candy bees.

"I created the frosting myself, but the honey cake was originally my grandmother's recipe." Spike grinned as he lifted his chin to the petite, silver-haired woman cheering for him in the audience. "Hey, Mee-maw."

"Hey, sugar," she called back.

Spike was close to a foot taller than her, so Sibia had to tilt her head back as she smiled up at him. "That's sweet. Seems like you're really close to your grandma."

"I am. Both my folks worked a lot, so she practically raised me. And she's the one who taught me how to cook."

"I love that," Sibia said. "And I can't wait to try your honey cupcakes." She moved to Evie's station next. "Speaking of being close to your grandma, I heard you run a coffee shop and bakery with your grandmother."

"I do," Evie said, shooting a proud smile at Rosa. "And I'm also adapting a recipe for a honey cake that came from my abuela. But mine will be a three-layer cake with a sweet-cream honey frosting, topped with a gorgeous, glistening honey butterscotch glaze that will drip off the sides like shiny raindrops."

"I can't wait to see how you do that," Sibia said. "It sounds incredible."

"It will taste incredible too," Evie said, offering the camera one of her charm-filled grins and a saucy wink.

The hall filled with the scents of baked sugar, vanilla, and the crushed and roasted nuts Charlotte had used in her baklava. Both Charlotte and Evie seemed a little off their game today, but Sibia shone as she enchanted the audience with clever anecdotes and sparkling wit. The audience in the hall seemed to hold its breath, then exhale, as each contestant placed their stunning desserts in front of the judges, who tasted each one.

The new mayor kept a poker face, but the delight of Leon, the medical examiner, was written all over his face as he groaned and gushed over the delicious flavors and mouthwatering dishes.

As before, Evie and Spike stood together, and Charlotte stood a little farther away. Her apron was a mess of sticky honey and cookie crumbs. She kept her eyes trained on the judges and clutched a glass measuring cup to her chest as if it were a security blanket.

Mayor Bracken stood to address the contestants, and a rustle sounded as the bulk of the audience leaned forward. "You all have outdone yourselves today. Every one of these desserts is a spectacular taste sensation. Judging this Bake-Off has been such a mixed blessing for us. The great part is that we get to try all these amazing dishes, but the terrible part is that we have to choose which ones are the best when, honestly, they have all been so good."

The medical examiner stood up next to the mayor. "We want you all to know that every single thing you've prepared has been incredible." Leon turned to the audience. "And we want to encourage you all to go to the contestants' restaurants because they are all remarkable chefs."

"Just tell us who won," someone yelled from the audience. Bailey couldn't be sure, but it sounded a little like Charlotte's husband, Ben.

The mayor raised his hand to the crowd. "Okay, okay. Today was especially difficult." He turned to face Spike and Evie. "You both made a version of a honey cake, and both recipes were incredible. The cakes were moist, the frostings were unique but equally delicious, and none of us had ever tasted anything like that butterscotch glaze. But the standout today was the salted honey cheesecake." He changed his focus to Charlotte. "The cheesecake was sweet and smooth, and the crust was crispy, but the salted honey glaze just put it over the top. Congratulations, Charlotte—you took today's round."

Bailey was expecting Charlotte to jump up and down or burst out in song or do a cartwheel—or just do something that showed the joy she must be feeling, but she just stood there, clutching the measuring cup. Her eyes were wide and glistened with tears, but she didn't move. She blinked, as if in shock, as she whispered, "I won?"

For all her sass, Evie had always had a tender heart, and she wrapped an arm gently around Charlotte's shoulder and kept her voice soft. "Congratulations, Charlotte."

"Today's win has made our job even harder," the mayor continued, seemingly oblivious to Charlotte's odd state of shock. "You have each won a round, and like we said, you are all outstanding chefs and created the most wonderful dishes, but there can only be *one* winner. So, after much deliberation, the winner of this year's Bee Festival Bake-Off is—"

Mayor Bracken's announcement was cut off by a bloodcurdling scream coming from backstage.

"Somebody help," Imani yelled as she came running around the curtain from backstage. "He's dead! Rex is dead."

Chapter Nine

Rex is dead?

Bailey couldn't quite grasp what Imani had said. How could Rex be dead? She'd just seen him the night before. She realized she'd put her hand in front of Daisy, using the universal mom motion of a seat belt. Although Bailey wasn't sure even an actual seat belt could protect her daughter from a dead body.

The hall had gone deathly quiet, as if the whole room were holding its collective breath.

Then Charlotte dropped the glass measuring cup she was holding. It shattered as it hit the floor, spraying broken shards of glass across the stage. As if the crash released them from their stupor, the room broke into pandemonium. Some people started crying while others ran for the exits, as if death might be contagious, or perhaps in terror of becoming the next victim. They'd all seen the news stories of active shooters, but there hadn't been any shots.

And that was Bailey's best friend on the stage.

Griffin was the only one who hadn't frozen at Imani's announcement. He'd shot out of his seat like a cannon firing and leaped onto the stage to get to Evie.

Bailey moved her arm from in front of Daisy to behind her as she wrapped her daughter in a hug. "Are you okay?"

Daisy nodded. Then as though reading her mother's mind, she said, "Yes, I'm fine. Go be with Aunt Evie."

She pressed her daughter into the waiting arms of her great-aunts. "Stay here." She glanced from her daughter to Marigold and Aster. "And if I yell for you to run, you run."

"We'll protect her with our lives," Marigold said.

And Bailey knew she meant it. She ran up onto the stage to be with Evie, but her friend and Griff were already heading backstage with Spike. Toby had set down his camera in order to be able to fold Sibia into his arms in a big bear hug.

Charlotte stood frozen in place, her mouth opening and closing like that of a shellshocked fish. Her husband ran up the steps in front of Bailey, and Charlotte let out a sob as she clung to Ben's chest.

Bailey clambered after Evie and Griff, following them backstage and toward the open door of the supply closet. Gregory had been the first to reach the closet after Imani, and Bailey assumed Rex must be inside, from the way Gregory's face turned green and he turned and sprinted to the nearest trash can.

Griff and Spike were the next to arrive, and the bartender held his arms out to protect Bailey and Evie from seeing what was inside the closet.

"I've seen a dead person before," Bailey said, peering around him to where Rex lay on the floor of the closet.

Yikes. She *had* seen a dead body, but not one whose skull had been partially crushed by a yellow KitchenAid mixer.

She covered her mouth and swallowed down the bile rising in her throat.

Drawing in a deep breath, she tried not to focus on the lifeless corpse but instead on the details of the scene. A man had died, which was horrible, but this was still a great opportunity for a mystery writer to observe a dead body and what looked to be a crime scene. Unless Rex had whacked himself on the head with a mixer.

The celebrity host was lying on the floor of the closet, a pool of blood circling his shattered skull. She avoided looking at his open, unseeing eyes and let her gaze travel down his body. He was wearing tan shorts and a blue golf shirt. She tried to remember what clothes he'd had on the last time she'd seen him, but he'd been wearing a bear suit then.

His arms were outstretched, and Bailey gasped as she saw the black leather spiked bracelet he clutched in one hand. Where would he have gotten a hold of that? Her heart raced in her chest. No way—not from Evie. She hazarded a quick look at her friend, who was staring in horror at something just beyond the body.

Bailey followed her gaze and bit back a cry as she recognized the gold spike-heeled sandal that lay on its side at the edge of the pool of blood. Drops of red were splattered across the heel and the thin straps. But why was there only *one* shoe? Where was the other sandal?

Her gaze traveled around the rest of the room, which was about the size of an average walk-in closet. The shelves were lined with paper products and cleaning supplies, and one whole side had been dedicated to supplies for the Bake-Off. The top two shelves held mixing bowls and the various tools needed for baking, like blenders, food processors, and extra mixers. The lower shelves held the needed ingredients called for in the contestant's recipes. Bailey had stacked the jars of spices and bags of sugar and flour herself. But she hadn't been in the closet since yesterday afternoon, when she'd help gather all the ingredients needed for today's dessert round.

The Bake-Off volunteers had filled a tub the night before with each contestant's required ingredients for the next day. They kept them on the tables set up backstage, ready to move to the kitchen stations each morning before the contestants arrived. So there was a chance that no one had been in the closet since yesterday afternoon.

Although, if Spike hadn't loaned Evie his sugar cannister, someone might have discovered Rex's body sooner.

They'd all seen Rex at the Bear Run, but Bailey couldn't recall if he'd met up with the group for ice cream in the park. She couldn't remember seeing him at all after the race had started.

She looked up at the empty space on the shelf where the KitchenAid mixer had been sitting the last time she'd been in the supply closet. Had Rex been in here all night? Or had the mixer fallen on him this morning? She remembered Sibia saying it looked like his bed hadn't been slept in.

Bile threatened her throat again as she thought about his dead body being in here all night. Had the hit from the mixer killed him right away, or had he called for help in the empty hall? There was only one person who could answer those questions.

"We need to call the coroner," she said to no one in particular.

"I'm here," a voice said from behind them.

Bailey turned to see Leon Foster, the medical examiner, who had also been serving as a judge for the Bake-Off.

"Thank goodness," she told him. The two of them had developed a rapport the last time they'd hung out with a dead body.

He leaned down close to Bailey's ear. "It's a good thing I was here. I heard this guy was just *dying* to meet me."

Bailey let out a soft chuckle. She really did like this guy. Inappropriate coroner humor and all.

"Everyone please step back and refrain from touching anything," Leon said, lowering his tone as he took charge of the scene. "One of my assistants was here at the fairgrounds, getting a corn dog, so I've asked her to bring my kit from the car. Until then, I need you all to return to your seats and wait for the sheriff's department to arrive. I'm sure they're going to want to get a statement from each of you."

Careful not to touch anything, he knelt next to the body and started taking pictures with his phone. Bailey thought she heard him mutter something about wishing he'd asked her to bring him a corndog too. How could he even think of eating at a time like this?

Bailey pulled her phone from her pocket. "We need to call Sawyer."

"I'm here," he said from behind her.

She turned to see Sawyer walking toward the closet. "How'd you get here so fast?"

"I was already heading this way, to check on who won the Bake-Off, when I heard all the commotion. Doesn't take long for news like this to spread around here."

Hmm. So far everyone Bailey had said they should call immediately had showed up behind her. Would it be bad form for her to nonchalantly suggest calling Chris Hemsworth? Or perhaps to say that Hugh Jackman was needed at the scene? He'd played a detective in a movie once, hadn't he?

Stop it. They'd already had one celebrity show up in Humble Hills, and things weren't working out so well for him. Best to leave Chris and Hugh alone. *For now.*

Sawyer leaned his head into the closet. "Hey, Doc," he said to Leon, "this doesn't look good."

"Not for this guy. I've got my assistant bringing my other camera, but I thought I'd grab a few shots with my phone. I took a few angles of his black eye and that scratch on his cheek. Looks like maybe he was drinking a protein shake or something chocolaty in that water bottle by his hand. Also took some shots of the mixer, the bracelet, and the shoe." Leon pointed to the blood-splattered sandal.

Bailey watched Sawyer's expression. Maybe he wouldn't recognize it.

The sheriff looked from the sandal to Bailey and raised one eyebrow. Of course he recognized it. He had unbuckled the thing and seductively slid it off her foot just a couple days before. Well, maybe not *seductively* . . . but he had unbuckled it and removed it from her foot.

"I gotta get out of here," Gregory said, wiping the sweat from the top of his lip on the corner of his sleeve. "I may get sick again."

"Imani, the makeup artist, is the one who found Rex," Bailey told Sawyer. "Then Gregory was the next person who saw him."

Sawyer nodded to the stage director. "You can go out to the other side of the curtain, but I'll need you to stick around and give your statement to myself or one of my deputies." He pointed to Imani, Gregory, Sibia, and Toby, who were all standing together. "In fact, I'm going to need statements from all of you. And I wouldn't book your plane tickets home either. Not until we have a better handle on this situation."

Gregory groaned, and Bailey offered him a conciliatory frown. "Sorry you all have to stay longer."

He shrugged. "It's not that big of a deal. Especially considering the circumstances. And we were planning to stay for the entire festival anyway. At least the hotel has comfortable beds." He jerked a thumb at the cameraman. "Although that guy can sleep anywhere. Once he's out, nothing wakes him up. Whether he's napping on the office sofa or curled up in the back of the van, I swear he sleeps like the dead." He winced and glanced toward the supply closet door. "No offense."

"I'm sure there's none taken," Bailey assured him.

She watched him and the other crew members head around the curtain. Sibia had her arm around Imani's shoulder. They passed a petite, dark-haired woman heading backstage, carrying a sturdy black plastic case in one hand and a greasy paper sack in the other. She moved toward Leon and passed him both items.

Looks like he may have gotten a corndog after all.

Leon opened the case, and the two of them pulled out gloves and a stack of clear bags and began to work, collecting evidence and photographing the scene.

Bailey didn't realize Sawyer was right behind her again until he spoke next to her ear.

"That's Jin Nakamura. She's the assistant medical examiner," he told her.

"I figured."

"She's not the only assistant around here. When I walked in, your great-aunts told me they haven't let anyone leave and have been recording the names and numbers of everyone in the building."

A grin pulled at the corner of her lip. "Of course they have."

"Aster asked if I would consider deputizing them."

"Would you?"

"I'm thinking about it." He grinned down at her, then his expression turned serious. "You know this is going to be an active crime scene. So we need to talk about calling off the festival."

Bailey's grin died on her lips. "We *can't* call off the festival. There're too many people involved. The vendors count on the income, and we have paid advertisers, not to mention all the kids who have entries on display. There's still *three* days left. Nothing else is going on in here. Can't we just close off this one building and let the rest of the festival continue?"

Two deputies arrived just then, drawing away Sawyer's attention as he got them started taking statements from everyone in the building.

Spike had kept anyone else from coming backstage. And no one was going to try to get by the broad-shouldered bartender. He might have seemed sweet when he was frosting yellow honey cupcakes in the shapes of beehives, but no one wanted to mess with him when he growled out instructions to stay back.

Leon approached the sheriff and lowered his voice as he leaned in to talk to him. Bailey kept her eyes averted, but she may have nonchalantly leaned a little closer too.

"It's gonna take me an hour or so to process the body and the closet. Jin's helping so it will go a little quicker. I'll send her to get the truck here in a bit, then we'll transport the body over to the morgue," Leon told Sawyer. "I'll need to do a full autopsy, but it's not a stretch to say he probably died from blunt force trauma to the head. And from the blood, hair, and skin on the mixer, I'm going to unofficially hazard a guess that *that* was the blunt instrument. Jin and I bagged the bracelet, the shoe, and the mixer. And this was clutched in the deceased's hand." He held up a clear evidence bag, and Bailey forced herself not to gasp at the tiny black and yellow ceramic bee attached to a bouncy spring inside.

Chapter Ten

Bailey waited backstage, mentally taking notes of the procedures of the medical assistant and the sheriff's department as they processed the body and the scene. She could already imagine how she was going to use everything she was learning in her next book. And she cringed as she realized she'd gotten a few things wrong in a few of her previous books.

It took well over an hour to process the scene, and Leon and his assistant amassed quite a stack of evidence bags. Jin had left and come back with a stretcher, and the two of them had zipped Rex's body into a large black bag, then wheeled him out of the hall.

Marigold, Aster, and Daisy were waiting for them when Bailey and Sawyer came out from backstage.

Marigold handed him a stack of papers. "Here you go, Sawyer—I mean, Sheriff. We collected everyone's names, addresses, and phone numbers, and took notes on anything pertinent that they might know about what happened to Rex."

"Anything *pertinent*?" Sawyer asked.

"Don't worry," Aster told him. "We watch plenty of crime shows, so we didn't 'lead' any witnesses. We just wrote down what they told us."

Marigold frowned at her sister. "How could we *lead* anyone to say anything? We don't know anything ourselves." This time, she raised her eyebrow at Sawyer. "Although we did assume that if the host of the show was found dead behind the stage, and the person who found him was in shock and murmuring about 'so much blood,' he probably didn't die of natural causes."

"No comment," Sawyer said, pressing his lips together in a firm line.

"Did you tell the audience Rex had been murdered?" Bailey asked her aunts.

"Shh." Aster swept the room with a furtive glance, but no one seemed to be paying attention to them. "Of course not. We really only asked them for their names and contact info, but people love to talk. Especially during a crisis. Most people just told us where they've been since the last show. Some were crying. But more over the shock of the thing because we did ask those people if they knew Rex. But no one admitted to knowing him personally. Most of them said they just *felt* like they knew him because they'd watched the morning show so often, with him and Rachel Ward."

"I thought I knew him too," Bailey said. "Or at least imagined what his personality would be like. But the real Rex Rafferty was nothing like the sweet, funny guy I've seen on television."

Marigold harrumphed. She'd heard *all* about him putting the moves on Evie. "They say you should never meet your heroes."

"I wouldn't call Rex anyone's hero," Bailey muttered.

"You'd be surprised," Marigold said, pointing to the information they'd collected. "A lot of people loved him. Most people are just shocked or saddened. Not one person acted like Rex was a pig who got what he deserved."

Daisy's eyes widened. "Aunt Marigold."

Bailey's great-aunt looked chagrined. "Well, I didn't mean that he deserved to *die*. But he wasn't a good man. And he acted like a big turd to our Evie. So, he at least deserved a good swift kick in his famous walnuts."

Daisy covered her mouth as a giggle escaped.

"I agree," Bailey said.

Sawyer looked over at her.

She shrugged. "Sorry. But he did. Deserve the swift kick, not the dying thing."

A small growl sounded at the back of Sawyer's throat, but he didn't comment further.

Marigold tapped a page with her pen. "One pertinent piece of information we discovered was that several people mentioned seeing someone in a bear costume going into Edwards Hall."

"That sounds helpful," Bailey said.

"Sure. That narrows it down to just a few hundred people." Sawyer scrubbed a hand over his jaw. "Did anyone happen to mention any *pertinent* characteristics of the bear they saw?"

"That's the thing that makes this information so important. Four different people mentioned seeing someone in a bear suit, but every single one of them had a different description of the bear. One said it was short, one said it was tall, and two said it was medium height."

"That sounds about right for an eye-witness account. Everyone always seems to see the same thing in a different way. And everyone interprets height differently, usually depending on how tall *they* are."

Marigold offered him a pert nod. "I see your point, Sheriff. But I found it interesting that all four gave a different *time* that they saw the bear go into the building. And on that fact, three of them were absolutely sure. A couple of them had their watches ping with a one-mile notification right around the time they saw the bear. So, one swears it was seven fifteen, and the other one claims it was eight thirty. One guy said he was supposed to meet his wife at ten o'clock at the building across from Edwards, and he was mad that it was already five after. He'd just checked his watch when he saw the bear go into the building."

Sawyer shook his head. "What the heck were all those bears going into that building for?"

"There's a restroom in there. And a drinking fountain," Bailey offered. "Or they might have wanted to see the setup for the Bake-Off."

"Could be."

Aster held her phone up to him. "We also took pictures of every person in here, Sheriff. We can send them to your email."

"That was smart," he said, passing her a business card with his email on it.

She tucked the card in her handbag. "We saw them do it on an episode of *Homicide Hunter*. They took pictures of everyone at the scene, then later found on the body a distinctive orange fiber that matched the jacket of one of the guys in a photo. Totally solved the case."

The crowd seemed to be growing restless. Sawyer excused himself and stepped up onto the stage to address the crowd. "Hey, folks, I appreciate your patience. But I'm going to have to ask for just a little more of it."

"Is Rex really dead?" A man with a thick beard, wearing a faded green John Deere hat, called out from his seat at the front of the audience.

The woman next to him elbowed him in the ribs. "Of course he's dead. We just watched 'em wheel him outta here on a stretcher. They don't usually zip the live ones into a body bag."

The man raised his chin toward Sawyer. "I just wanted him to confirm it."

Another murmur went through the crowd, and Sawyer held up his hands to quiet them and the bickering couple. "At this point, I can't confirm or deny anything other than to say there *has* been a fatality, but next of kin will need to be notified before we release any names or information. For now, I need everyone to stay calm and remain in their seats until my deputies clear you to leave. We're just about finished, so if you can bear with us a little longer, we'll try to get you out of here as soon as we can."

Bailey checked her watch as she walked over to meet Sawyer stepping off the stage. "I need to go tell Granny Bee what happened," she told him. "She was giving a class on killer bees, and I can only assume it's still going and she hasn't heard about Rex yet. Otherwise, she would be here. Are you okay if I run across the fairgrounds to let her know what's happening. I'll be back in, like, ten minutes. I promise."

Sawyer frowned but finally relented. "Fine. But everyone else stays here."

"But . . . what about Daisy?" She didn't really want to leave her daughter behind when there was possibly a killer on the loose.

Sawyer's gaze was sincere as he reached for her hand. "I'll keep an eye on her. She'll be safe here with me."

Bailey nodded and then turned away before he caught the tears that had sprung to her eyes.

What was wrong with her? Must be her allergies acting up.

He was just being nice. But it meant something to her that he cared about her daughter.

She told Daisy to wait while she went to get Gran, then hurried across the fairgrounds to the building where the killer bee program was being held.

Granny was still presenting when Bailey slipped into the back of the room. Her audience was small but seemed to be held captive by the interesting subject. "So, remember what I told you," Granny was saying. "A single killer bee is no deadlier than your average honeybee. They have less venom, shorter wings, and are smaller. But their major difference is the way they defend their nest. When an average honeybee's colony is threatened, about ten percent of the bees come out to defend their home. When a killer bee's colony is threatened, they empty the nest to attack their assailant. With every sting, they release a pheromone that signals more bees to join them in the attack."

A teenage boy in the front row raised his hand. "How many bees does it take to kill someone?"

"Good question," Granny said. "It takes about a thousand stings to kill an average adult. But they've been known to have hundreds of thousands of bees in their swarms. You can see why they get their nickname." She winked at the boy. "And don't think you can outsmart them by hiding underwater. Those bees are determined, and they'll wait you out and continue their onslaught when you come up for air."

"Cool," the boy said.

Granny concluded her program, and Bailey waited as she took a few more questions from the audience. As the questions wound down, Bailey caught her grandmother's eye and waved.

Granny smiled, but then her expression turned to concern as she hurried toward her.

"What's going on?" Granny Bee's brows knit together as she took Bailey's hands and squeezed them in hers. "You're pale, and your hands are freezing."

Bailey leaned closer to her grandmother and lowered her voice. "It's Rex."

Bee huffed. "What about him? Does he need the festival committee to iron his underwear now or maybe pick the raisins out of his Raisin Bran?"

Bailey shook her head. "No, it's not that. He's dead."

"Dead?" Granny repeated.

"Shh. Keep your voice down. We don't want to cause a panic or give Sawyer a reason to shut the festival down."

"Shut the festival down? He can't do that. There's still three days left. We haven't even crowned the Queen Bee in the pageant yet. And so many people are counting on this festival."

Somehow Bailey didn't think Sawyer's decision about shutting down the festival would hinge on the crowning of the Queen Bee.

"I know. That's what I told him," she said. "I'm trying to convince him to just seal off the crime scene in Edwards Hall and let the festival continue."

Granny's eyes widened. "Crime scene?"

Oops. Apparently, she'd buried the lede.

"Yeah. It looks like Rex was *murdered*."

Chapter Eleven

Bailey and Granny Bee hurried back to Edwards Hall. A deputy let them in, but the hall seemed much quieter than when Bailey had left. It looked like they'd released most of the people in the audience. The news crew were sitting together in a cluster of chairs by the stage. Marigold, Aster, and Daisy appeared to be compiling their paperwork with the deputies. And Sawyer was talking to Evie and Griffin. His expression was grim, and Evie looked scared, an emotion that Bailey hadn't seen often on her friend's face.

"What's going on?" Bailey said as she approached the tightly huddled group.

Griffin's mouth was set in a tight line. "The sheriff was just telling us that he needs to take Evie down to the station for questioning."

Bailey looked at Sawyer. "What? Why?"

The sheriff sighed. "Bailey, you know why. Besides the fact that Rex was holding *her* bracelet, and one of *her* shoes was sitting in his blood, she had an altercation with him two days ago and threatened to kill the guy."

"Who told you that?"

"It doesn't matter. But I know *you* were there too. And you heard her say it."

Who blabbed their big fat mouth?

"Come on, Sawyer. That was just a figure of speech. She didn't mean she was actually going to *kill* him." Although she had been pretty angry.

"It sounds to me like she was pretty mad at the guy."

"With good reason," Bailey hissed.

Sawyer gave her a sideways glance. "Now don't go giving me a reason to take you in too."

"It's fine, Bailey. I want to go. Really. I know I didn't do this, and I want to do what I can to clear my name. So, I'm happy to go down and answer Sawyer's questions. It's not that big of a deal."

But they all knew it *was* a big deal. A dead guy had just been found holding Evie's bracelet. And her shoe was resting in a pool of his blood.

Bailey knew in her heart that Evie hadn't killed Rex. She *hoped* Sawyer knew that too. But he was the sheriff, and he had to follow the evidence. And right now, the evidence was pointing straight at her best friend.

"Okay. But if you're going to the sheriff's office, I'm coming with you," Bailey said.

Griff reached for Evie's hand and twined his fingers with hers. "I'm coming too."

Bailey stopped for a second on their way out of the building, to talk to Granny Bee. "They're taking Evie down to the station for questioning. I want to go with her. Can you take Daisy home with you?"

"Of course. I'll call Lyle to come pick us up. And then I'm calling an emergency meeting of The Hive, so bring Evie back to the ranch with you when she's finished. We won't let her go through this alone. Tell her we won't stop until we figure this out."

* * *

Later that night, after Evie had given her statement and a voluntary DNA swab, she, Bailey, and Griff headed back to the ranch house where Granny and The Hive were waiting.

Aster, Marigold, Rosa, and Daisy were seated around the kitchen table when they walked in. Cooper had been under Daisy's chair, but he came out and padded over to greet Bailey. She bent down, sinking to her knees, to hug the furry golden retriever.

Granny came in from the kitchen, carrying a simple charcuterie board covered with crackers, meats, and cheeses. Little bunches of grapes were interspersed among the cheeses, and a small bowl of olives sat on one corner of the board while a similar-sized bowl of almonds sat on the other.

"I figured we'd need the protein," Granny said, setting the board in the center of the table. "I think we have a long night ahead of us."

"I feel like I've already had a long night," Evie said, sinking into the seat next to her abuela.

Rosa put an arm around her shoulder and rubbed her back. "I'm so sorry, mi vida. We all know you didn't kill anyone, even if the estupido police don't."

Evie sighed. "They aren't stupid. They're just doing their jobs. Of course they're going to question me. *My* things were found with the body. And I really did threaten to kill the guy."

"You know, I was thinking about that. Not about you threatening to kill Rex, but about your things being found with the body." Bailey slid into the chair next to her daughter and reached for a cracker. "We can't deny that the sandal belonged to you. That's a given. And you did have a leather bracelet like that, but so did Spike. And the coroner found a small ceramic bee on a spring, just like the ones Charlotte wore on her headbands, clutched in Rex's hand. So, if the bracelet belonged to Spike, and the bee belonged to Charlotte, then it would appear that Rex was holding one item from each contestant. Which seems like just too much of a coincidence for him to have grabbed all three of those as he was getting whacked in the head with a KitchenAid."

"And I don't believe in coincidences," Griff interjected.

"Neither do I," Bailey said. "It just seems so obvious that all three of those things were planted to point suspicion at the Bake-Off contestants. And if *we* can see that so clearly, Sawyer will too." She turned to Evie. "I mean, come on—are we supposed to believe you dressed up in your fancy heels, lured Rex to a supply closet to kill him, and then fled the scene, leaving one sandal behind, like some kind of murderous Cinderella?"

"I hope not," Evie replied. "Because we all know that size nine sandal is going to fit my big foot perfectly."

"We all know you didn't kill Rex, honey." Granny repeated what Bailey had already said. "Now we just need to prove it."

Evie quirked an eyebrow at her. "How do you suggest we do that?"

"I agree with Bee," Marigold said. "We're a group of smart and resourceful women, so we'll use those smarts and our ingenuity to prove you're innocent. We've already solved one murder this summer. We can solve another. We just need to do some digging and see what we can unearth."

Granny found a spiral notebook and a pen. She wrote *Rex's Murder Notebook* on the front.

"Umm . . . maybe you should rethink that title," Bailey told her. "That makes it look like we're creating a *plan* to kill him."

"Oops. You're right." Granny wrote the words *Ideas to Solve* above the others. "There. That ought to fix it. Now, we just need to think through this logically." She opened the notebook to a clean page. "We should start with a list of suspects. I'll write down everyone we can think of who had a reason to want Rex dead."

"Good," Marigold agreed. "Then we can go through each one and figure out if they had the MMO to kill him."

"What's MMO?" Daisy asked, leaning forward to get a better look at the notebook.

"Means, motive, and opportunity," Aster filled in. "We heard that term on a true crime podcast last week. But it makes perfect sense. Then, I say that after we make the list, we go through all the suspects and interview or question each one, and either move them higher up the list if they seem guilty or cross them off if they're innocent." She looked at Griffin, who used to be a police officer and was the only one in the room who actually had any real investigative experience in solving a homicide. "What do you think, Griff?"

He shrugged. "Sounds like a reasonable place to start. And I plan to do a little digging into Rex's background after I get back to the hotel and can access my laptop."

"Good," Granny said, holding her pen poised over the paper. "Now, who should we list first?"

Evie picked up an olive. "I think we should start with the most obvious suspects first—myself, Spike, and Charlotte—since our things were found with the body. Then the television crew should be next. No one in town even knew Rex. But the crew have all been working with him and would have the most incentive to murder the guy. I know if I had to work as closely with him as they do, I probably *would* end up killing him."

Bailey smacked her forehead. "Please don't say that in front of Sawyer." She turned to her grandmother. "Can you think of any of the festival volunteers that he might've upset?"

Granny Bee shook her head. "Not enough to kill him. I mean MaryAnn Sanders complained about having to cut up all those lemon wedges, but Aster and Marigold were the ones who took on the job of removing all those dad-blamed red M&M's, which seemed much more of a pain in the tush."

Aster nodded. "It was a pain. But not enough of one to consider offing the guy over."

Bailey cringed. Her great-aunt sounded like an Italian mobster. Although most mobsters probably didn't discuss "offing" someone over chocolate candies.

Granny ticked off the names on the list. "Evie, Spike, Charlotte, Toby, Sibia, Gregory, and Imani. That's a pretty short list."

"It only took *one* person to murder him." Bailey rolled a slice of salami and balanced it on a cracker. "Now we just need to go through and figure out where everyone was when Rex was murdered, and discern who had a motive to kill him."

Marigold looked at Evie. "Since you're at the top of the list, we might as well start with you. Can you tell us where you were when Rex was murdered?"

Aster held up her hand. "Wait. Do we even know *when* he was killed?"

"Not exactly," Bailey said. "I know the last time I saw him was before the Bear Run. So, until we find someone who saw him after that, we have to assume it was sometime between seven o'clock last night and eight o'clock this morning, when everyone started arriving for the Bake-Off."

"I went back to Griff's for a bit after the Bear Run," Evie said, and Bailey noted the way her cheeks went a little pink with color. "I went home around ten and went straight to my room. I spent about an hour prepping for this morning, then went to bed."

Granny looked over at Evie's grandmother. "Rosa, did you talk to her? Or hear her come in?"

Rosa shook her head. "No. I'm sorry, my sweet. After volunteering all day, I was beat. I went home after the Bear Run and fell into bed. I didn't even wash my face. I didn't hear anything or wake up until this morning. I was so tired, I slept like the dead." She winced. "Maybe that wasn't the best word choice."

Marigold frowned as she turned back to Evie. "So, basically what you're saying is that you have no alibi."

Chapter Twelve

Bailey's heart broke for her friend as Evie slumped farther down into her chair.

"I guess not," Evie said.

Aster patted her on the arm. "Well, I'm sure you're not the only one. Now it's up to us to figure out who else was unaccounted for. And who had a better motive for wanting him dead."

"And this list is a great place to start," Bailey assured her.

Daisy pushed back from her chair. "I'm going to go start a file on my laptop for each suspect, where we can record everything we find." Cooper followed at her heels as she ran up the kitchen stairs.

A knock sounded on the front screen door, followed by a greeting in Sawyer's deep voice. "Hey, everybody," he said, sauntering into the kitchen. "Looks like I'm missing a party."

"Oh, sugar," Granny tutted, "don't you know that every day you get to spend with us is a party?"

Sawyer smiled, but Bailey saw the weariness in his eyes. She motioned to the seat next to hers that Daisy had just vacated. "You want to sit down? Have some cheese and crackers?"

He shook his head. "I don't have time to stay and chat. I have to get back to the station. I was just stopping by on my way out to my place, to grab a fresh shirt. Me and my coffee had a little disagreement over whether it should go in my mouth or down my front. Apparently, the coffee won." He looked down at the dried brown stain on the front of his uniform.

Marigold stood up and headed for the kitchen. "I'll make you a plate to go."

"That'd be mighty nice of you," he said, then narrowed his eyes suspiciously at the group. "So, what prompted this little get-together? Seems a little late for book club."

Granny huffed. "It's never too late for book club."

"Yeah, we were just discussing what book we should read next." Aster's hand fluttered nervously to her neck.

"Really?" Sawyer's tone conveyed that he didn't believe them for a second. "Seems strange to be talking books when you're in the middle of the Bee Festival and a dead body was just discovered during the Bake-Off today."

Marigold pointed a finger at him. "Oh, that's right. Have you found the person who did it yet?"

The sheriff's gorgeous blue eyes narrowed even further. "No. Not yet. But you all don't fool me for a minute. That's another reason I stopped by—to remind you all that *I* am the sheriff, and my department of *trained investigators* will be working this case."

Marigold huffed. "*You* might be trained, Sawyer, but that Deputy Crawford—he's Pearl's youngest boy, and I don't think he could investigate himself out of a paper bag. He didn't even learn to tie his own shoes until the fourth grade."

"Now, don't be hateful, sister," Aster said. "A lot of kids have trouble with that nowadays, what with Velcro sneakers and all those funny crocodile shoes."

"I love my Crocs," Evie said. "They're super comfortable. Especially at the restaurant."

"Really?" Aster asked. "I'll admit I've never worn them. Do you think I should try a pair?"

"For sure," Evie told her. "They have them in all sorts of fun colors. Even glittery ones."

"Ohh, I love glitter."

Sawyer took off his cowboy hat and scrubbed a hand through his hair. "Ladies, please. As much as I love a good discussion about comfortable glittery shoes, my point is that *my* department will be handling the investigation. And we do not need you all's help or interference."

"Why, Sawyer." Granny waved a dismissive hand in his direction. "We wouldn't *dream* of interfering with an investigation."

"We weren't even thinking about the murder," Aster told him.

Daisy's voice carried as she came pounding back down the stairs and into the kitchen.

"I printed off our list of suspects . . ." She stopped mid-step as she saw Sawyer. Then, without missing a beat, she smiled sweetly and handed the sheet of paper to him. "For you, of course."

"Of course," he repeated dryly as he took the offered page. He let his gaze travel over every woman in the room, pausing just long enough on Bailey to make the back of her neck heat. "I'm only going to say this *once*. I do *not* need your help with this investigation." He shook his head and let out an exasperated sigh. "Aw, hell. Who am I kidding? I've *already* said it twice. And I'm sure I'll be saying it more times again. But I am asking you—no, I'm begging you—to please keep your noses out of this case."

This time, the look Granny Bee offered him was more shrewd than mock innocent. "Like I said, Sawyer, we wouldn't dream of interfering. Just tell us that Evie is no longer on your list of suspects."

He sighed again. "You know I can't do that."

"Then I'm afraid you'll have to get used to our noses."

He muttered something that sounded like "Incorrigible," then dismissed them with a wave of his hand as he turned and headed for the door. "I have to get back to the station."

"Sawyer," Bailey called, pushing out of her chair to go after him. She caught up to him on the front porch. It wasn't much of a run to the porch, but she felt breathless just the same. Maybe that was more to do with the broad-shouldered man who had turned to stare at her with a set of the most gorgeous, smoldering blue eyes. But she couldn't think about that smolder now. "She's my best friend," Bailey told him. "You know I have to help her if I can."

Her eyes widened, and a tiny gasp escaped her as he took a step forward and swept her into his arms. He held her tightly against him, then pressed a hard kiss against the side of her forehead.

His breath was warm against her ear, sending even warmer tingles throughout her body. "When I heard someone had been found dead at the Bake-Off, I thought my heart would stop. I couldn't get there fast enough to make sure you and Daisy were okay." He swallowed and his voice came out huskier than before. "Not much scares me anymore, but the thought of something happening to you . . . now . . . after we finally found each other again . . . that terrifies me."

She blinked back tears as she looked up at him. He gently brushed her bangs from her forehead, and his eyes held hers as if trying to convey the feelings he couldn't figure out how to say. Then his gaze dropped to her mouth, and she knew exactly what he was feeling. And all those warm tingles she'd been having a minute ago now turned to molten lava in her veins.

He leaned closer, and Bailey inhaled a soft breath as her lips parted in anticipation. She could already feel the warm press of his lips to hers. But instead of taking her mouth in a passionate kiss, he only leaned his forehead against hers, and she died a little inside.

"Please, Bailey," he whispered. And she knew she would do just about anything for him—whatever he asked. "Please stay safe. And don't try to solve this murder."

Anything but that.

* * *

It was close to nine that night when Bailey drove Evie back to the fairgrounds to get her car. She'd left it there earlier, when Griff had driven her to the sheriff's office for questioning. He'd offered to bring her back to get it that night, but Bailey had needed to run into town for milk anyway, so she'd said she would do it. They'd promised to be extra careful and stay together, until they both drove away.

Bailey pulled up next to Evie's red convertible Mustang, and they both stared through the windshield at Edwards Hall in front of them. The appearance of two small strips of yellow caution tape crisscrossed over the handle of the door was the only indication that something had happened in the building.

"It's weird that we saw a dead guy today, right?" Evie asked.

Bailey nodded. "So weird."

"Who do *you* think killed him?"

"I have no idea. It seems like our list of suspects should be longer since the guy was such a douche canoe."

Evie huffed out a small laugh, but then her breath hitched as she let out a sigh. "Do you really think we can figure out who did it?"

"We're going to try." Bailey picked up her friend's hand and gave it a quick squeeze. "Look, we've got a solid plan and a list of suspects, and we'll start interviewing them tomorrow. That's what the detectives do in my books to solve crimes."

"Yeah, but your books are fictional. That was a *real* dead body in there. With *real* blood. And *my* very real shoe sitting in it."

"I know. And that part is scary, but this is how the real police do it too. They start by asking questions and piecing together the facts of the victim's life and then figuring out who had a motive and the means to kill him."

A tiny grin formed at the corner of Evie's mouth. "MMO?"

"Exactly."

"But we don't know anything about the guy. Certainly not enough to know who had it in for him."

"Okay. So, what *do* we know?"

"We know he liked drinking fancy water and was a super freak about red M&M's."

Bailey laughed. "Check and check. What else?"

"We know he made seriously inappropriate advances toward me. And Imani hinted to you that he'd done the same—or maybe worse—to others."

Bailey had told her about the conversation she'd had with the makeup artist regarding Rex's behavior. "Yeah, it's the 'maybe worse' part that gets to me. What if he went too far with one of the women on the crew?"

"But there's only Imani and Sibia here."

"So, we'll just ask them tomorrow—point blank—if Rex ever got physical or crossed the line with them."

Evie nodded. "I think their reactions will tell us a lot."

"Good. That's another step in our plan. What else do we know about Rex?"

"He wears expensive cologne and likes lavish surroundings, like a half-a-million-dollar luxury motor home."

"I wonder how long it will take Helen Dobbs to come get it," Bailey mused. They both seemed lost in thought as they stared through the windshield. Suddenly, Bailey turned and quirked an eyebrow at her friend. "Are you thinking what I'm thinking?"

Evie offered her an innocent shrug. "I am if you're thinking that we need to get inside that trailer before Helen reclaims it and hauls it off the fairgrounds."

Chapter Thirteen

Bailey scanned the empty parking lot and even emptier fairgrounds. She could see the corner of the motor home sticking out around the side of the building. "We could just take a quick peek."

Evie nodded. "In and out. Wouldn't take but a minute."

"We could wear gloves."

"I have some in my purse."

"What harm could it do?"

"It won't hurt anything to just look."

They reached for their purses at the same time then gave each other a nod before slipping out of the car and quietly closing the doors. No sense drawing attention to themselves, just in case someone was still hanging around the fairgrounds.

Bailey slipped her crossbody purse over her neck, not sure what she had brought her bag for. It was not like she was going to go shopping or make a purchase while they were breaking into a murder victim's residence.

She looked up at the neighboring buildings. "I hope there aren't any cameras on the fairgrounds."

"We should have brought our disguises."

"Ugh, no. We should *not*. In fact, I hope you burned that red hooker wig you made me wear last time we broke into a house."

"It belonged to my nieces. Of course I didn't burn it."

"Somebody should have." Bailey let out a shudder at the memory of wearing the long-haired wig and how it made her look like a prostitute with a bad dye job. So, of course that's when Sawyer had caught her in the house. She was lucky he hadn't shot her. Or tried to shoot the roadkill-looking thing off her head.

The two women walked casually across the fairgrounds, as if they had every right to be there. They approached the motor home quietly, and both surveyed the area around it. There was a small light shining inside, but no movement in or around the RV.

A few pairs of plastic gloves from the café were usually rolling around in Evie's bag. She and Bailey pulled them on, and then Evie pulled a rectangular pouch from her purse. "You shine the flashlight on the doorhandle, and I'll pick the lock."

Bailey tapped her phone's flashlight on and aimed it at the door. "Since when do you know how to pick a lock?"

Evie set her purse on the ground, took two picks from the pouch, and squatted in front of the door. "Since Griff's been teaching me."

"Why in the heck is he teaching you that?"

"Because I asked him to. I thought it looked like a fun skill to have."

"Most men just take their girlfriends to the movies or out to dinner."

"Griffin Yates is not *most* men."

Good point. And Evie Delgado was not most women.

Griff was obviously a good teacher because Evie sprung the lock within seconds. "Got it," she said with a satisfied grin. She pushed open the door and called softly inside, "Hello? Anybody home?"

They listened for a second, neither expecting anyone to answer, before they slipped inside and pulled the door closed behind them. Two stairs up led them into the living area of the motor home. The kitchen was in front of them, with a counter that doubled as an island and an eating area. A leather sofa sat on one side of the motor home, and two leather recliners sat across from it. Lush carpeting led down a hallway to the bedroom and bath.

Bailey let out a low whistle. "Wow. This thing is nicer than my last apartment."

"I know. Everything in here is total luxury." She gestured to the dishes in the sink and covering the counter. "Too bad Rex was a slob. Who did he think was going to come in and clean this up for him?"

"Probably Sibia."

They ventured farther into the trailer, and Bailey shone her light across the eating area. She pointed to an elaborately decorated apple pie, with one piece missing, that was sitting on the counter next to an empty plate. "Do you see that apple pie?" she asked Evie.

"Yeah, I do."

"Do you see where it came from?" She tilted her phone and lit up a bright yellow box that read "Sunshine Café" on the top.

"Do you think Charlotte was trying to bribe him? Or maybe just butter him up?"

"To do what? He wasn't a judge. He couldn't affect the outcome of the Bake-Off."

"No, but he could spend more time talking to her during the contest. Which might get her more airtime on Rex's show."

They moved down the hall and peeked into the bathroom. Nothing amiss in there—just way too many hair products for one man to be using—although Bailey was surprised at how small the bathroom was in comparison to the rest of the motor home. The tiny space barely held a compact shower, toilet, and small sink.

In the bedroom, the bed was still made, like Sibia had said. But Evie directed her flashlight at the white pillowcase. "Doesn't look like Rex was the only one in this bed. See that mascara and foundation smeared on the pillow?"

Bailey frowned. "You don't think Charlotte would go *that* far to win?"

"No way. I mean, I believe she obviously brought him a pie, but I can't see her doing *this*." She grimaced as she waved her hand toward the bed. "She and Ben have been together since they were sixteen. And they've always seemed happy to me."

"I agree. But there are plenty of women in this town who would jump at the chance to get in bed with a celebrity. Just because *we* know he's a smarmy bastard doesn't mean everyone else does. He might've been an asshat. But he was still a good-looking asshat."

Evie shuddered. "Look around. Besides knowing we're looking for someone with questionable taste in men, and who doesn't know about the spritzer that keeps your foundation off your pillow, is there anything else in here that looks like a clue?" She pointed to the small bedside table. "You check that drawer, and I'll search the pockets of the clothes lying on the floor."

Bailey eased open the drawer, dreading what she would find. She did *not* want to know what Rex Rafferty kept in the drawer of his bedside table. But thankfully, the contents were a mix of the dull and useless—a flat box of Kleenex, a tube of lip balm, a jar of Vicks VapoRub, and a book of matches from Harv's House of Pizza.

"Jackpot," Evie cried, waving a piece of paper in her direction. "I found something."

"Is it a confession from the murderer?"

"No. It's a list."

"What kind of list?"

"I don't know. It's just a list of names. But I feel like it's important."

Bailey scooched around the bed and shone her light on the page. It was creased down the center from being folded over, and looked like it may have been in Rex's pocket for a while. The heading read simply "Humble Hills." Underneath was a list:

1. Carl's Hardware—Carl Davis
2. Harv's House of Pizza—Harvey McCormack
3. Humble Hills Hot Tubs & Spas—Gordy Russell
4. P. J.

Bailey read the names out loud and said, "Okay, we know Carl from the hardware store, and we obviously know Harv. I don't really know Gordy Russell—I think he and Carl were both a few years ahead of us in school. But who's P. J.?"

"I have no idea." Evie frowned. "And I have no idea why Rex would have a list of Humble Hills residents in his pocket. How would he know any of these people if he'd never been here before?"

"Maybe it was just a list of errands he needed to run. Like he wanted to grab a hammer, a slice, and check out a new hot tub. And then eat a peanut butter and jelly sandwich. Or buy some pajamas." Bailey shrugged. "Okay, I'm reaching here. But maybe this list isn't as ominous as it looks."

"Maybe it is."

"We should take a picture of it, then put it back where we found it so Sawyer can find it later."

"You take it," Evie said. "I'm in enough trouble as it is, without having evidence of a B&E on my phone."

Bailey laughed as she tapped her phone's flashlight off and turned the camera on. "You sound like the aunts with all their crime show slang." She snapped a couple of pictures. "Got it. Now let's put that thing back and get out of here. This place is giving me the creeps."

Evie folded the note and carefully slid it back into Rex's jacket pocket as Bailey tucked her phone into her own pocket. Her eyes had adjusted to the dark enough that she could see to get back to the living area of the RV.

They were halfway down the hallway when they froze.

They weren't alone.

Someone was jiggling the door of the motor home.

Chapter Fourteen

Bailey's heart raced as her head whipped from the bedroom back toward the living area. "Hide," she whispered.

Evie clutched her arm as she whispered back, "Where?"

There was literally *nowhere* to hide. Motor homes like this were made to use every conceivable space. They couldn't hide under the bed or in a closet.

The bathroom was on their left. It was a tight space, but it would have to do.

Bailey opened the door and shoved Evie inside then pushed in behind her. Evie crammed herself into the tiny shower, and Bailey crouched on the toilet as she tried to slide the door closed as quietly as possible.

Bailey swallowed, and it felt like the sound of doing so was loud enough to be heard throughout the whole RV. Her muscles were already cramping from the crouching position, and she suddenly had to sneeze. She wiggled her nose as she leaned forward, straining to hear what was happening outside the door.

The camper's door creaked open, followed by the thud of footsteps coming up the two stairs and into the living area. Praying that the intruder didn't come down the hallway or—heaven forbid—have to use the bathroom, she tried to hold as still as possible. Had she always breathed this loud? And why did her leg suddenly itch?

She was tempted to open the door a crack, just to see if they could identify the intruder, but she was afraid the sound of the door would make too much noise and alert the trespasser. More thuds, then the door of the motor home slammed shut.

Bailey let out her breath. "I think they're gone."

"So is the feeling in my arm," Evie said.

Bailey looked over to see Evie pushed back against the wall of the compact shower, her right arm raised above her head and the circular water faucet jammed into her side. As her friend tried to wiggle out of the shower, she knocked into Bailey, who was trying to step down off the toilet. But her legs had cramped up and she fell sideways, right into Evie, whose arm came down and hit the single faucet handle of the shower.

Both women shrieked as cold water shot out of the sprayer nozzle.

"Turn it off," Bailey cried, holding her hands over her face.

"I'm trying," Evie squealed. But as she raised her hand to block the water, she accidentally knocked the sprayer from its holder. Like a snake uncoiling, the hose whipped around, the sprayer shooting water all over the bathroom *and* Evie and Bailey.

Amid more shrieking and some creative swearing, they managed to get the water turned off, but they both got soaked in the process. Bailey's wet hand slipped off the handle as she tried to open the door. She managed it on the second try, and both women fell out of the door, sputtering and soaking wet.

Bailey pushed her sopping bangs from her forehead and looked at Evie, whose hair hung in equally drenched curls. She peered down at her T-shirt clinging to her skin, then back up at Evie's similarly soaked clothes.

A giggle bubbled up in her throat, and she tried to hold it back, but Evie let out a snort of laughter, and that was all it took. They both dissolved into chortling, belly-clutching shrieks of laughter.

Evie pointed at Bailey. "Your hair. It's sticking up like . . ." She couldn't even finish her sentence because she was laughing so hard again.

Bailey crossed her legs and held up her hands as she wheezed out, "Stop. I'm going to wet my pants. Or I'm going to have to squeeze back into that bathroom. Either way, I don't want to leave DNA behind."

"Let's get out of here," Evie said between more bouts of laughter.

They tried to get their giggles under control as they stumbled out of the hallway and into the kitchen area.

Evie stopped, and Bailey smacked into her back. "What's wrong?"

Her friend pointed to the table. Bailey gasped. The pie *and* the Sunshine Bakery box were both gone.

Their laughter had died, and in their haste to get out of the motor home, they practically fell out of the door.

Then they froze again as a bright light blinded them and a deep voice commanded, "Hold it right there."

Bailey held her hand up to shield her eyes as she blinked against the light. Cold water from her hair dripped down her face, and she sputtered, "Sawyer?"

The sheriff lowered the light, but the scowl on his face was almost as glaring. "What in the Sam Hill are you two doing here? And how many margaritas were involved this time?"

"We're totally sober. No margaritas," Bailey assured him, holding her hands up and wiggling her gloved fingers at him. "And I promise, we didn't touch or take anything."

Evie gestured to their wet clothes. "Except the faucet handle when we were hiding in the shower. We did touch that."

"Why were you hiding in the shower?"

"Because someone else came in there while we were searching . . . um . . . I mean looking around the place," Bailey explained.

"Have your guys already been in there?" Evie asked before Sawyer had a chance to inquire about *how* they got into the trailer.

Sawyer nodded. "Yes. Of course we checked out the victim's trailer. My men already went in there this morning and photographed and searched the whole thing."

"Then maybe you should go inside now and look at what's missing from the kitchen table," Bailey told him. "And note that neither one of us is carrying a pie or a yellow takeout bakery box."

"And you should also search the pockets of the jacket lying on the floor in the bedroom." Evie wiggled her fingers. "And again, note that we did *not* take anything."

Technically, they *had* taken a picture. Or two. But this didn't seem the time to point out the technicality.

"Okay, but did you leave something behind?" Sawyer narrowed his eyes. "How do I know you didn't just plant something in the pocket in that jacket?"

Bailey huffed. "Why would we do that?"

"Come on, Bailey." Sawyer sighed and spoke in a tone that conveyed his patience was waning. "Because Evie is a suspect in Rex's murder."

"That may be true," Evie said. "But I didn't do it. And all we're trying to do is figure out who did."

"Well breaking into the victim's trailer is not the way to do that."

"We know. We're sorry. We really are," Bailey said, reaching for Evie's arm and pulling her away from Sawyer. Water squished up through the toes of her tennis shoes. "And we're going to walk straight to our cars and both go immediately home and think about what we've done. Right now."

His scowl stayed in place, but he didn't move to stop them, so they turned and made a break for their cars.

"Call you later," Bailey called as she slid into her driver's seat. She started the engine and followed Evie's Mustang out of the parking lot. Grabbing some napkins from her glovebox, she blotted at her wet hair.

She was halfway home before she remembered she'd forgotten to get the milk.

* * *

The next morning, Bailey had just finished blow-drying her hair when her phone dinged with a text from Evie.

Bakery is buzzing like mad this morning. Can't keep us with the customers. Send help. Need more milk. And eggs, the text read.

On our way, Bailey typed back, then shot a quick text to Granny Bee, who was already at the festival, that she and Daisy were going to help Evie and Rosa at the café.

Twenty minutes later, Bailey and her daughter pushed their way past the line of people on the sidewalk, to get into the restaurant. They'd had to park three blocks away because Main Street was so clogged with cars.

The Spill the Beans Coffee Shop was located on the east side of the downtown area of Humble Hills. The town was laid out in a square, with the courthouse in the center and four streets of shops facing it. The rest of the town spread out from there, with a large park and a neighborhood of old Victorian homes, like Lavender Manor, the one Marigold and Aster lived in, on one end and the fairgrounds and swimming pool on the other end.

The main streets of downtown had been revitalized several years before to embrace the charm and nature of the mountains by adding more cedar and log cabin–style exteriors, stacked pine planters filled with colorful wildflowers, more pine trees, old-fashioned gas lamps, and sage-green awnings over most of the business's front doors. With the mountain range in the background, it was a pretty little town, and seeing the huge bronze statue of the bear that had held court in the town square since she was a little girl always filled Bailey with nostalgia.

The Sunshine Café was on the other side of the square, and a similar line was forming along the sidewalk outside of it.

News travels fast. Bailey figured their restaurants were crowded more from the notoriety of one of their owners being a murder suspect than from word of the delicious dishes they'd made at the Bake-Off.

Evie's brother, Mateo, was manning the coffee bar with Olive Green, a redheaded girl they'd hired that summer after she'd been fired from her job keeping house for the mayor. Griff, wearing a smile and his normal jeans and black T-shirt, with a white apron tied around his waist, held a notepad and was taking orders at a table in the corner.

Bailey blinked. Yes, she was right; he was *smiling*. And apparently charming the three middle-aged women sitting at the table, if their giggly laughter was any indication. Who was this man, and what had he done with her usually grumpy friend?

"Glad you're here," Griff said, striding past her to hand the order through the window to Rosa. "This place is a madhouse. My face hurts from trying to smile at people who are only here to gossip about the murder and get a glimpse of Evie. Like she might be wearing a friggin' T-shirt that says, 'You caught me. I did it.'"

Aww. There was the gruff guy she knew.

She held up the box with the three gallons of milk and six dozen eggs they'd just picked up from the grocery store. "What can we do to help?"

Griff took the box from her. "Rosa, Evie, and the cook are manning the kitchen. Thank goodness Rosa had the foresight to come in early today and make triple the number of pastries she normally does." He nodded to the row of cups lined up on the counter behind Mateo and Olive. "I think they could use help making coffee drinks. And I could use help taking orders and bussing tables."

"We're on it," Bailey said, stashing her purse under the counter and reaching for a couple of clean aprons.

Daisy took one from her and tied it around her waist. "I'll start on the coffee orders." She'd been working at the coffee shop part-time throughout the summer, so she was familiar with the drink recipes and how the coffee bar was set up.

"I'm on waitress duty then." Bailey grabbed an order pad as Griffin filled her in on who had already been helped and who needed something next. She'd done her time as a waitress and had also pitched in at the bakery when Evie was short-staffed, so she was well versed in taking orders, delivering plates, filling coffee cups and water glasses, and bussing tables.

The café itself was an adorable mix of pink, yellows, and teals. Smaller bistro tables for two were spread among wooden four-tops painted bubblegum pink. Small touches of honey and bumblebees were everywhere around the café, from the tiny bee decals on the top rails of the chair backs, to the bumblebees buzzing along the gold wallpaper border at the top of the walls. The dishes had cute bees on the rims of the plates and the sides of the teacups. Small jars of Granny Bee's honey were on every table, and a row of pink-framed bee pictures formed a vertical line in the space next to the front door. It was all so cheery and cute, and it made Bailey smile every time she walked into the bakery.

Someone had left a copy of the *Humble Hills Herald* on a table. Bailey wasn't smiling as she turned the paper to read the headline. "Death by a Bundt Instrument?" was followed by the line "Was there murder on the menu? Could the Bake-Off host have been offed by a contestant?" No wonder Evie and Charlotte's restaurants were crowded. She imagined Spike was having the same rush of business at Hog Wild.

As chaotic as the bakery was, Bailey was glad for the extra business for Rosa and Evie. But she almost lost them a customer when she considered pouring coffee into the lap of a gossipy couple who were laying odds on whether Evie had actually killed Rex.

The morning flew by with a steady line of customers. The topic of the murder seemed to be on everyone's lips, and it was constantly on Bailey's mind as she twisted and turned their list of suspects in her brain, as if they were pieces she was trying to fit into a homicidal puzzle.

She knew one thing for sure: interviewing their list of suspects was going to have to wait.

Chapter Fifteen

Bailey would have liked to take two Advil and a nap after helping to close down the bakery after the lunch rush, but she'd have to settle for ibuprofen and the half a bottle of warm Diet Coke that was still in her cupholder from the day before. The Bee Festival pageant was in full swing, and Granny still needed her help and Daisy's.

She'd hoped she and Evie might be able to talk to Charlotte, but her diner had longer hours and was still hopping when they were leaving.

The pageant was being held in Norris Hall, and Bailey and Daisy slipped into the back of the building just as Marigold was walking out onto the stage.

"This afternoon is the talent competition," Daisy told her as they took a couple of seats toward the back.

Marigold was wearing a long black dress and sensible one-inch platform heels. Her silver hair was smoothed straight and held back in a black clip at her neck. Her expression was somber, and she held her head high and her back straight as she approached the table where a piano keyboard had been set up, in the center of the stage.

She paused, her hands held above the keys, to look out over the audience for a moment before launching into a beautiful, haunting piece of classical music. Bailey couldn't tell a Bach piece from one by Beethoven, but she knew it was a classical number.

"She's really good," Evie whispered as she took the seat next to Bailey.

"She's been playing since she was a girl," Bailey whispered back.

About three-fourths of the way through the sound, the tempo of the music changed. The pace picked up, then Marigold reached below the table and pulled out a flat-brimmed baseball cap as she pushed a button on the keyboard.

"Oh. My. Gosh." Bailey covered her mouth to keep from bursting out in laughter as her great-aunt put the hat on . . . then turned it around, so the brim faced the back.

The keyboard thumped out a hip-hop rhythm as Marigold leaned back, crossed her arms over her chest . . . and proceeded to rap. "I like big books and I cannot lie; my name is Marigold, and I'm pretty fly. Flies like honey, and I like bees. I may be old, but I still got my own knees. I play piano and garden like a boss. I make my own jelly and a mean hot sauce. Don't think I'm soft— named for a flower, 'cause I've got skills and believe in girl power."

The audience was on its feet, cheering and whooping as Marigold tossed her hat into the audience, then hit the button on the synthesizer and went immediately back into the serene strains of the classical piece she'd been playing. She finished with a flourish as she ran her fingers down the keyboard, then stepped back, offering the audience a sly wink. Then she took a bow and marched off the stage.

Bailey, Daisy, and Evie were all on their feet too, jumping up and down as they joined in the wild applause.

"That was amazing," Daisy called over the roar of the crowd.

Evie nudged Bailey's arm. "Did you know your great-aunt could rap?"

"I had no idea. I'm just as surprised as you are." Bailey shook her head, still in shock but loving that Aunt Marigold had just floored the audience.

The crowd took their seats as the next performer came out on stage.

"Oh no." This time Bailey covered her eyes, leaving just enough space to see through them as her Aunt Aster took the stage wearing a glittery red, white, and blue sequined dress and twirling a baton.

Well, not exactly twirling. More like just waving it around. She held the bar firmly in one hand, but rather than twirl it around her arm, she sort of just tilted it back and forth. All the laughter died in the audience, and they cringed as one when the baton slipped out of Aster's hand and went rolling across the stage.

"Darn it," Aster cried, racing after it. She grabbed it off the floor as she murmured, "You know, when you're twenty and you drop something, you pick it up. When you're my age and you drop something, sometimes you just decide you don't need it anymore."

A few people snickered as if they weren't sure if she'd been trying to make a joke or not.

"You know you're getting old when your doctor refers you to an archeologist." She twisted the baton a little more, then spoke directly to the audience. "I tell ya, a lot changes when you get old. You know with age comes wisdom"—she wrinkled her pert nose as she winced—"and hair in really weird places."

That one garnered a few more laughs.

Aster tossed the baton up a few inches and caught it. "I'm actually pretty spry for a gal my age. Although lately my favorite exercises are raising my eyebrows and running out of patience." She tossed the baton again as the audience chuckled. "You know the secret to having a smoking hot body as a senior?" She paused, then went in for the zinger. "Cremation."

As the audience laughed, she put the baton behind her back with one hand, then grabbed it with the other and brought it out in front of her with a flourish, as if she'd just performed a magic trick. "Dating *is* hard at our age, though. You know, my back goes out more often than I do. And as we get older, we tend to get more forgetful. I met a fella on a blind date a few weeks ago. He sat down at the bar next to me and asked, 'So, do I come here often?'"

The audience was really getting into it and laughing with her now.

She set one end of the baton on the stage and leaned on it as if it were a cane and she were doing an old vaudeville act. "I went shopping with my sister last week, and she asked me which underwear I liked best." Aster shrugged. "I told her it *Depends*." She paused for more laughter. "Baton twirling isn't my *only* talent. Really. I'm a great multitasker. In fact, I can sneeze and pee all at the same time. I imagine you all think that's funny, but it's true. And I don't know what to do about it. I tried calling the incontinence hotline the other day. They asked if I could *hold*."

The baton slipped from her hand, and she turned around and bent over to pick it up. The stiff layers of crinoline netting under her dress caused the back of it to flip up when she bent forward, revealing a big smiley face on the seat of her glittery red Spanx.

As the audience roared with laughter and applause, she turned back around and this time did a real twirl with the baton, circling her arm, then tossing the baton high into the air and catching it with ease. She took a bow, waved, and pranced off the stage.

Bailey, Evie, and Daisy exploded with the audience, rising to their feet as they all clapped and cheered for Aster. Evie put her fingers between her lips and let out a loud whistle.

Her great-aunts apparently had more talents than she'd realized.

Bailey told them so a few minutes later, after the pageant had ended for the day and Marigold and Aster came out into the audience to join them. They had changed out of their pageant dresses and were both wearing pastel-colored T-shirts, black capris, and sneakers.

"You guys were awesome," Daisy told them.

"I hope so," Aster said. "We have some pretty stiff competition. One of those young gals was juggling fire sticks."

"And the other could sing like a bird," Marigold added. "I thought it was Carrie Underwood on the stage."

"You all *have* to be in the running with those acts you just did," Bailey said. "Are you wiped out from the competition?"

"It doesn't matter if we are," Aster said. "Your grandmother has us selling honey lemonade at the Busy Bee stand for the next two hours."

Marigold checked her watch. "Speaking of which, we should probably get over there."

"I'm free if you want me to come help," Daisy told them.

"You are a godsend, child," Aster told her, putting an arm around Daisy. "That would be wonderful."

"You gals want to help too?" Marigold asked Bailey and Evie.

Bailey shook her head and lowered her voice. "We can't. We're off to track down some of the suspects on our list and see if we can find out anything about Rex's murder."

Daisy's shoulders fell, as if she suddenly wished she could take back her offer to help the aunts.

"I promise we'll tell you everything we find out," Bailey assured her. "We'll meet you all back at the ranch after the festival shuts down tonight."

"We've kept our ears open today and heard a gal talking about how she saw someone wearing a bear suit going into Edwards Hall the night of the murder," Marigold said.

Bailey frowned. "I thought *several* people told you they saw someone wearing a bear suit going into Edwards Hall."

"They did. And all at different times. But none of them could tell us much beyond the height of the person in the suit. This woman saw something else."

Aster picked up the story as her sister paused for a breath. "This woman said the person in the bear suit was wearing bright red high-top sneakers."

Bailey looked over at Evie, who nodded.

"Does that mean something to you?" Marigold asked.

"It might," Bailey told her. "The makeup artist for the show wears bright red high-top sneakers."

"Then it sounds like she might be the first person you need to talk to."

* * *

Evie and Bailey found Imani and Gregory at the end of Vendor Row. They were sitting at a picnic table, sharing a funnel cake drizzled with honey as they people-watched.

Gregory looked the height of preppy fashion, wearing black golf shorts, a light blue polo shirt, a navy sweater tied around his neck, and loafers with no socks. Imani had on cut-off jean shorts, a black Ramones T-shirt, and the red high-tops.

"How's the funnel cake?" Bailey asked as she and Evie sat down across from them.

"I think it's the best one I've ever had," Imani said. "Seriously, I gained ten pounds just looking at it."

"At least you're sharing it, so you're splitting the calories," Evie offered.

Gregory offered them a sheepish grin. "This is our second one."

They laughed together, as if they were old friends instead of having just met each other a few days before.

Bailey really liked them. But just because they were both funny and sweet didn't mean they hadn't committed murder. They knew Gregory had gone back into Edwards Hall at the beginning of the Bear Run, when he claimed he had forgotten his phone, and now they knew Imani had gone back into the building at some time that night too. She tried to think of the best way to ease into the conversation about Rex and casually ask them what they were doing in Edwards Hall the night their boss had been killed.

"So, this thing with Rex is nutso, right?" Evie said. Leave it to her best friend to just jump right into the deep end. "Who do you think killed him?"

Gregory shrugged. "I don't know. It's weird that he would get whacked in this tiny town. If we were back in LA, the list of people who hated Rex would fill an auditorium. But nobody even knows him here."

"Except us," Imani said. She looked from Evie to Gregory. "And I think we all three made the list of suspects."

"I know I did," Evie said. "That article in the paper practically accused me of doing it. I wish that reporter hadn't been there when I got into it with Rex. I practically handed her that story."

"But that was one tiny skirmish with him," Imani said. "The rest of us have history with the guy. And we *all* had a reason to want him gone."

Gregory cocked an eyebrow. "Speak for yourself, honey. It's true that I wanted him off the show, but not badly enough to *kill* him."

Bailey's Spidey-senses were tingling. This was exactly the thing she was hoping they could get them to talk about. She only wished she had a tape recorder or a notepad to jot down what Gregory and Imani were telling her and Evie. "Why did *you* want him off the show?"

Gregory huffed. "You mean besides that he was an arrogant, selfish, chauvinist pig?"

"Rex got Gregory's partner fired from the show," Imani explained.

"That's where we met," Gregory said. "Anders was the day-time newscaster and had been vying for the spot on the morning show with Rachel Ward. It wasn't enough that Rex got the spot; he had to publicly humiliate Anders and then start a campaign to get him fired."

"That's terrible. How did he humiliate him?" Evie asked.

"It wasn't one thing. It was a series of small things that added up—like messing with his dialogue on the teleprompter and starting rumors that he was talking about people behind their backs."

"We don't have any actual evidence that Rex got him fired," Imani said.

"But we *know* he was responsible." Gregory's brows knit together. "Losing that job just about destroyed Anders. We'd moved in together by that time, and all of a sudden, this sweet, fun-loving guy could barely get out of bed in the morning. He was so depressed. And I swear Rex black-balled him, and then Anders couldn't get hired on with another station and burned through all his savings."

"That's awful," Bailey said. *And sounds suspiciously like motive.* "How could you stand working with Rex after that?"

Gregory shrugged. "It wasn't easy. Honestly, I couldn't stand the guy. But one of us needed to be bringing home some bacon. And the show pays well. So, I just sucked it up and did my job." He lifted his chin. "And it helps that I'm a trained actor. And a danged good one. I can make anyone believe anything." He must have realized how his boast sounded because he quickly changed his focus to tearing off a new piece of funnel cake. "But like I said, I didn't kill him."

Or at least that's what he wanted them to believe.

Chapter Sixteen

B ailey tried to think of a way to ask Gregory and Imani if they had an alibi. She figured she'd try Evie's tactic of talking about herself first and then go for a casual offhand remark. "I'm just thankful that I was with my daughter and my grandmother for most of the night. So at least I have an alibi."

"Lucky you," Gregory said. "I was alone in my hotel room."

Imani nodded. "Me too."

"But I did call my husband and we talked on the phone for an hour while we watched *The Bachelor*. So, depending on what time the murder happened," Gregory said, "I may be covered."

"I was so tired after that crazy day of production, and then doing the Bear Run, that I just took a shower and went to bed."

Gregory took another hunk of funnel cake. "Has your hunky sheriff boyfriend told you when the time of death was?"

"He's not my boyfriend," Bailey stuttered. Although he *used* to be. "And no, he hasn't told me anything about the case. Except to butt out of it."

Evie reached over and snagged a small bite of funnel cake. "We're hearing most of our information from Bailey's great-aunts.

They were collecting contact information from everyone at the Bake-Off."

"Oh yeah, they talked to me," Imani said. "Have they heard anything useful?"

Evie lifted one shoulder in a relaxed shrug, as if she weren't just about to drop a truth bomb on them. But Bailey knew her friend, and she already saw it coming. "Apparently several people claim they saw someone in a bear suit going into Edwards Hall the night before Rex was murdered. And one of those someones was wearing bright red high-top sneakers." She stole a glance at Imani's shoes.

Imani jerked her head back and narrowed her eyes. "What are you trying to say?"

Evie shrugged again, portraying the picture of innocence. "I'm not trying to say anything. I'm just repeating what I heard someone else say."

"Well, for your information," Imani said. "I *did* go back into Edwards Hall that night. I remembered that I'd left a jar of foundation sitting on the back counter and forgotten to put the lid back on it."

"You went all the way back into the building for some foundation?" The question popped out before Bailey could stop herself from asking it.

"You would too if that foundation were specially ordered from Paris and cost three hundred dollars. *And* it was the only one your boss would use," Imani countered.

Bailey gasped, thinking of her six-dollar bottle of foundation that she'd found in the clearance bin at Walgreens two months ago. Three hundred dollars was her car payment. And the studio spent that on Rex's *face*? Did it come attached to a gold bar?

"And his majesty would have pitched a royal fit if he didn't have it," Gregory chimed in. "I've seen him tear into Imani for having the gall to offer him the wrong kind of bottled water." He pointed a piece of fried dough at his coworker. "Remember that time he dumped a full bottle of soda all over your entire makeup kit and then knocked if off the counter after you offered him it instead of his hoity-toity brand of water?"

The makeup artist's eyes narrowed, and she pulled her hands into her lap, but not before Bailey caught sight of one of them shaking. "Yes, Gregory, I remember. It took me five years to put together that entire collection. And Rex destroyed it in one five-second temper tantrum. It cost me almost ten thousand dollars to replace everything in it. I had to take a second mortgage out on my house."

So maybe the studio *hadn't* paid for Rex's expensive taste in makeup. But was ten thousand dollars and a second mortgage worth killing someone over? Maybe, if that were combined with the sexual advances Imani had referred to earlier.

"We should go," Imani said, pushing herself up from the picnic table.

"It wasn't our intention to offend you," Bailey said, always the one who worried about everyone's happiness over her own. *We just wanted to know if you killed your boss.*

Imani sighed. "I'm not offended. It was an honest question. I did go back into the building. But for as many times as I've imagined doing it, I *didn't* kill him."

"Later, gaters." Gregory stood up too and tossed the empty paper plate in the trash as he followed Imani toward the parking lot.

It wasn't until they were halfway there that Bailey realized they'd never gotten a chance to ask Gregory about what *he'd* been doing when he was in Edwards Hall.

* * *

The funnel cake had made Bailey hungry, so she and Evie split one as they walked toward her car.

"Who should we interrogate next?" Evie asked around a mouthful of fried dough.

"I wouldn't call what we just did much of an interrogation."

"Okay, so we didn't get to play good cop/bad cop or pull out anyone's fingernails, but we still got in some good questions."

"First of all, eww. No matter how many people we question, I'm not planning on pulling out anyone's fingernails."

"Let's leave it as an option." Evie winked as she shoved another hunk of funnel cake into her mouth.

"Speaking of torture, I think we've tormented the crew enough for now. Maybe we go try to talk to Charlotte or Spike. Or we could work on checking out the people on the list we found in Rex's pocket."

"Let's try Charlotte," Evie said. "Even though the diner is technically closed, I'm sure she's probably still there."

Downtown was still fairly busy, but they found a parking spot within a few blocks of the diner. Through the front window, they could see Charlotte wiping down the counter and resetting the coffee machines, but the front door was locked. Like two kids staring at a puppy in a pet shop window, Bailey and Evie cupped their hands around their eyes and pressed the sides of their palms to the window.

Evie tapped against the glass. Charlotte jumped and tossed the stack of coffee filters she was holding into the air. Pressing her hand to her chest, she turned toward the window. Her face crumpled into a pained expression, and she whipped back around, then dropped below the counter.

"We can see you," Bailey called through the glass as they watched Charlotte crawling around the corner of the counter and into the kitchen. She knocked again, and they waited several minutes, but she never came back out of the kitchen.

"I think she's trying to avoid us," Evie said.

"Ya think? You might already be a detective."

Evie gave her shoulder a good-natured nudge.

Bailey backed away from the window. "I guess we go try to talk to Spike."

"Or, as long as we're downtown, maybe we should check in at the hardware store or Harv's House of Pizza."

They had no luck at either place. Harv was out doing a delivery. And Carl from the hardware store was manning a booth at the Bee Festival.

"I guess we go back to the fairgrounds and try to find Carl. And now that I'm thinking about it, there was a hot tub vendor out there too. I wonder if he's the same one that's on the list." Bailey had her hand on the car door, when she spotted a familiar couple coming out of the coffee shop. But the way they were acting with each other wasn't familiar at all. Bailey nodded toward the couple.

Evie let out a low whistle. "Since when do Toby and Sibia hold hands? And . . . oh my . . . have you ever seen him *kiss* her?"

"Um . . . no. And especially not with tongue."

"Is he trying to swallow her face?"

"He probably could. The guy is well over six feet tall, and Sibia's maybe five six in a pair of heels." Her face went mushy as she watched the sweet cameraman smile down at the personal assistant as if she'd just hung the moon and offered him the sky. "They're so cute."

Evie leaned her elbows on the top of the car. "Yeah, but are they rom-com cute like *When Harry Met Sally*, or are they cute like Bonnie and Clyde on a murderous rampage that just took out their boss?"

"Do you think Bonnie and Clyde went out for caramel macchiatos after their murderous rampages?"

Evie shrugged. "They could have."

"Let's see what they're up to," Bailey said, already turning away from the car and heading toward the production crew couple. She waved as they came closer. "Hey, you two."

The couple looked up as one, but Bailey couldn't tell if the surprised look on their faces had more to do with seeing her and Evie away from the Bee Festival or the fact that they might have just seen them kissing.

Sibia dropped Toby's hand and reached up to wave. Again, was that just her normal waving hand? Or did she not want them to see her holding hands with the cameraman?

"Fancy seeing you here," Bailey said, trying to sound casual instead of like she was about to question whether they had an alibi for their boss's murder. "What are you two up to?"

"Just grabbing some coffee," Toby said without missing a beat. He didn't seem as concerned about getting caught holding Sibia's hand. "What are you two up to?"

Just trying to figure out who murdered the celebrity host and keep my bestie out of prison.

"Just came into town to grab a gallon of milk," Bailey told them. She really did need to get that milk. Her poor daughter had

had to suffer through dry Cheerios again that morning. "We just saw Gregory and Imani out at the fairgrounds."

"Oh no," Sibia said. "I forgot to get Gregory's chai tea. I told him I'd bring him one. If you'll excuse me, I'll be right back." She turned and hurried back into the coffee shop.

"You two seem pretty chummy," Evie said, grinning as she nudged the cameraman in the side.

Toby couldn't seem to help the grin that spread across his face. "Yeah, we got to talking the other night after the Bear Run, and one thing led to another and . . . well, let's just say things have been going really well."

"That's great," Evie told him. "I'm really happy for you."

"Me too."

"Any chance they went well enough that night that you all can alibi each other?" Evie asked.

"Huh?"

Bailey kept silent. Evie was doing fine on her own getting information from the cameraman, and she didn't want to hinder the flow of conversation.

Evie shrugged. "Don't get me wrong. I'm not accusing you of anything. We were just talking to Imani and Gregory about where we all were the night of Rex's . . . you know. So, alibis were on my mind."

"Well, I don't like to kiss and tell, but since you put it that way, I guess I can tell you that Sib came back to my hotel room that night and spent the night. So, I guess we do alibi each other."

Gregory's words came back to Bailey about Toby sleeping like the dead. Would he have even noticed if Sibia had slipped out of his room sometime in the night?

"Are you sure? Is there any chance either of you could have left the room while the other one was asleep?" Bailey asked. So much for keeping her mouth shut.

Toby's brow wrinkled. "I don't think so. I guess all I know is that she was there when I fell asleep around eleven, and she was still there when I woke up in the morning."

Sibia came back out, holding a takeout cup in her hand. "We should probably get going," she told Toby. "Nice to see you both."

Evie and Bailey watched them get in their rental car and pull away.

"Did that seem weird to you?" Evie asked.

"Totally weird," Bailey agreed. "Sibia is usually really friendly."

"One more mystery to add to this odd production-crew business."

They agreed to head back to the fairgrounds. Ten minutes later, they pulled into the parking lot, and Bailey realized she had forgotten the blasted milk. Again.

Chapter Seventeen

B ailey and Evie walked down Vendor Row, the scent of funnel cakes and corn dogs heavy in the air. The vendors ranged from booths with homemade soup mixes to stands that sold solar panels. They tried to walk by most of the booths, but Bailey couldn't pass up a cute notebook and stopped to purchase a three-pack of decorated journals she saw, and Evie found a pair of earrings she had to have in another booth.

Both women had been curious as to what kind of booth the hardware store would have, but it made perfect sense when they walked up and saw the displays and equipment for beehive starter kits. The booth had premade hive boxes, beekeeper suits, smokers, long gloves, and veiled hats. There were also numerous hive tools, uncapping forks, and bee brushes.

Carl Davis was in his mid-thirties, but he seemed much older. He and his wife had four kids, and his parents and grandparents all lived in town, so Bailey imagined he didn't get a lot of rest. His father, Carl Sr., had been the one to open the hardware store downtown originally, but Carl had worked there since he was a kid and had inherited the business several years ago. He was tall and still had the solid build of the high school football player he'd once been, but his shoulders now seemed to sag, as if carrying the weight of heavy burdens; his face usually looked tired; and what hair he had left was already going gray.

His back was to them when they walked up to the booth, and he had his phone up to his ear. His tone sounded angry and frustrated as his voice rose. "I understand that. But what do you expect me to do about it?"

Bailey and Evie waited, both listening and hoping he might just utter a helpful clue to the case. Or an admission of guilt would be even better.

"You're the one—" Carl said, then stopped as if the person on the other end of the call had cut him off.

Bailey leaned forward to try to hear better, and her crossbody bag accidentally hit a display of smokers and knocked one to the floor. It hit the cement with a clang, startling her, Evie, and Carl.

He whipped around, his eyes wide, a guilty expression written all over his face as he said, "I gotta go" into the phone and disconnected the call. His expression changed to one of recognition as he stepped toward them, dropping the phone into his front shirt pocket. "Hi, ladies. Something I can help you with?"

Maybe it hadn't been a guilty expression. Maybe Bailey was just hoping to project guilt on someone other than her best friend. He could have been arguing with his wife.

"Hi, Carl. Hope there's no trouble at home," Evie said, almost as if reading Bailey's thoughts.

Carl looked confused. "Trouble?"

Evie pointed to the phone in his pocket. "We didn't mean to interrupt your call."

His eyes cut down to his phone, then back to them, and Bailey swore a look of guilt passed over his face again. He was definitely uncomfortable as he shifted his shoulders and shook his head. "Oh, that. No. That was nothin'." He looked to the side for a second, like he was trying to come up with a plausible explanation for the heated conversation. "Just something with the shop," he murmured as he leaned down to pick up the fallen smoker. "You need something for your grandma?" he asked Bailey as he positioned the smoker back on the display.

"No, we're just looking around the vendor booths." She held up the decorative journals. "Doing a little shopping. How's business been for you out here?"

He shrugged. "I hate to say it, but it's picked up quite a bit since yesterday. I think everyone wants to come out to the fairgrounds to see if they can get a glimpse of the trouble we had going on."

That "trouble" being a murder.

But he couldn't have given them a better opening.

Step into my web said the spider to the fly.

"Yeah, that sure was something." Bailey looked around at the honeycomb extraction tools and tried to keep her voice casual. "Did you know Rex?"

Carl jerked his head back and took two steps away from them. "Me? No. Why would I know him?"

Interesting reaction.

"I guess I meant did you watch him on television? Or get a chance to meet him while he was here?"

"No. Never met the guy. Wife occasionally watches the show. She likes that Rachel Ward. But I've never met the man."

So you said. Repeatedly.

Carl cocked his head and narrowed his eyes at her. "What makes you think I knew him?"

She shrugged, hoping to convey innocence. "Oh, nothing in particular. I just remember hearing he'd visited some local businesses, and I thought he'd dropped by the hardware store. Everyone was in quite a tizzy about meeting such a big celebrity."

Carl huffed. "I don't know that he was *that* big of a celebrity. Seemed like kind of a blowhard to me."

Interesting opinion of someone he'd just said he'd never met.

"He was," Evie said. She'd been letting Bailey lead the conversation while she looked around at the display as if she were actually contemplating starting a beehive. She lowered her voice and leaned in toward Carl like they were the only ones in conversation. "Personally, I wasn't really impressed with the guy. He seemed like an arrogant jerk to me."

Evie had set the hook, and Bailey waited for Carl to take the bait. But he just repeated that he wouldn't know because he'd never met the guy. Then another customer walked up, and Carl excused himself to go help them.

"Well, that netted us a fat lot of nothing," Evie said as they walked away from the hardware store booth.

"I don't know." Bailey kept her voice low just in case they were still in earshot. "The guy seemed pretty squirrelly to me."

"Yeah, he was acting kinda jumpy."

The booth selling hot tubs was at the end of Vendor Row, but no one was at the welcome table. Instead, there was an "Out to Lunch" sign saying that someone would be back in half an hour.

"H-E-double hockey sticks," Evie swore. "I guess we're not gonna talk to Gordon Russell."

"We could wait for him to come back," Bailey suggested.

"Or . . . we could go get some kettle corn and check back in fifteen."

Bailey laughed and hooked her elbow through Evie's. "I like the way you think." Their noses led them toward the sweet and salty kettle corn stand, and she pointed toward the tall bartender who was waiting in line. "Hey. There's Spike. Now's our chance to talk to him."

They waved as they took their place in line behind him.

"Hey there. What kind of trouble are you two getting into today?" he asked.

Evie tsked. "Who? Us? Trouble? Never."

Spike laughed, then turned to order two large bags of kettle corn. He handed one woman a twenty-dollar bill as the other woman in the stand scooped fresh popcorn into two bags. She passed them to Spike, and he handed one to Evie. "My treat."

Bailey had never seen her friend turn down free food.

"Oh, thanks," Evie said. "I just love this stuff." She took a handful and held out the bag to Bailey as they followed Spike to an empty picnic table in the shade. "So, what are you doing out here this afternoon, besides generously passing out bags of kettle corn to unsuspecting women?"

"I only give kettle corn to the pretty ones," he said with a smile that could charm a stripe off a tiger.

Evie laughed and they both stuffed more popcorn in their mouths so they didn't have to come up with another response.

"I actually stopped by because I was trying to get my jacket that I left in Edwards Hall yesterday," he told them.

Evie fanned her face. "It's eighty degrees out here. Why do you need a jacket?"

"Because it has the keys to my supply shed in the pocket."

"Oh poop. How'd you get into the shed yesterday?" Evie asked.

"I didn't need to. I didn't even remember I'd left the keys in the pocket until I was at the bar earlier, and the shift manager told me we'd run out of cups and napkins. We were insanely busy last night. And not just with our regulars. There were lots of folks that I'd never seen before."

"We were crazy too. And so was Charlotte's place. And I think those new folks you're seeing are the reporters that have been coming into town," Evie told him. "There were several having breakfast at my place this morning too."

Bailey nodded. "I waited on one guy who'd driven up from Denver and another who'd flown in from LA. But I made Griff wait on Jane, that reporter from the *Humble Hills Herald*."

Evie turned to her, a handful of popcorn paused in midair. "Wait. I didn't see Jane Johnson in the bakery this morning."

"Well, she was there. And after the article she'd written that didn't paint you in the best light, I wasn't about to serve her coffee. I was afraid I might pour it in her lap." Bailey gestured toward Edwards Hall. "I'm amazed that you could get in there to get your jacket," she told Spike. "Don't they have it all locked up?"

"Surprisingly, no. But there was a deputy posted there, and he let me in when I told him what I needed. He went with me to find the keys and let me take just them. I had to leave the jacket behind." Spike rubbed a hand across his bearded jaw. "But it did get me to thinking about those bags they let us bring in with our stuff in them. You know how they allowed us to bring one duffel or tote bag backstage?"

Evie nodded. "Although I didn't bring mine back. Sibia went into the audience and found mine after I'd been announced as a contestant."

"Mine too. And I saw her grab that pink bag of Charlotte's as well. But do you know where those bags were stored backstage?"

"In the supply closet," Evie answered. "Sibia told me they kept our stuff in there to keep it safe and out of the way."

"But those tote bags *had* to be where the killer found all that stuff to plant on Rex." Spike paused and narrowed his eyes at Evie. "You *do* think the killer planted all that stuff to make you, me, and Charlotte look guilty, don't you?"

Evie nodded again. "Absolutely. I never even wore those sandals around Rex. I'd stuffed them in my bag before the first show even started and never took them out again."

"Same with one of my leather bracelets. And we both know that Charlotte had extras of those little springy bees. She stuck two of them on our kitchen stations. I don't know for sure, but it's not a stretch to imagine she had some in her tote bag." Spike picked a stray kernel of popcorn off the front of his shirt and tossed it to the ground. "It would have been easy enough for the killer to have grabbed something out of each of our bags and planted it on Rex's body."

And it would be easy enough for Spike to plant the idea in their heads if he'd been the one who'd actually killed Rex and then placed their things strategically in the dead man's hand and around his body.

"You know, I had a pair of earbuds in my bag," Evie said. "I wonder if the deputy would let me in there to get them too."

"Probably," Spike said. "He let Charlotte in to get something."

"Charlotte was there today too?"

"Yeah. She came in as I was leaving, so I don't know if it was something she wanted from her tote bag or from her kitchen station, but she seemed pretty desperate to get in there to get it. I heard her practically begging the deputy to let her in."

Bailey nibbled at a piece of popcorn. "That's weird."

"True," Spike agreed. "But that lady's been acting nothing *but* weird lately. Remember the first day of the show? She seemed so put together and organized, but by the last day, she seemed scattered and kept dropping things."

"I noticed that too," Evie said, acting as if she'd just thought of it now with Spike's observation, when really, she and Bailey had talked over all the weird ways that Charlotte had been acting. "Why do you think she was so stressed?"

Spike shrugged. "I don't know, man. I mean the Bake-Off was cool, and I was really honored to be chosen and all, but winning wasn't gonna make or break my joint. Do you think she and Ben were in some kind of financial trouble?"

"Not that I know of. But even if she won, the cash prize for the Bake-Off was only five hundred dollars. That wouldn't get anyone out of much trouble."

"Although the television exposure would have probably helped. Not so much with the locals, because everyone knows our restaurants around here," Spike said. "Hell, there's only about ten dining places to choose from, and that's counting the pizza and hotdogs they serve at the gas station. But maybe she thought the TV thing would bring in more tourists."

Evie shook her head. "I don't know. But she really wanted to win."

Spike leaned closer and lowered his voice. "Yeah, one of the crew members told me she even took Rex a homemade pie. Like that might sweeten him up to her. But he wasn't even a judge."

"Rex didn't need a pie," Evie said, her mouth twisting into a grimace. "He'd sweeten up to anything with a pulse. The guy was a perv."

"Yeah, I noticed he was getting pretty creepy with you."

Evie shuddered as if a chill had just run up her back. "Did you notice if he was acting creepy like that with anyone else? Did he get handsy with Charlotte?"

Spike cocked an eyebrow at Evie. "I can practically hear the gears of your brain working. What you really want to know is did Rex give Charlotte a reason to want to kill him."

Evie offered him an innocent shrug. "Well? Did he?"

"I don't know. I didn't see anything like that. But I do know that she went back to Edwards Hall after the Bear Run. Like *way* after."

"How do you know?"

"Because I left my bike at the fairgrounds earlier, and had a buddy drop me off to pick it up around ten thirty. And that's when I saw Charlotte coming out of the Bake-Off building."

Chapter Eighteen

Bailey almost choked on a popcorn kernel. "Charlotte was in Edwards Hall at ten thirty at night?"

Spike nodded.

"What was she doing there?"

"I have no idea," he said. "I called her name, but she must not have heard me. And I don't think she wanted anyone to see her, because once she snuck out the door, she practically ran toward her car in the parking lot. It was weird, though. Because she's usually so friendly. But she looked like she'd been crying, so maybe she just didn't want to talk."

Spike Larsen seemed to have given them way more than just a free bag of kettle corn. He was chock-full of noteworthy information. So much that Bailey was dying to break into one of those new journals she'd just bought and write down everything he'd said.

"Well, that was interesting," she told Evie as they watched Spike amble away from the picnic table and toward his motorcycle. He straddled the bike, and she gave him a little wave as he started the engine and roared out of the parking lot.

"Yeah, it was," Evie said. "What the heck do you think Charlotte was doing in that building so late at night?"

"And why was she crying? And hurrying away?"

"Maybe because she'd just murdered the host of the Bake-Off."

Bailey cringed. "Sweet Charlotte? I don't know. I have a hard time picturing her whacking anyone on the head with a mixer. She seems more like the 'kill 'em with kindness' type."

"They say it's always the nice ones that you least expect."

Bailey had pulled a pen from her purse and was making notes on all the things they'd found out that day. "So, I guess we're not the only ones who know about the pie in Rex's trailer that came from the Sunshine Café—although this is the first confirmation we've heard that Charlotte was for sure the one who gave it to him." She kept her head down as she started a new page. "What time did Spike say he saw Charlotte coming out of the building?"

"Around ten thirty."

"I wonder if he told Sawyer that he saw her?"

"You can ask him yourself."

Bailey jerked her head up to see Evie pointing toward the tall lawman, who'd just come out of the admin building and was walking toward them.

"What are you working on there?" he asked Bailey as he came closer. "Looks like you're scribbling so fast your pen's gonna burn a hole through your paper."

Bailey snapped the notebook shut and slid it under her rump just in case he tried to make a grab for it. *Don't be ridiculous.* They weren't in the fourth grade. He wasn't going to steal her notebook. But she was still sitting on it, just in case.

"Just making some notes for a new book I'm working on. Had a thought and didn't want it to slip away before I got it written down," she told him, hoping the lie wasn't written all over her face.

"Oh yeah. I'd love to see how your writing process works. Mind if I take a look?" He held his hand out for the notebook.

Apparently, she wasn't fooling him a bit.

"Maybe another time," she said, sliding the notebook farther under her bum. "This is just a bunch of gibberish. Probably wouldn't make any sense to you."

"I'm a pretty smart guy."

"I know you are. And I'm glad you're here, because I had a thought about the case and wanted to talk to you."

"Of course you did." He sighed and slid onto the picnic bench next to her. She was wearing khaki shorts and tried not to think about the warmth of his denim-clad thigh as it pressed against her bare leg. "The case that you and your bestie are supposed to be keeping your cute little noses out of?"

Evie pushed up from the picnic bench. "That popcorn sure made me thirsty. I'm going to go find some lemonade. You guys want anything?"

Sawyer shook his head as he leaned back against the table and stretched his arm out behind Bailey.

She nodded. "I'd love a Diet Coke." Anything to cool her off. And keep her thoughts from how easy it would be to just lean back into the crook of his arm.

Evie must have been thinking the same thing because she did a quick head nod in the direction of Sawyer's shoulder as if urging Bailey to go for it. "Be right back," she said, her voice a little too singsongy.

"All right," Sawyer said. "Out with it. I know you're dying to tell me something."

"I'm dying to tell you *so many* things. But if I did, you might think we've been snooping around instead of just innocently happening upon interesting conversations."

"Why don't you just go ahead and tell me what you've heard in these *innocently interesting conversations.*"

"Will you tell me some things *you've* heard in interesting conversations?"

He raised an eyebrow in reply.

"I have to ask."

"And I have to say that I think you look real pretty in this color blue." He leaned forward and touched the edge of her tank top. Her arm burned where the back of his fingers rested. "It makes your eyes look like the color of the lake on a hot summer day."

She swallowed, her mouth suddenly going dry as his gaze dropped to her lips. "Are you trying to distract me?"

"Is it working?"

Oh gosh yes.

"Um . . . maybe . . . a little." Why did the day suddenly feel warmer? "But I really do have some stuff to tell you."

His lips curved into a wry grin, and he leaned back against the table again. "All right, darlin'. Tell me."

She filled him in on all the things they'd learned, watching his expressions to see if anything she said seemed to surprise him. His head tilted to the side when she told him how weird Charlotte had been acting, but he didn't seem surprised to hear that she'd been in the building the night before the murder.

"I *have* interviewed everyone who was there," he told her. "Give me a little credit for knowing how to do my job."

"I do give you credit. Of course I do," she said. "I'm just try-ing to make sure you know there are other people out there who seem *way more* suspicious than Evie."

"I appreciate that."

"And another thing. I got to thinking about the gold sandal and how that's kind of the key piece of evidence against Evie, but I think it needs to be thrown out completely."

"That's not the only piece of evidence," he said. "But go on. I'm kind of interested in hearing this one."

"We can all agree that the sandal does belong to Evie, but hers isn't the only DNA you're going to find on it. I was actually the last person to wear those shoes. So mine will be on it too. And so will yours."

"Mine?"

"Yeah, remember how you took those shoes off me when we got to the car? Your DNA will be on them too." She was talking fast now, trying to get past the part about him taking her shoes off. Something about it sounded flirty, and she was trying to stick to the point, and not get distracted by the cords of muscles in his forearm. What was it about a muscular forearm that seemed so delicious? And made her think about him sweeping her into his arms and carrying her off to his . . . *Gah. Stop. Need. To. Focus.* "So, that's why I think we should just throw that shoe out of evi-dence. Because it's been contaminated or whatever with the DNA from all three of us."

His lips curved into a wider smile the longer she talked, almost as if he could read her racy thoughts about how hot his forearms were. "Is that what you think?"

"Yes," she said, her voice coming out a little too breathy.

"I'll take it into consideration then."

"You will?"

"Sure, I will. I don't think I'll actually throw it out of evidence, but I promise to consider it."

She narrowed her eyes. "Are you just teasing me now?"

"I wouldn't dream of it." But his grin told her a different story.

"Fine," she said, leaning back against his arm.

"You sure learned a lot for someone who's *not* looking into the case. You have anything else to share?"

"That's it," she said, feeling defeated as she realized how little they'd actually learned. She leaned forward as a new thought struck her. "Hey, speaking of when I was wearing those sandals, I just remembered you saying you were at the fairgrounds because you'd been called out about a vendor being vandalized. Who was the vendor?"

"What does that have to do with anything?"

"Maybe nothing. But it was unusual. We don't usually have vandalism happen at the Bee Festival, so maybe it's something. What happened?"

"It wasn't really vandalism. The guy at the booth just got worked up about it."

"What happened?"

"Somebody snuck into the display where all the hot tubs are and put dish soap in one of spas. So when the owner turned it on the next morning, the jets caused a ton of bubbles. Didn't really hurt anything. But made a heck of a mess."

Bailey already knew the answer. Her Spidey-senses were tingling that this wasn't a coincidence. "Who was the guy?"

"Gordon Russell."

Chapter Nineteen

Bailey filled Evie in on her conversation with Sawyer after the sheriff left. Storm clouds were rolling in, and the sun had already dipped behind the mountain. The festival only had another hour left, but there were still plenty of people milling about the fairgrounds.

"Sounds like we need to go back to the hot tub booth and try to talk to Gordon Russell," Evie said.

They walked back down Vendor Row. It was getting close to six, and Carl's Hardware Store had already shut down their display.

"There's a good chance Gordon isn't coming back for the night either," Bailey said when they found the hot tub booth still vacant.

Just then, a bright blue convertible pulled up next to the hot tubs, and a guy in his mid-thirties climbed out and sauntered toward them. He took off his aviator sunglasses and had the gleam in his eye of a used-car salesman with a potential fish on the hook. "You ladies in the market for a hot tub? You can always come back in your bikinis and try a couple out."

Bailey stared at the man. First of all . . . *ew*. And second of all, she had a thirteen-year-old daughter, *and* she loved ice cream, which meant she'd graduated to a tankini almost a decade ago. Although Evie could still get away with a two-piece, and the way the slimeball was eyeing her made Bailey think he was picturing her in one now.

She took a protective step in front of her friend. She wanted to throw her arms out like an offensive lineman shielding a bikini-clad quarterback—but they were here to get information from the guy, so she needed to not be too obnoxious.

"We're just looking for right now," she told him. "But we're hoping to buy a spa this fall." *Ha*. She was months away from her next royalty check, so she could barely afford to go to a spa right now, let alone buy one.

"Well, Gordon's my name and hot tubs are my game," he told them, passing them each a business card. "You can call me Gordy, though."

"Nice to meet you, Gordy," Bailey said, taking the card. *Not really.*

Evie pointed to the convertible. "Nice car. You don't see a lot of Toyota Solaras around anymore. What year is it? A 2003 or 2004?"

Gordy let out a low whistle. "A lady who knows her cars. Pretty *and* smart."

"My brothers are into cars more than me, but I can appreciate a classic. I have an old Mustang. Cherry red. But I always thought the Solara was a neat car."

"Me too. And this one's special. That electric blue is a custom paint job. You'll probably never see another one this color."

"Cool. Have you had it since it was new then?"

"Nah. I always wanted a convertible, but this one's a recent acquisition." His face beamed with a proud smile, as if he'd won the car in the lottery. But there was something more than pride behind his eyes, something darker, like the kind of look the maniacal villain in the movies gets right before he rubs his hands together and reveals his evil plot to take over the city.

That might be a little over the top, but so far, Bailey was not impressed with Gordon Russell. He wore black slacks, a black polo shirt, and not just one or even two, but *four* gold chains around his neck. He wore loafers without socks and a fake designer watch. Bailey had done a book with a jewelry heist and now knew how to spot a fake.

And his watch wasn't the only thing about Gordon Russell that was phony. He seemed to be trying to give the impression of appearing wealthy but wasn't quite pulling it off. His scuffed "Italian" loafers were also knockoffs, and the cologne he wore was way too strong and cloying to be expensive. Unlike Carl, who seemed to be around the same age, Gordon still had a thick head of dark hair but wore it in an outdated style with too-long bangs and too much hair gel. He wasn't fat but had a paunchy middle that hung over his belt and indicated too much fried food and too many beers. He reminded Bailey of one of the guys in *The Sopranos.*

"This seems like a nice model," Bailey said, pointing to a gray hot tub with a seafoam green interior.

"Oh yeah, she's a beauty," Gordy said, back in salesman mode. "That one has an acrylic shell, sixty massage jets, and multicolored LED lighting. You get that baby, and I'll even throw in the floating spa and drink holder." He offered them a lecherous wink that made Bailey want to throw up in her mouth. "You girls look like you know how to party."

Bailey looked down at her khaki shorts, plain tank top, and sensible sporty Teva hiking sandals . . . well, okay, more like *walking* sandals . . . but still, she couldn't see what about the chunky soles or thick straps would give off the "party" vibe. Maybe it was her crossbody purse with the small grease stain from their earlier funnel cake that said she was a real party girl.

Using all her powers of patience, she ignored the offensive remark and pointed to the small hot tub in the corner. Most of the other spas were full and bubbling with water, but this one was empty and had two towels crumpled inside it. "What happened to that one?"

Gordy's brows knit together, and his fingers curled into fists. "Some jerks thought they were being funny and vandalized my booth the other night."

"Oh no," Evie said, appearing to show genuine concern. Apparently, she was a better actress than Bailey. "What happened?"

"They put dish soap in the water, and the thing bubbled over and made a royal mess."

"Do you know who did it?" Bailey asked.

Gordy shook his head. "Not yet. But I'm gonna find out. Probably somebody who's jealous of me."

"Jealous?" It took everything Bailey had to stop at the one word and not add "of what?"

"Heck yeah. I'm quite a legend around here. I played football, you know. All four years at Humble Hills High. I was the quarterback that took our team to State back in '03."

"Impressive," she murmured.

He puffed up his chest. "Yeah, it was. And these jerks don't realize that putting that crap in the water can cause a lot of damage. And this is my livelihood we're talking about here."

Evie nodded. "That's terrible. And I get it. Owning your own business is no joke. Our place was in a frenzy this morning. And so were the other restaurants. Although we can't complain about all the extra business. Even if we do have to put up with a bunch of reporters hanging out in town."

He jerked his head toward her. "What reporters?"

"You know, the ones coming here because of the"—she lowered her voice to a stage whisper—"murder."

Gordy's shoulders tensed. "I don't know anything about that. I didn't even know the guy."

Hmm. Interesting that he answered their questions before they'd even asked.

"Why would you?" Evie asked. "*Nobody* knew him. He was some big shot newscaster from California."

"Yeah, he was from California. Why would I know him? I don't even know his name."

Methinks thou doth protest too much.

"Yeah, you said that," Bailey said. Then she couldn't help but poke the bear a little. "You seem kind of defensive, though. What's up with that?"

"I'm not being *defensive.*" He huffed out a breath. His shoulders were tight, and his brows were knit together. "I just told you that I didn't know the guy. And I don't know anything about any murder."

He took two steps toward them, and those steps felt just menacing enough that both women stepped back in unison.

His eyes narrowed, and his voice changed from Mr. Friendly to suspicious. "What is this? Are you guys even interested in looking at hot tubs?" A dawning look crossed his face. He stepped closer, his expression angry now as his arms bulked out at his sides.

This guy was nuts. And he definitely knew something.

They took another few steps back.

His voice rose to an angry pitch, and he raised his hands. "Are you two reporters? Do you think there's some kind of story here? Are you trying to frame me or something?"

Now he was getting out of hand. His reaction seemed way too over the top for the situation at hand. Bailey was sorry she'd poked this bear. But also not sorry, because this guy obviously had something to hide. This just might not be the best time to figure out what that something was.

Bailey reached for her friend's arm, to get them out of there, but Evie had taken another step back, and the back of her knees bumped against one of the inflatable plug-and-play hot tubs. Her arms pinwheeled, and she lost her balance and fell backward.

She grabbed Bailey's arm as she tried to stop herself from falling, but instead pulled Bailey with her, and they both splashed into the hot water.

They came up splashing and spluttering, and water cascaded over the side of the tub as they tried to crawl out of it.

Gordy was really pissed now. "What the hell? Are you *trying* to ruin my business? Were you two bitches the ones who vandalized my tub the other night?" He was looming over them now, yelling down at them as Evie made her way out, but Bailey slipped back into the water.

"Get away from us," Evie yelled back. "You're the reason we fell in. You think you're some kind of macho stud. You're just a creep who's trying to throw his weight around."

"Who are you calling a creep, you little bitch? I was just trying to sell you a hot tub!"

Evie had pushed to her feet and was yelling right into Gordon's face. "We wouldn't buy a hot tub from you if you were the last man on earth selling them."

Bailey was still trying to get out of the water, but her hands kept slipping on the slick sides. She would definitely never buy *this* hot tub. She couldn't even get out of it.

Evie was tall, but Gordy was broad shouldered and seemed used to pushing people around. He swung his arm out, narrowly missing her face, but close enough that she flinched and jerked back. "You need to get the hell out of here. And you're gonna pay for the damage to that spa."

"What damage?" Evie yelled back. "*We're* the ones who fell in. So, you're gonna pay for the damage to *us*."

"I'm not paying for shit. You're the stupid bitches who fell in."

Evie pushed back her shoulders and got right in Gordy's face. Her jaw was set, and she glared right into his beady eyes. "Call me a bitch one . . . more . . . time."

Gordy stabbed a finger at Evie's chest. "I'll call you whatever I want. And I just figured out who you are. You run that little coffee shop downtown. So now we'll see how you like it when someone comes into your business and tries to wreck it."

Chapter Twenty

B ailey gasped.

Instead of backing down, Evie leaned closer and narrowed her eyes. The girl had grown up with five brothers. And she'd *never* let one of them push her around. "Are you threatening me?"

"I'm gonna need you to take a step back, Gordon," the sheriff's deep voice said from behind the hot tub. "And I think we all need to calm down."

Bailey floundered in the hot tub, splashing water on Sawyer's cowboy boots as he leaned down to grab her arm and pull her to her feet. "You all right, darlin'?"

"I am now." How did he always seem to show up when she needed him? Or when she and Evie had gotten themselves into another embarrassing scrape?

"You okay, Evie?" Sawyer asked as he held Bailey's arm so she could finally climb over the side of the tub.

"I will be," Evie told him, her eyes still flashing with anger. "When we get away from this jerk."

"You're the jerk," Gordy spat back.

Evie whipped her head toward Sawyer. "You heard him threaten me, right? He said he was going to come down and try to destroy my business."

Gordy shook his head at Sawyer and gave Evie a look like she was overacting. "That's not what I said."

"That's *exactly* what you said."

Water was dripping from Bailey's clothes and hair, and she wrapped her arms around her stomach to stop herself from shivering. "I h-h-heard you," she said, her teeth chattering as she spoke.

Evie planted her hands on her hips, impervious to the fact that she was soaking wet, and glared at Gordy. She was shaking too, but it seemed more from anger than from the cool evening air against her wet clothes.

Gordy made a scoffing sound as he turned toward Sawyer, as if they were just a couple of good ol' boys. "Women—am I right? Always overreacting."

Sawyer grabbed a couple of rolled-up towels that were being used as part of the display next to an eight-person hot tub, and tossed one to Evie before wrapping the other around Bailey's shoulders. "Let's get you two out of here and find you some dry clothes." He pointed a finger at Gordy, the soothing tone he had used with the women now replaced with a hardened edge. "You go on home too. I'll stop by in a bit. And you and I are gonna have ourselves a little chat about what went on here."

"But—" Gordy started to say, but the sheriff cut his next words off with one steely glare. "Yeah, fine. Sure, Sheriff. That sounds good. I'll rustle us up a couple of beers, and we can hash out this little misunderstanding."

A small crowd of people had gathered around the hot tub display, drawn in by the shouting and the appearance of the sheriff.

"Nothin' to see here, folks," Sawyer told them. "Everything's under control." He still had his arm around Bailey as they squished their way back up Vendor Row. Marigold and Aster came hurrying toward them, each holding a blanket. They were dressed in matching black tights and black and yellow striped leotards. Black tutus were cinched around their waists.

"We just heard what happened," Aster said, shaking out the blanket and handing it to Sawyer to wrap around Bailey's shoulders. "Are you girls okay?"

"We're fine," Evie said, accepting the other blanket from Marigold. "What did you hear?"

"That you and Gordy Russell got into a fight, and he pushed you into a hot tub and tried to drown you," Marigold said.

"That's not exactly what happened," Evie said. "But I kind of like that version of the story better than the real one."

"Why?" Aster asked, rubbing the blanket on Bailey's arm.

"Because he didn't *push* us into the hot tub," Bailey said. "We fell in. Or rather, Evie fell in and pulled me in with her. But then she did get in a fight with Gordy."

"But no one was ever in danger of drowning," Sawyer clarified.

Evie pulled the blanket around her shoulders. "I think the more important question is why are you two dressed like you're going to a honeybee jazzercise class?"

"These are our costumes for the grand finale number of the Queen Bee Pageant tomorrow. All the contestants are dressed like bees, and we're going to do a dance routine to that Blake Shelton song that says, 'I'll be your honeybee,'" Aster explained.

"It was another one of our sister's grand ideas." Marigold rolled her eyes. "I swear I do not know how she talks us into these things."

* * *

An hour later, Bailey, Evie, and the rest of the women of The Hive were gathered around the table at the farmhouse. Griffin had just brought in two buckets of fried chicken and all the fixings, and he and Granny Bee were in the kitchen, gathering plates and silverware. Daisy was pouring water into glasses and helped carry all the food to the table. Thankfully, Marigold and Aster had changed out of their bee leotards and tutus and back into their normal attire of capri pants and pastel-hued cotton shirts.

"So, tell us," Marigold said to Bailey and Evie as everyone sat down and started passing the food around and filling their plates, "what did you find out in all your investigating today?"

Bailey took a chicken leg, her favorite, and passed the bucket to Daisy, who sat next to her. "Honestly, not much."

"That's not true," Evie said. "We did find out some. We know that several people went into Edwards Hall last night, including half the production crew, Spike, Charlotte, and numerous people dressed in bear suits." She filled them in on their conversations with Rex's staff and with Spike. "We also found out that Toby finally won Sibia over, and they spent the night together at the hotel." She made the sound of bedsprings creaking, then stopped as she looked from Daisy to Bailey, then back to Daisy. "Sorry, kid. That was just a funny sound I sometimes make when I'm happy that two people have fallen in love."

Daisy rolled her eyes. "I'm practically a teenager. I know stuff."

Bailey whipped her head toward her daughter. "What stuff?"

Evie kept talking because there was no way she wanted to start *that* conversation. "So, we know that pretty much everyone on Rex's staff had a reason to want to kill him."

"And none of them have a real alibi," Bailey added, although she hadn't forgotten Daisy's comment. She just planned to circle back to that later tonight when they were alone. What kind of *stuff* could her sweet innocent twelve-year-old girl know about? And would it be frowned upon if she considered locking her daughter in the house until she was eighteen?

Evie waved a chicken wing in front of her. "I don't really have an alibi either. So maybe we don't want to focus too much on that."

Bailey and Evie filled the others in on the rest of the people they'd talked to.

"It was super weird that Charlotte avoided us like that," Bailey said when they'd finished. "And we're pretty sure Carl from the hardware store lied about knowing Rex. And Gordy Russell acted like he was out of his dang mind when we brought up Rex."

"He kept telling us he didn't know him," Evie said.

"But he said it so many times, we're pretty sure he *did* know him."

Granny Bee leaned forward. "But how could these two local hometown guys know a famous celebrity from California?"

"Good question." Bailey tapped her chin. "I think Rex had been here before. I didn't pay attention at the time because I was just so excited about the Bake-Off starting, but now that I'm thinking about it, some of the things he said at the beginning of the show make me think he *had* been to Humble Hills. Remember he said something about having a slice of Toni-Roni pizza? Only locals call it that."

Griffin frowned. "That's a little shaky. He could have heard that term standing in line at the restaurant."

"True. But he also talked about that old stone cabin off highway 24, and that place was torn down ten years ago."

"So maybe he visited here at some point?" Aster offered.

"But you're the one who told us he'd never been here before," Bailey pointed out.

Aster shrugged. "That's what he said. Well, he said he'd never seen the mountains, which I guess made me assume he'd never been here." She pointed toward the front bay window of the house. "Because you can see the mountains from just about everywhere in town."

"Maybe he knew someone who lives here," Granny Bee suggested.

"No one came to the set to visit him. Or no one that I saw anyway," Evie said. She turned to Griffin. "You were checking into him today. What did *you* find out?"

"Not much. The guy had one of the most boring life histories you can imagine. Everything about his past from before he started in broadcasting appears to be humdrum little facts, like where he attended school and that he lived in the same house growing up in a small town in Iowa. He'd done all sorts of things since he became a star on television, but everything before he moved to California just seems too neatly packaged. And usually when a life looks too neat, there's something else going on."

"What does that mean?" Daisy asked. Whenever Griffin was around, she soaked up every aspect of his job, sometimes acting like his private eye apprentice. Bailey loved her daughter's curiosity and eagerness to learn, but wasn't too sure she wanted her twelve-year-old to know quite so much about the seedy underbelly of criminal life.

"Good question," he said, earning a proud grin from Daisy. "It means that most people have messy lives. And that mess shows up in their history. There's usually a move or two, several cars, a home loan, somewhere they've gotten a divorce or been involved in a neighborhood dispute or done something stupid in college. Or heck, had at least a speeding ticket or two. This guy's got nothing. On paper, it just looks too perfect. When I see this kind of history in my line of work, it usually means somebody bought themselves a nice, neat vanilla background."

Daisy frowned. "Why would someone do that?"

Griff quirked an eyebrow at her. "Well, usually, my young Padawan, it means they have something in their *actual* background that they're trying to hide."

Chapter
Twenty-One

B ailey loved giving her characters a sordid backstory, but she had a hard time believing one had generated in their sleepy little town. "What could someone be trying to hide that happened in Humble Hills? Nothing of note ever happens here. And if it does, everyone and their dog knows about it by suppertime."

Granny Bee tsked. "Plenty of things happen in small towns."

Aster nodded. "Don't you watch true crime shows? There's always something sinister lurking beneath the sweet tranquility of the sleepy small town."

Bailey held up her hands. "You're right. I stand corrected. But what would Rex be trying to hide?"

"That's what we need to find out," Griffin said.

"And what do Carl and Gordy know about it?" Evie asked. "Because I guarantee those two dudes know something."

"I agree," Bailey said, reaching for another biscuit. "Why else would Gordy get so mad? And start accusing us of vandalizing his booth?"

Griffin scowled. "Vandalizing his booth? I didn't hear about this."

"It happened the first night of the festival." Bailey's focus was on dripping honey on the perfectly buttered biscuit on her plate. "I guess someone put dish soap in one of the hot tubs and turned on the jets. Apparently, it made a heck of a mess. And Gordy said that can really damage the hot tub."

Bailey jerked her head up as Daisy's glass tipped over with a crash, and milk spilled across the table.

"Oh gosh. I'm sorry." Daisy grabbed a stack of napkins and tried to sop up the milk before it poured off the side of the table. Her voice shook, and she sounded as if she might cry. "I'm really sorry."

Granny Bee sopped up the milk coming in her direction. "It's fine, honey. There's no need to get upset. It's just a little spilled milk."

"But I didn't mean to." Daisy's face was tilted to the table as she focused on cleaning up the mess.

"Of course you didn't, sugar," Aster said, already coming back from the sink with a wet dishcloth.

"It's okay." Bailey put a hand on her daughter's shoulder. Daisy didn't usually get this upset about a little spill.

Daisy carried the wet napkins to the kitchen trashcan. Cooper followed behind her, licking up any errant drops of milk that hit the floor. "I think I'm just going to go to my room," Daisy muttered before heading up the back staircase.

Granny Bee frowned at Bailey. "Is she okay?"

Bailey shrugged. "I have no idea what that was about. I assume she was embarrassed that she spilled her drink in front of Griffin."

"That was no big deal. I knock stuff over all the time." Griffin pushed up from his chair. "Should I go talk to her?"

"No," said every woman at the table at the same time.

Griffin eased himself back into his chair. "Oh-kay. I'll just stay here, then."

Bailey put a hand on his arm. "You're sweet for asking. But if she's already embarrassed, you showing up in her room to tell her it's okay would completely mortify her."

"Understood."

"I'll go check on her in a bit," Bailey said as she went back to pouring honey on her biscuit.

Granny Bee stood up. "I'll check on her. I need to go upstairs anyway. Tomorrow is the last day of the festival, and there's still a lot to do. I have one more presentation tomorrow with the Colorado Beekeeper's Guild, and the Queen Bee Pageant concludes in the morning."

"Come on, Sister. We should go too." Marigold stood and motioned for Aster. "We need our beauty rest if we're going to face those judges tomorrow and hold our heads high when they *don't* announce our names."

"Speak for yourself," Aster said, picking up her plate and carrying it to the kitchen. "I still think I have a solid chance."

Marigold shook her head at Bailey. "Our daddy instilled way too much confidence in his children."

Bailey laughed as she gestured to the table. "Leave all this. I'll clean it up."

"I can help," Evie said.

Bailey shook her head. "You all go on home. I'm working on a new scene in my book, and I do some of my best thinking with my hands in a sink full of soapy water."

* * *

"And the third runner up is . . ."

Bailey held her breath the next morning as she squeezed Daisy's hand. They'd already sat through the pageant contestants talking about their personal commitments to their social projects—Bailey almost choked on her coffee when one girl said her plan to help the environment was to eat more beans and encourage others to do so as well, which, according to her, would help reduce greenhouse gas emissions. But Bailey worried if they all started eating more beans, there might be too much of another kind of gas emission. Marigold and Aster had gone with more traditional projects like composting and recycling efforts.

They had also endured the final song and dance production and now waited breathlessly to hear the winners announced. The eight contestants had changed from their honeybee costumes into formal wear and were lined up on stage to hear the final results. Aster and Marigold stood next to each other, both wearing gorgeous evening dresses in two different shades of blue.

"Oh, don't they look beautiful," Granny Bee said, sliding into the chair next to them. She'd had to leave after the honeybee number, to take care of a festival issue, but Bailey was glad she'd made it back in time to see the final results.

The announcer called out the name of a girl Bailey hadn't met, but she knew her parents both worked as teachers at the high school. The girl graciously accepted her trophy, a check for two hundred and fifty dollars, and a huge bouquet of flowers before stepping back into line.

"The second runner up is . . ." the announcer said, then paused for dramatic effect. Bailey grabbed her grandmother's hand too. "Aster Briggs."

The crowd went wild as they cheered and applauded for Aster, who marched across the stage and accepted her trophy and bouquet of roses as one of the attendants placed a small tiara on her head.

"She did it," Daisy said, jumping up and down next to her mother. "She practically won!"

Daisy had been in bed by the time Bailey had gone upstairs the night before, and hadn't seemed to want to talk about the spilt milk incident, so Bailey was glad to see her acting like her normal self and cheering for her great-great-aunt.

Bailey was yelling her head off too. She turned to Daisy. "The prize is a *thousand* dollars."

"And bragging rights." Granny Bee's proud smile beamed across her face. "I'm so very proud of her. And she gets to keep that tiara."

Bailey couldn't stop smiling. "She's going to be so thrilled."

Daisy's brows knit together. "I hope Aunt Marigold won't be sad if she doesn't win too."

"I don't think we have to worry about that." Bailey nodded at her aunt Marigold, and her heart melted at the look of joy and pride for her sister on her face.

A drum roll sounded as Aster took her place back in the lineup of contestants.

"And the winner of this year's annual Queen Bee Festival Pageant is . . ." The announcer hesitated, offering the audience a dramatic pause, then practically shouted out the name: "Shelby Martinez!"

"She deserves it," Daisy said as she and Bailey stood to applaud the excited girl. "She's the one who juggled the firesticks. And she made her formal dress herself—and it was so pretty."

They stayed on their feet, clapping and cheering for all the contestants as the event wound down. The great-aunts came out from behind the stage curtains and accepted congratulations from the crowd and hugs from Bailey, Daisy, and Granny Bee.

"I told you we had a good chance of taking this thing," Aster said, nudging her sister.

"Yes, Sister, I should have listened to you," Aunt Marigold said. "I'll go home and start packing my bags for that trip to Hawaii."

Aster blew a raspberry her direction. "Okay, so I didn't take the *whole* thing and win us the beach vacation, but look at this gorgeous tiara." She tilted her head from side to side so the rhinestones sparkled in the light.

Marigold's expression softened as she put an arm around Aster's shoulder. "It *is* gorgeous, and so are you. I'm very proud of you."

Aster grinned like a little girl who'd just been handed her first kitten. "I'm proud of me too."

"You both did an amazing job," Bailey told them.

"Thank you, honey," Marigold said. "We did have fun, but now I'm ready to go home and take a four-hour nap. Being a beauty contestant has plum wore me out."

* * *

Aster and Marigold went backstage to collect their things and finalize their participation in the pageant.

"We need to head out," Granny Bee told Daisy. "The workshop starts in twenty minutes, and I want to be there when people start showing up."

Evie and Griffin strode into the hall as Bailey, Daisy, and Granny Bee were walking out.

"Oh poo," Evie said. "We were racing over here to catch the end of the pageant. How did the aunts do?"

"Aunt Aster took second place," Daisy told them.

A grin spread across Griff's face. "You're kidding!"

"No. I'm not," Daisy said. "Isn't that awesome?"

"Yeah, it is," Evie said. "A little funny and unexpected, but still totally awesome."

"We were cheering our heads off," Bailey said. She nodded at her friend. "I'm surprised you made it at all. I figured you'd be at the restaurant all morning. Have things slowed down?"

"No. But my abuela hired four of my cousins to help with the extra work, so I took a break to come see the pageant before the lunch rush started."

"Good idea. I'm sorry you missed seeing Aster when her name was announced. She was adorable."

"I'm sorry we missed it too," Evie agreed. "What are you all doing now?"

"Granny Bee is leading a workshop with the Beekeepers Guild. She's teaching them how to make queen cages and queen candy," Daisy explained.

Griffin frowned. "Why would they want to put the queen in a cage?"

"So the hive doesn't murder her," Daisy said.

"Why would they murder her? I thought bees basically worshiped their queen."

Bailey nodded. "They do. They love her. But sometimes if the current queen dies or if a beekeeper wants to start a new hive, they have to introduce a new queen into a colony."

"But the bees know she's an imposter and not their real queen, so they try to kill her," Daisy explained. "So you put the new queen in this little cage, which is a box with mesh on at least one side so the workers can smell her pheromones. Then you plug the cage with some queen candy, which is like a sugary pasty substance, and then the bees will try to eat through that candy to get to the queen."

"To kill her?" Griff asked.

Daisy nodded.

He shook his head. "That's ruthless, dude."

"Yeah, it is. And bees are determined little buggers," Daisy continued. "But in the time it takes them to eat through all the candy, they've usually become used to the pheromones she's emitting through the little screens. And then they accept her."

Bailey and Granny Bee watched Daisy as she explained the queen cages to Griffin, and Bailey knew the proud grin on her grandmother's face matched her own. Daisy had been learning so much on the ranch this summer, and it made Bailey's heart happy.

Granny put her arm around Daisy's shoulder. "Daisy is helping me teach the class this afternoon."

"I thought you were hanging out with that new friend of yours today," Bailey said. "What's her name? The one you were running around with the other day. Rosie?"

Daisy shook her head and looked just miserable enough that Bailey wondered if the two friends had had a falling out already. "No. Her name's Josie. And we're not hanging out today. She's . . . um . . . too busy today . . . and well . . . it doesn't even matter. We're not that good of friends anyway."

"Oh. I'm sorry."

Daisy lifted one shoulder in a shrug. "That's okay. I'd rather help Granny with the bee stuff anyway."

Bailey hoped that was true. Daisy had experienced some trouble at her last school, with some of the girls picking on her because she preferred books to boys. But she was only twelve, for goodness sake. Not every girl is boy crazy from the time she enters grade school. And there would always be plenty of time for boys. For now, Bailey was happy to have her daughter's nose buried in a book and for Daisy to still think it was fun to hang out with her great-grandma.

"I can see why you're helping out with the class," Griff said. "You really know your stuff. You taught me something new. That was pretty cool."

Thanks, buddy, for changing the conversation.

"You're great with kids," Bailey told him after Daisy and Granny Bee had left. "You're gonna be a great dad someday."

"I think so too," Evie said.

Griff looked like he might choke. "All I said was that she did a good job," he sputtered.

Evie and Bailey grinned at each other as Bailey nudged him in the side. "You're too easy."

His phone rang, and he looked relieved by the interruption as he pulled his phone from his pocket and held up his hand. "Sorry, I've been waiting for this call. I gotta take it." He tapped the screen and held the phone to his ear. "This is Griffin."

Bailey's ears perked up, and she and Evie made no disguise of eavesdropping on his call. Unfortunately, all they heard him say was a bunch of "yeses" and "uh-huhs" and one "that's what I thought."

"Sounds good. Thanks, Dan. I owe you one." Griff chuckled at the other person's response. "Yeah, that *and* a beer." He ended the call and stuck the phone back in his pocket. "I kept thinking about Rex's background and knew there had to be more to it, so I just kept digging. I got a couple of interesting hits in Iowa and California, which made me think Rex had changed his name."

Bailey nodded. "Smart. Rex Rafferty just sounds like a stage name."

"It is. He registered it with the Screen Actors Guild. His real name is John Stone. At least that's what's on his driver's license. But everything I dug up on John Stone was the same bland background information, which only made me want to dig deeper to see what this guy was hiding. I know some of these people who create fake backgrounds for a price, and they usually have the person keep some truth in their history so it's easier for them to remember."

"That makes sense," Evie said.

"So, I called this guy, Dan, who works in county records down in Denver to see if he could track down a legal name change. There isn't a database for name changes. You typically have to know where the name was legally changed and then search in that county's records. I figured we'd start the search in Iowa since that's where John Stone had some background. And Dan happened to know a guy in records in Iowa. These guys love a mystery, so they've been working on the name 'John Stone,' and he just called to tell me they got a hit."

"They found a record of someone legally changing their name to John Stone?" Bailey asked.

Griffin nodded. "Yeah. It was done about sixteen years ago, so probably right after he turned eighteen."

"So, tell us. What was his name before?"

"Eugene Dix."

Evie winced. "Oh geez. That's unfortunate. No wonder he changed it."

"My friend is emailing me everything they found, so now I have a new place to start digging again. And something tells me that even though Rex Rafferty said he'd never been to Humble Hills, I'd bet a thousand dollars that Eugene Dix has."

"I'll bet you're right," Bailey said, excited that they had a new lead.

"I'm itching to start working on this, so I'm gonna head back to my hotel." Griffin looked at Evie. "Can I drop you by the restaurant?"

"That'd be great." Evie turned to Bailey. "I'll catch up with you later this afternoon, and we can go try to visit Carl and Charlotte again. But don't go talk to them without me."

"I won't," Bailey assured her. "But I do have an idea, so I may run by the county coroner's office and talk to Leon Foster, the medical examiner."

"You mean you're going to the *morgue*?" Evie asked.

Bailey nodded. "Leon has offered several times to help me out with research for my books. Maybe I'll have some questions that might *hypothetically* be for my book, but also might possibly be similar to what's happening with Rex."

Evie's shoulders gave a shiver. "It's okay if you go *there* without me."

Chapter Twenty-Two

The county morgue was located in the basement of the police station and smelled like formaldehyde and old lunch meat. This was the first time Bailey had been there, and her writer brain was cataloging every detail.

She'd brought a notebook and a pen along, just to make her reason for being there seem more legitimate, but she couldn't help herself and was furiously scribbling notes as she walked down the deserted hallway. She wanted to get down the feel of the place. The way the air became cooler as she walked down the stairs, the antiseptic smell, and the occasional ting of metal against metal.

Several of the old buildings downtown, including the courthouse, the library, and the police station, were all built of stone. Bailey had done a book-signing event in Paris several years ago and had taken a tour of the catacombs that ran under the city, and the walls of this basement, with their exposed blocks of cream-colored stone, reminded her of walking down into those ancient crypts.

She let out a shiver. That was a little macabre. No need to get all morbid. These weren't the ancient tombs of Paris. This was just a normal basement in the mountains of Colorado.

Where dead bodies are stored. And their insides are removed, weighed, and examined.

The hallway was lined with closed doors that Bailey assumed were offices or supply closets. There was a set of swinging double doors at the end, and she heard the distinct sound of the Eagles coming from that direction. She took a deep breath and followed the strains of "Take It Easy," trying to tell herself to do the same thing as she prayed she wouldn't find Leon standing elbows deep in the stomach cavity of a dead body. Although that would certainly add some depth to her next book.

"Hello," she called as she pushed through the double doors, then froze as she saw Leon. Not elbows deep in a corpse, but sitting at a desk stacked with neat piles of file folders and working at a computer.

She'd walked into what appeared to be a smaller office area in front of the larger examination room. Tall windows separated it from the office space, so she could still see into the lab, which was neat and perfectly clean—no bloody body parts, no dead bodies, just three gleamingly spotless metal exam tables, a long sink area, a lot of medical equipment, and the back wall lined with closed freezer doors.

She sent up a prayer of thanks that she hadn't walked into an autopsy in progress, but still, this suddenly felt like a very bad idea. The public probably wasn't supposed to just wander into the morgue—although no one had stopped her. But then again, she might have slipped past the security guard when he was talking to an elderly couple.

This room smelled like a combination of bathroom air freshener and fresh popcorn, but her nose wrinkled at an underlying scent that reminded her of the smell of that package of old hamburger she'd found in the back of the refrigerator that had gone well past its expiration date.

"Bailey," Leon said, smiling as he stood up from his desk.

"Hey, Dr. Foster." She spied a puffed microwave bag of popcorn sitting on his desk. "I hope it's okay I just stopped by. I didn't mean to interrupt your lunch."

He waved a dismissive hand at his desk. "No problem at all. I'm happy to see you. And I told you to stop by anytime." He pointed a finger at her. "As long as you agree to call me 'Leon' or 'Doc.' 'Doctor Foster' still feels like my dad."

She grinned. "Okay. Leon."

"Glad that's settled." He held up the bag. "Can I offer you some popcorn?"

She shook her head. Her appetite had disappeared with that comparison to the smell of rotten meat. And she wasn't sure it would ever come back. "No, I'm fine."

"I'm glad you're here. I haven't had anyone to talk to." He jerked a thumb toward the row of freezer drawers. "These guys have been giving me the cold shoulder all day."

She laughed but wasn't sure how to respond.

He leaned on the corner of his desk. "So, what can I do you for?"

"I'm adding a new character to my next book. A medical examiner."

Leon fist-punched the air. "Yes. Will you please name him Leon?"

"I'll consider it," she told him, laughing again. "I'm working on a scene that takes place in the morgue during an autopsy, and I was hoping to ask you some questions to make sure that I get the details right. I figured talking to a real coroner would lend some authenticity to the scene."

Leon pulled his shoulders back. "Yeah. Awesome. I'd be honored to help. You want something to drink?" He waved a hand toward the freezers. "Or we could just crack open a cold one."

She barked out a laugh, then shook her head. This was why she loved this guy. And she hoped she could capture his personality in the new character she was introducing to her story. She'd been so impressed with Leon when she'd first met him, even though it hadn't been in the best of circumstances. She hoped not to ever meet anyone else while staring at a dead body. But after she'd met him, she'd known she had to add a coroner to her mystery series.

She held up her notebook. "Okay if I take some notes?"

"I'd be disappointed if you didn't," he said with a grin. He gestured to the chair in front of his desk. "Have a seat. And tell me, what do you want to know about the wonderful world of corpses?"

She chuckled again as he sat back down at his desk, and she settled into the chair across from him. She really did have a lot of questions, and she spent the next thirty minutes devouring every detail he shared about the life of a small-town medical examiner.

"The majority of my work is fairly boring," he told her. "I do a lot of research and work in the lab. And because I cover three counties, I usually have plenty of things to keep me busy. Busy enough that the county coughed up the budget to let me hire an assistant this last year, and Jin has been a lifesaver. She's an outstanding assistant."

"I only met her briefly the one time, but she does seem great."

"She's amazing. And I have to admit we don't often get to work a homicide, so we're both pretty excited." He frowned and raised one shoulder in a shrug. "I mean, not excited that somebody murdered the guy, but you know what I mean."

Yes, she knew *exactly* what he meant. And was thrilled that he'd just given her the opening she was hoping for. "Speaking of the murder," she said as casually as she could, "do you have any theories yet? Or anything you'd be willing to share?"

Leon offered her a knowing grin. "I was wondering when you were going to get around to asking me about the murder."

She held up her notebook, already filled with pages of notes. "I really am adding a medical examiner to my novel."

"But you'd still like to know what's going on with Rex's murder."

She lifted her shoulders in a casual shrug. "I may have a *few* questions that could pertain to either the book *or* Rex's case. Just hypothetically, of course."

"Of course. What do you want to know? Hypothetically, of course."

"I guess one thing I was wondering is if perhaps someone had legally changed their name, would their fingerprints show up in the system under their new name or their old one?"

"Hypothetically speaking . . . first of all, their fingerprints would have to already be in the system for us to get a match. I'm not saying the person would need to have had a record or been arrested—these days there are plenty of other ways for folks to have their fingerprints on file. Whether that's a background check for a job, or even submitting your fingerprints for TSA pre-check in order to be able to skip the security lines."

"So, say for instance, I have a character in my book who gets murdered, and he goes by one name, but it's discovered that he legally changed his name at some point in his life. Would that be something the medical examiner would know?"

"If the fingerprints are on file, they will most likely match all the aliases associated with that name and have them listed on the record." He nodded his head and kept nodding as he said, "Most likely the medical examiner would know *all* the aliases that the victim goes by."

"And *all* the places the victim had might have lived? Say *here* in Humble Hills, for example?"

Leon nodded. "Yep. The medical examiner would know that too."

They were staring at each other as Bailey tried to think of another pertinent question to ask, when the door swung open and Leon's assistant, Jin, barreled through.

She was already speaking as she came into the office and dropped a folder on his desk. "The lab reports just came through for that protein shake or whatever that weird chocolaty stuff was in Rex's water bottle. And you were right, Doc. It *was* laced with senna glycosides."

Bailey's eyes widened.

Rex was poisoned too?

Chapter
Twenty-Three

B ailey held perfectly still, hoping Leon's assistant wouldn't notice her.

It must have worked because Jin kept talking as if Bailey weren't there. "They also found a considerable amount of it in Rex's blood. And we both know there's no way he would've taken that much on purpose, especially right before he was going to tape the show."

Leon gestured to Bailey. "Jin, have you met Bailey Briggs? She's a local author and stopped by to ask me some questions about a scene in her new book."

Jin clapped her hand over her mouth. "Oh my gosh. I'm so sorry, Doc. I didn't see her sitting there."

Bailey waved at dismissive hand her in her direction. "Don't worry. I didn't hear a thing. I don't even know who this Rex person is."

Jin looked from Bailey to Leon, then back to Bailey again. "I thought I saw you backstage at the Bake-Off."

Busted.

"Oh yeah, you did. But still, my lips are sealed." She pressed her lips together and mimed the motion of locking them and tossing away the key.

"I am *so sorry*," Jin mouthed as she backed out of the room. "Nice to meet you, Miss Briggs. I'll come back later, Doc, when you're not busy."

After she was gone, Bailey readied her pen as she glanced at the folder, then back at Leon. "So, Doc, hypothetically speaking, if a character in my book was murdered and senna glycosides were found on the toxicology report, what would that tell my medical examiner about the murder?"

Leon's lips curved into a grin. "Isn't that an amazing coincidence? That the character in your book would also have considerable amounts of senna glycosides in them."

"That's what I was thinking too. Just a crazy coincidence."

Leon narrowed his eyes at Bailey. "Do you even *know* what senna glycosides are?"

She arched one eyebrow, trying her best to look condescending. "Do *you*?"

Leon let out a loud laugh. "I do like you, Bailey. And yes, I do know what they are. And since I know that you're just going to google it anyway, I might as well tell you that senna glycosides are the common element found in stimulant laxatives."

"Laxatives?" She wrinkled her nose. "You mean like Ex-Lax?"

"I mean *exactly* like Ex-Lax."

She shook her head. "Wait. You're saying someone laced Rex's water bottle with Ex-Lax? Why would someone *do* that?"

He steepled his fingers as he leaned back in his chair. "You tell me, Miss Briggs. Why do *you* think someone might do that?"

Bailey tapped her pen against her chin. "Well, I mean, people take laxatives all the time. And Rex was traveling *and* in a new environment. But Jin said there were *considerable* amounts in his blood, so I don't think Rex would do that, especially not the night before he was taping the last show. Which means someone else must have put a bunch of it in his water bottle. And if it was a chocolatey drink, it would probably disguise the taste. Right?"

Leon nodded. "Probably."

"The only reasons I can think of for someone to do that to him would be to either make him super sick as a punishment or to embarrass him during the show. Or maybe it was to keep him from doing the show altogether. And the only reason I could think for doing that was if maybe someone else wanted to take his place." Bailey sucked in a breath. "Wait. Just how much *is* a considerable amount? Was there enough to kill him? *Can* you die from taking too many laxatives?"

Leon opened the file and gave it a quick glance. "You can. But not in this case. There wasn't enough to kill him, but there was enough to make him pretty miserable." He raised his chin at Bailey. "Of course, we're both still speaking hypotheticals here, but can you think of anyone who would have any of those reasons you just mentioned?"

Bailey huffed. "I know that Rex made a lot of people mad. And there are *plenty* of them who might just enjoy seeing him miserable."

She told him about how Rex had humiliated Gregory's partner and gotten him fired from the show. "So I could totally see Gregory slipping him the laxatives and hoping he would get sick on camera as a way to pay him back for the humiliation he inflicted on his husband. Then again, Sibia *seems* really sweet, but she has access to all of Rex's food and could have easily slipped it into his drink. In fact, now that I'm thinking about it, she offered him a drink the other day, and he turned it down because he said something about it wasn't right. And Sibia would have something to gain because she's the one who took his place on the show and got her shot in front of the camera."

"That makes sense," Leon said. "I like your reasoning. A revenge scenario or bumping someone out of the way makes sense. Any other theories?"

"I'm not sure those were theories. Just ideas. But I can't think of any reason for any of the contestants to have done anything to Rex." Although if she were going with a revenge scenario, the only one who would have any reason to humiliate Rex as payback would be Evie.

She kept that idea to herself.

"Do any of those theories make sense to you?" she asked Leon, hoping to hear *his* thoughts on the murder.

He shrugged. "I don't get paid to have theories. I just get paid to present the evidence."

"That's not how it seems on television. The medical examiner is always the one solving the murders."

He rubbed his bushy salt and pepper hair. "Yeah, and those medical examiners are also usually handsome and have great hair." He quirked an eyebrow at her. "Promise me you're going to give the coroner great hair. And a great sense of humor. And maybe a Scottish accent. He's got to be a real character."

"I can't promise an accent, but I guarantee he'll be handsome. And a real character." She offered him a coy grin and dramatically batted her eyelashes. "Just like you."

He laughed and affected a Scottish brogue. "Why Miss Briggs, are ye flirtin' with me, lass?"

She laughed and shook her head. "Definitely *not* an accent."

"Maybe he could be British," he said, switching accents. "He could offer someone a spot of tea and a biscuit. That would be bloody cool."

*　*　*

Bailey was still smiling as she slipped out the morgue door and ran right into Sawyer.

He grabbed her shoulders to steady her but didn't look real excited to see her. His brow creased as he peered down at her. "Well, hello, Bailey. What are you doing here?"

She smiled with what she hoped looked like innocence. "I'm adding in a medical examiner as a new character in my book, so I stopped in to ask Leon a few questions."

His stare remained steely. "Questions about your fictional story? Or questions about Rex's murder?"

Dang. He knew her too well. This time she tried for an innocent shrug. "Maybe both?" He didn't seem to appreciate her attempt at humor, so she quickly changed the subject. "Where are you headed?"

He pointed across the street. "Just going over to the Tasty Freez to grab some lunch. You want to join me?"

"Sure," she said falling into step beside him.

They approached the walk-up window, and Bailey was overcome with memories of the millions of times they'd been there together. They may have been thirteen years older than when they were a teenage couple, but the feelings she had for him were still just as strong.

Her stomach flipped, just like it used to, when he turned and smiled down at her. "You still like mini corn dogs and Tater Tots?"

"Of course." She couldn't believe he remembered. "Do you still like a cheeseburger with ketchup only and a chocolate shake?"

He laughed as he nodded. "You remembered." He stepped up to the window and placed their order. He shot her a quick glance. "You want me to order you a milkshake too? Or do you just want to act like you don't want one and then drink half of mine?"

She just grinned for an answer.

He chuckled. "Half of mine it is, then."

She wasn't the only one who remembered how they used to be.

They picked up their food, and without saying anything, both walked across the street to the park and to their favorite bench, where they always used to sit. Being with Sawyer felt as familiar as sliding her feet into a worn pair of slippers. But at times, it also still felt new and exciting.

They sat down on the bench, and Sawyer handed her his shake and her bag of food. "So, what kind of information did you trick Doc into giving you?"

"He didn't tell me anything." Which was essentially true. Jin had been the one to tell her something. Doc had just let her spin her own ideas. "I did learn something of importance earlier today, though."

"Oh yeah? What's that?"

"Did you know that Rex Rafferty was just a stage name for John Stone."

Sawyer nodded. "I did."

"But did you know that John Stone legally changed his name from Eugene Dix?"

Sawyer's eyes widened. *Yes.* She gave herself an imaginary high five. She had found out something he hadn't. "Yes, I did know that," he said. "But I'm surprised that you do."

Oh. She tried not to feel disappointed as her bottom lip poked out in a pout. "How did you know?"

Sawyer quirked an eyebrow. "You do realize I *am* the sheriff? Which means they give me access to all sorts of fancy law enforcement equipment. I knew that the minute I ran his fingerprints through the database."

That made sense. And it made sense why he wouldn't tell her. But she still felt disappointed that he'd already known.

She took a sip of his shake, then passed it back to him. "Did you know that Eugene Dix used to live in Humble Hills?" She was totally fishing here but was hoping Sawyer might take the bait.

He shook his head as he chewed on a fry. "That I did *not* know. Are you sure?"

Her shoulders slumped. "No. I'm just guessing. But I was hoping you would confirm one of my theories."

He laughed. "Just *one* of your theories. Bailey, darlin', I do enjoy hearing how your brain works. And I know you're chompin' at the bit to tell me what you know." He handed her back the shake. "So why don't you fill me in on *all* your theories."

She took a sip of the shake and savored the cool chocolaty taste. She was dying to tell him what she thought. She popped another Tater Tot in her mouth and filled him in on everything she'd found out as they finished their lunch.

Sawyer didn't confirm or deny any of her notions, but he was a good listener and occasionally asked a question that had her thinking she might be on the right track with some of her deductions.

They tossed their trash and fell into step together again as they walked back to the police station. A thrill ran up Bailey's spine as Sawyer's hand brushed hers.

That small thrill turned into a tsunami of sensation as the next time their hands brushed, he took hers and twined their fingers together. Holding his hand did make her heart beat faster, but it also felt perfectly right, as if she'd just been in limbo, suspended in time, waiting for him to take her hand again. As they walked, she let out a breath that felt like she'd been holding for years.

He kept her hand clasped in his all the way back to her car and only let go so she could dig her keys out of her purse.

He turned and leaned his back against the car as he tipped up his cowboy hat. "Will it do me any good to beg you to stop asking questions and just let me work this case my way?"

"Probably not."

He sighed. "Don't you have a novel you're supposed to be working on?"

"I do. But all this investigating just gives me more material for my latest book."

He raised one eyebrow. "So what you're saying is that I need to give you something else to take your mind off this case. Something to distract you."

"My best friend is in trouble. I can't think of anything that could distract me from trying to solve this murder."

"Well, I know what's been distracting me," he muttered as he reached up to cup the back of her neck in his palm.

Pulling her toward him, he leaned in and pressed his lips to hers, capturing her mouth in a kiss that stole her breath and every coherent thought from her head.

Chapter
Twenty-Four

Bailey's arms automatically wrapped around Sawyer's neck, and she melted into him as he deepened the kiss. His mouth was warm, and he tasted like chocolate shake. The familiar smell and feel of him wrapped around her like a cozy blanket on a cold night, and she could have kissed him forever.

Which they might have done. It was hard to tell since it felt like time stood still and everything else fell away. They could have been kissing for one minute or ten, but he looked as dazed as she felt when he finally pulled away.

He blinked, then swallowed, as if trying to regain his composure. "I'll call ya later," he said before turning away and walking back to the station.

Bailey slid into the front seat of her car but couldn't remember what she'd been going to do next. Heck, she wasn't sure she could even remember her own name. And she didn't care. She just sat there, staring into nothing, reliving every moment of the last thirty minutes.

Reaching up, she touched the tips of her fingers to her lips, recalling the exact feel of his mouth as it had pressed to hers.

She jumped at a hard knock on her window and looked up to see Evie peering through the windshield. Bailey finally turned on the car and hit the button to roll the window down.

"Wow. You look like a woman who's been thoroughly kissed," Evie said, leaning into the car.

Bailey pressed her hand to her mouth. "Are you serious? Can you tell?"

Her friend laughed. "No, I can't tell. Although the absolutely guilty look on your face right now makes me wonder if *you're* the one who just murdered someone?"

"Um . . . I . . . then how did you know?"

Evie shook her head. "Because I saw you guys making out next to your car as I was walking over here."

Bailey's head whipped from side to side. "Do you think anyone else saw?"

Evie laughed again. "I think *everyone* else saw. But who cares? We all know that it's just a matter of time before you two get out of your own way and get back together."

Bailey sighed at the thought. Was she ready to completely leap in and try again with Sawyer? Her brain might have been telling her to take it slow, but her lips were weighing in with a resounding *"Yes!"*

"Are you on a break?" Bailey asked, trying to change the focus of the conversation to anything other than her and Sawyer and the future of their possible relationship.

Evie shook her head. "I'm off for the day. And I saw you over here and thought we could try to catch Charlotte again. Her lunch rush looks like it might be dying down too."

"Good idea."

They didn't want to take up a table or talk to her in front of a customer, so trying to catch Charlotte again meant loitering out on the sidewalk, casually glancing through the window and watching for an opportunity to catch her alone. They got their chance when they saw her head out the back door. Then they hightailed it around the building and caught her in the alley.

"Hey, Charlotte," Bailey called, trying to catch her breath. She really needed to work out more. Or just *start* working out period.

Charlotte let out a shriek and almost dropped what she was holding—which Bailey was surprised to see was a cigarette and lighter.

"I didn't know you smoked," Evie said.

"I don't. Usually," Charlotte said, dropping the single cigarette and lighter into her apron pocket. "Only when I'm stressed out."

Interesting.

"What are you so stressed out about?" Bailey asked. "The Bake-Off is over."

Was all that stress due to the fact that you just murdered the host?

"The Bake-Off is *not* over," Charlotte insisted. "They never declared a winner."

"I guess you're right." Bailey had forgotten that they'd discovered Rex's body just before announcing the winner. Surely *that* wasn't why Charlotte was acting so funny.

Although she wasn't just *acting* funny; she looked different too. She had on jeans, a faded yellow Sunshine Café T-shirt, and sneakers. Her hair was pulled up in what looked like a hurried ponytail and her eyeliner was smudged below one eye. She looked nothing like the put-together, crisply starched woman she'd been the first day of the show.

"Is there something I can help you with?" Charlotte said in an obvious attempt to get rid of them.

"We just wanted to talk to you about what happened with Rex," Evie said.

"I don't know *anything* about what happened to Rex." The shrillness of her voice told a different story.

"Look Charlotte, we're not here to accuse you of anything," Bailey said. "We just want to talk."

"Talk about what?" She chewed at the torn cuticle on the side of her thumbnail as she looked from Bailey to Evie, then a dawning expression crossed her face. "Oh my gosh. Do you think *I* had something to do with Rex's *murder*?"

"We know you went back into Edwards Hall at ten thirty that night," Bailey told her. "Did you kill him?"

Charlotte's eyes widened as she rapidly shook her head. "What? No. Absolutely not."

"Then why have you been acting so squirrelly around us?" Bailey asked. "We saw you yesterday when you dropped behind the counter and crawled into the kitchen after you spotted us outside."

"We know you've been avoiding us," Evie added.

Charlotte's shoulders slumped, and she let out a weary sigh. "Okay. Yes. I *have* been avoiding you. But it has nothing to do with Rex getting killed. It has to do with my disgraceful behavior at the Bake-Off."

"I don't understand," Bailey said.

She looked toward the back door and then lowered her voice so much that Bailey and Evie had to lean closer to hear her.

"Things haven't been going so great at the restaurant lately. We've gotten in a little over our heads. I really needed this. I thought if I had a chance to get on television, that might drive more business to the café. Otherwise, I never would have . . ." She paused to swallow as a single tear ran down her cheek. "If we hadn't been so desperate, I swear I never would've done it."

Bailey still didn't get it. "Done *what*?"

Charlotte stared at the ground, using the toe of her shoe to rub at a stain on the concrete. "I'm sorry. I really am."

Evie huffed in frustration. "Sorry for *what*?"

"For sabotaging your recipe."

"Sabotaging my recipe?" Evie looked questioningly at Bailey, then back at Charlotte. "What are you talking about?"

"I'm the one," Charlotte choked out. "I'm the one who switched the sugar in your canister for salt. I snuck into the building the night before and swapped them." She buried her face in her hands. Her shoulders shook as she sobbed. "I've never cheated at anything in my life. I just wanted this *one* thing. I just wanted to win."

"That's why you went back into Edwards Hall at ten thirty that night?" Bailey asked.

Charlotte nodded.

Bailey frowned at Evie. "Well, I have to say, this information is a little disappointing. Switching out sugar for salt is nothing compared to whacking a man over the head with a KitchenAid mixer."

"I agree." Evie turned back to Charlotte. "Did you see Rex at all when you were in there?"

"No. The last time I saw him was . . ." Another sob escaped her as Charlotte pressed her hand over her mouth.

"You might as well tell us," Bailey said. "We're going to find out anyway."

This was a lie. They probably wouldn't have found out anything. She was embarrassed to admit that their investigative skills in this case had been sorely lacking. They'd barely found any clues and didn't feel any closer to figuring out who the real killer was.

But Charlotte didn't need to know that.

"Okay. Okay," Charlotte relented. "I also took Rex a pie. I was trying to butter him up. You know, get him to like me." She narrowed her eyes at Evie. "He spent so much time talking to and paying attention to you. And look at me . . ." She paused to glance down at herself. "How could *I* possibly compete with someone like you?"

"First of all, you're gorgeous, so stop putting yourself down," Bailey said. She hated to hear women berate themselves. Even bake-off-cheating possible murderers. "And second of all, who cares if Rex paid attention to you? He wasn't even one of the judges."

"It didn't matter. He just needed to spend more time talking to *me* on camera. We've been working on a new idea of trying to sell our pies online. And I thought if I could find a way to work that into the conversation, and if Rex happened to mention that he had tried one of my pies and said something about how flaky the crust was or about the delicious filling, then maybe it would be the boost that our online business needed."

"So, I don't suppose you added any Ex-Lax to that pie?" Bailey asked.

Charlotte reared back, her expression horrified. "Ex-Lax? In my *pie*? No. Of course not. Why would I do that?"

"Great question," Bailey said. "Why *would* someone do that? We don't know the answer, but someone did. Rex's drink was laced with it, and I just wondered if it was you. Or if you added more of it to the pie."

Bailey didn't want to give away the fact that they knew Charlotte's pie had been stolen from Rex's trailer. It would make sense that if she had drugged the pie, then she'd want to get it back.

"No. I wasn't trying to make him sick," Charlotte insisted. "I wanted him to go crazy for that pie."

"You know, that's strange that you said you took a pie to his trailer," Evie said. "Because I seem to recall hearing Sawyer talking about searching the trailer, and I don't remember him saying that he saw a pie."

Way to go, Evie. It was a lie, but Sawyer would never know. Hopefully.

Charlotte looked back down at the spot on the ground, suddenly unable to meet either Bailey or Evie's eyes. She let out another hard sigh. "I guess that's *another* thing that I'm ashamed of. You know how small towns are—everyone knows everyone. Well, my husband knows someone at the medical examiner's office, and he heard that they thought Rex had ingested something bad. And he knew that I had taken him a pie. Which, frankly, really gets my goat, because I can't believe my husband thinks that I would use my culinary skills to cause harm. But he was so nervous about it that he snuck into Rex's trailer the night after the murder and stole back the pie and the box I delivered it in. He was just so worried that it would look incriminating to have something of mine and with our name on it in Rex's trailer."

It did look incriminating, Bailey thought. But it looks *more* incriminating that Ben broke into the trailer to remove the evidence.

Charlotte reached out to rest a hand on Evie's arm. "I'm really sorry, Evie. I feel terrible. I felt terrible right after I did it. And I felt even more guilty when I won that day's Bake-Off recipe. I can't even enjoy the victory because I know that it came at someone else's expense. I feel awful for what I did. Can you ever forgive me?"

Evie put her hand over Charlotte's. "Of course I can. I don't condone what you did, but I can see that you do feel bad about it. And you won that day's recipe, fair and square. I figured out the sugar switch after I'd tried to cream a cup of salt into my butter. It tasted terrible. That's why I accidentally spilled my canister and borrowed fresh sugar from Spike."

Bailey couldn't help wondering, if Spike hadn't offered his sugar, would they have discovered Rex's body sooner? Could Charlotte be a better actress than they were giving her credit for? Had she purposely switched the sugar, knowing that not only would Evie's recipe be ruined, but that if the switch was discovered during the show, then someone would go to the supply closet to get a fresh bag of sugar? And discover Rex's body. Which would place Charlotte on stage when it could have happened and give her a chance to play innocent.

But Rex hadn't been killed during the show. He'd been beaned with the mixer sometime during the night.

"When you were exchanging the sugar for salt, did you see anyone else in the building? Or did you know that Rex was already dead?"

Charlotte's eyes widened. "I know I sabotaged Evie's recipe, but do you really think I'm the kind of person who could just step over a dead body to grab a container of salt?"

Bailey held up her hands. "Sorry. Of course you wouldn't do that."

Or would you?

"I *know* that Rex hadn't been killed yet," Charlotte insisted. "I was *in* that closet. I brought my own salt because I didn't want the show's supply to be depleted or make the festival fund have to pay for my deceitfulness. But I tipped over a bottle of vanilla that didn't have the lid on tight enough, and it spilled across the counter, so I had to go into the closet to get some paper towels. And I *would* have noticed if there'd been a dead body in there."

"Did you see anyone else in the building?" Evie asked.

"No. Not at first. But someone else *was* in there."

Chapter
Twenty-Five

Bailey frowned. "What do you mean someone else was in there?"

"I know it sounds silly," Charlotte said, "but when I first went in the building, it just felt like someone was watching me. I thought I was just being paranoid because I was doing this horrible thing. But I called out a hello when I arrived, and no one answered. I was putting the paper towels back in the closet when I heard a door shut and then heard two people's voices. It sounded like they were arguing."

"What did their voices sound like? Was it two men arguing or a man and a woman?"

"Definitely a man and a woman."

This was new information. Bailey couldn't help but feel like they were finally getting a solid clue. "What were they arguing about?"

"I don't know. I was in the closet, so I just hunkered down and prayed they didn't find me in there. I held perfectly still, and I can tell you, you never know how loud your breathing is until you're worried that someone can actually hear you taking a breath. I was so scared."

"Did you think they would hurt you? Did they sound violent?" Evie asked.

Charlotte shook her head. "No. It wasn't that. I was scared they would find me and kick me off the Bake-Off. But when they started to come backstage, I backed into the mop bucket and the wheels squeaked. They must have heard something because they stopped talking, and then I heard their footsteps run out of the building."

"Did you ever see them?"

"No. But I was worried they'd see me or I'd run into them outside of the building, so I stayed hidden for at least ten minutes, and then I got my fanny out of there."

"Was anyone outside when you left?" Evie asked.

Charlotte shook her head.

Bailey chewed on her lower lip. "Okay, so you were in the closet before Rex was killed. Think back to what was in there. Did you see the KitchenAid mixer?"

"Yes. There were two of them, a black one and a yellow one. I remember seeing them on the shelf and thinking that I wished I'd gotten the yellow one for my station. It was so pretty. And it would've looked better on camera because it matched my outfits."

"Did you happen to notice if there was any blood or brain matter on the side of the mixer at the time?" Evie asked.

Charlotte made a gagging motion. "Ew. No."

"No, of course there wouldn't have been." Bailey gave Evie a look that she hoped her friend interpreted as "what the heck, dude?"

Evie wiggled her eyebrows and mouthed, "Shock value."

In a move that rivaled her daughter's, Bailey rolled her eyes. "The mixer was on the floor. The killer wouldn't have knocked Rex on the head with it and then put it back on the shelf. But you did give us an important piece of the puzzle, because we now know that Rex had to have been killed after ten thirty that night."

"After eleven," Charlotte corrected. "Or maybe ten forty-five. I was in and out of there as quickly as possible. Even with the time spent hiding and cleaning up the vanilla, there's no way I was in there more than fifteen or twenty minutes."

"We keep getting little pieces of the puzzle," Evie said after Charlotte went back inside the café and they were walking toward Bailey's car. "But none of them seem to fit together."

"That's because we're only getting a few of the pieces, and the ones we have feel like they've been half chewed up by the dog."

"So do you really think that we can cross Charlotte off our list of suspects?"

Bailey shrugged. "I don't know. It felt like she was telling the truth. And she did seem lighter after she confessed to swapping the sugar and the salt. Her story did make sense. But that doesn't mean she's not a clever mastermind who told us all that in order to cover up the real story of her going back and killing Rex."

"But why would she want Rex dead? That's what doesn't make sense to me."

"You're right. Charlotte needed him to be alive and paying attention to her to get her the on-camera attention she craved." Bailey sighed. "I keep feeling like we're taking one baby step forward and then two giant steps back."

"So, let's take another baby step," Evie said.

Bailey checked her watch, surprised that it was barely past one. She glanced back at Evie. "Feel like a slice?"

Evie offered her the kind of smile that best friends used when they knew *exactly* what the other was thinking without having to actually say it. "Yeah, that's exactly what I feel like. Let's go."

They took Bailey's car, and this time they caught Harvey on the sidewalk as he was returning from a delivery.

"Hey, Harv," Bailey called out.

He turned to them with a friendly smile. "Hey there. You coming in for a pie?" He pointed to Bailey. "I know the Toni-Roni is your favorite."

Bailey almost lost her nerve. This was Harvey McCormack. He'd been a few years ahead of her in school, but she'd known him since she was a kid. He'd spent a couple of summers helping Granny Bee bale and stack hay. He wasn't a killer.

He was a sweet guy who'd married his high school sweetheart and had three kids, one of them Daisy's age. She just couldn't imagine him being involved in a murder.

"We were actually hoping to talk to you," Evie told him.

He jammed the padded pizza carrier he was holding under one arm. "Yeah, of course. What's up?"

Harv's name had been on the list in Rex's pocket. Rex knew about the Toni-Roni. It didn't matter how nice of a guy he was, or that he knew she liked orange soda with her pizza, or how many kids he had. He was on the list. He *had* to be involved somehow.

And they wouldn't know how if they didn't ask him.

"We wanted to talk to you about Rex Rafferty," Bailey said.

Harv frowned. "That celebrity hotshot who was killed down at the fairgrounds? What do you want to ask *me* about?"

"Did you know him?"

Harvey shook his head, a look of what seemed to be genuine puzzlement on his face. "No, I don't think so. Not unless he came in for a slice. But I think I'd remember if I talked to a guy we watch on television."

"You've seen his show?" Evie asked.

Harvey nodded. "Yeah, sure. The wife loves it. She even tried to get her hair done like Rachel wears hers."

"And Rex never looked familiar to you?"

He frowned again. "No. Should he?"

Bailey took a deep breath. This was the moment. "What if I told you that Rex Rafferty was just a stage name and that he used to be Eugene Dix?"

The color drained from Harvey's face. He shook his head, the bewildered expression appearing to be authentic as he sputtered, "N-no, it can't be."

Yeah. He was involved.

Harvey clearly looked to be in shock. Bailey almost felt sorry for him, but she knew this was the best time to ask questions, hopefully catching him off guard as he processed the news. "So, you *did* know Eugene Dix?"

Harvey gave a small tip forward of his head. "It was a long time ago. We were just dumb kids. I never wanted anyone to get hurt."

Hurt?

"What happened?" Bailey asked softly.

But he seemed lost in his own memories. "It was Carl and Gordy's idea. No, I think Gordy's the one who came up with it. And Carl did whatever Gordy said. I played football with those guys and hung out with them sometimes, so it took me a while to see it, but there was something seriously wrong with Gordy Russell. He had a mean streak in him. I saw him kick a cat so hard once that it dang near killed the thing. He was a bully—the worst kind—picked on anyone weaker than him. But he terrorized Eugene."

"Why?"

Harvey shook his head, his expression a mix of shame and remorse. "I don't know. Because he could. Because Eugene was kind of a weird kid. He was overweight and wore glasses. He had terrible acne and liked comic books." He swallowed. "I guess I don't really know if he was weird or not. I'm ashamed to admit that I never really tried to get to know him. I think he only had one friend. He was a year below us in school, but all I cared about then was football and girls, and he was just a nerdy high school kid. But he didn't deserve what they did to him."

Bailey kept her voice low as she gently prodded. "What did they do?"

Harvey swiped at his cheek with the back of his hand, rubbing away a tear that had leaked out the corner of his eye. "I have kids now. Two girls and a boy. My son loves video games, and he wears glasses too. I can't bear the thought of someone treating him the way Gordy and Carl picked on poor Eugene. We were sophomores and he was a freshman—he only went to school here the one year. I think his mom cleaned rooms at the hotel. It was just the two of them, and they were dirt poor. I think they were living in their car for a while. They had nothin' and still Gordy tried to take away anything good in that kid's life. Stole his books, messed with his lunch, tripped him in the halls, called him names—anything to humiliate him. But it was that last week of school that things got really bad.

"Eugene showed up at school wearing this blue and white shirt and this red hoodie from Aeropostale that looked pretty new. Like I said, the kid didn't have much, and he usually wore the same few baggy T-shirts and faded jeans that probably came from a thrift store. He had this real curly hair, and that day he'd used some kind of gel or something to slick it back. But Gordy recognized that shirt and hoodie he was wearing because they used to be his. Said his mom had given them to Goodwill the week before."

Bailey sucked in a small breath. "Oh no."

Harvey nodded, and his brows pulled together as if just telling the story was causing him physical pain. "It was the second-to-last day of school, and it had rained that afternoon. We'd switched to baseball by then, so Coach called practice off early. That's the only reason we saw Eugene in the woods. We were walking home, me and Carl and Gordy. You know that path that goes through the woods behind the school. It dumps you out next to the park?"

Bailey and Evie both nodded.

"Eugene must have been walking home—he was all by himself. Kid probably thought he was safe because Gordy was usually in practice at that time. We caught up to him, and Gordy just couldn't get over the fact that he was wearing his old clothes. He started pushing him and telling him he wanted his stuff back. He yanked the hoodie off him, then hauled him up by the collar and ripped the shirt. Eugene was a chunky kid, but he wasn't very tall, and he was terrified."

Harvey choked on his last word, the emotion of the story clogging his throat. "I should have done something. Should have stopped him. But it escalated so fast. One minute Gordy was just kind of pushing Eugene around, and then the next, he was pulling the shirt over his head. Gordy started punching Eugene in the face, yelling at him that he didn't deserve to wear his clothes.

"Eugene was crying, and he stumbled back and fell over this tree branch. That's when Gordy started kicking him. The kid was half naked, slathered in mud, just curled into a ball, with his arms covering his head. And Gordy was telling him what a loser he was. I did try then—I swear I did. I told Gordy to leave Eugene alone and tried to pull Gordy away from him, but Gordy was so worked up, he shoved me away and told Carl to hold me back. But I took off running, back to the school. Everyone was gone by then, but the custodian was still there. He was outside, putting some stuff in the sports shed.

"I told him Gordy and Carl were beating up Eugene in the woods, and Mr. Jenkins didn't think twice, just grabbed a bat from the shed and started running. By the time we got back to them, Eugene was still on the ground, but he was just wearing his underwear and covered in mud. His lip was split and bleeding, and his eye was swollen shut. Mr. Jenkins lost it, yelling and swinging that bat, and Gordy and Carl took off running. Mr. Jenkins took off his jacket and wrapped Eugene in it. I found his clothes, and we took him back to the school. He was crying and hunched over in pain, but he could walk. The school was empty, but Mr. Jenkins had keys to everything, so we took him to the nurse's station.

"Mr. Jenkins told me to call my mom and tell her what happened. She came to the school and had Eugene's mom with her, so she must have picked her up on her way. His mom was already crying a little, but when she saw Eugene lying on that cot, she just fell down next to him, hugging him, and started sobbing. My mom took me home, and I never saw Eugene again."

Bailey brushed the tears from her cheeks and had to swallow before she could speak. What kind of monster could do that to another child? "What happened to Gordy and Carl?"

Harvey lifted one shoulder. "I don't know. There was only one day left of school, and neither of them showed up. My mom and I packed up a bunch of my old clothes and took some food to Eugene's. They were renting this little house in the country. The place looked like it was all but falling down. Eugene's mom was loading up their car when we got there. I told her I wanted to apologize to Eugene, but she said he was sleeping. My mom gave her the stuff, hugged her, and we left. I saw my mom stuff a couple hundred dollars into an envelope and tuck it in with the food, but we never talked about it. I never heard of any charges or anything coming against Gordy or Carl. Maybe because Eugene and his mom moved away. I kept my distance from those guys that summer, and by the time school started in the fall, I'd made new friends and I guess I just wanted to forget it ever happened. I'm cordial, but I still do my best to steer clear of those guys now."

The door opened behind him, and Harvey's wife poked her head out. "Hate to interrupt you, hon, but I have another delivery that's ready to go out."

Harvey coughed and scrubbed at the wetness on his cheeks. "Yeah, I'll be right in."

She smiled and waved at Evie and Bailey before disappearing back into the restaurant.

"My wife knows about this, of course, but I haven't talked about it in years," Harvey told them. "It's not something I'm proud of."

Bailey put a comforting hand on his shoulder. "We understand. And we appreciate you telling us. In light of what's happened though, I think we need to share this with Sawyer. I'm sure he's going to want to talk to Carl and Gordy."

Harv frowned. "You don't think they had something to do with the murder?"

"I don't know. Rex had a list in his pocket with four names on it, and it included yours, Carl's, and Gordy's. Your story ties all those names together."

"*My* name was on a list? I swear, I didn't even talk to Rex Rafferty. And I sure didn't know that he was Eugene." He tilted his head as if a thought had come to him. "You said there were four names. Who was the fourth?"

"We don't know," Bailey said. "It was just initials. P. J."

"Then the list *has* to be about that day."

"Why?"

"Because those are the custodian's initials. His name was Paul Jenkins."

Chapter Twenty-Six

After hearing Harv's story, Bailey and Evie decided to take another run at trying to talk to Carl.

There were no customers in the hardware store when they walked in, but they found Carl in the back of the shop, stocking a shelf with small boxes of screws.

He didn't look surprised to see them, more like resigned, as if he'd been expecting them to show up again. "You two are like a couple of bad pennies," he said.

Bailey winced. "Sorry to bug you at work, but we just wanted to ask you a couple more questions." After what she'd just heard, she actually *wasn't* that sorry to bug him. In fact, she kind of wanted to punch him in the throat.

He pointed to the open box next to him. It was full of the small cardboard boxes he was stocking. He held one up and fixed a sticker on it from the pricing gun he held in his other hand, then stacked it on the shelf. "Decking screws. We go through them like crazy this time of year." He pointed to the box, then to the shelf. "You wanna talk, you gotta work." He passed Bailey the pricing gun and turned to open another box. "What do you want to know?"

Bailey had worked plenty of retail jobs and was no stranger to how a pricing gun worked. She fixed a sticker on every carton of the top level in the box, and then Evie scooped them up and stacked them neatly on the shelves.

"I know you told us before that you didn't know Rex Rafferty," Bailey said, labeling the next row with stickers. "But we don't think you were being completely honest."

Carl kept his gaze trained on the shelf in front of him. "I told you the truth. I didn't know that Rex guy."

"No, but maybe you knew him before he was Rex Rafferty."

Evie arranged a new stack of boxes on the shelf. "Did you know him when he was Eugene Dix?"

Carl was reaching for a new box, but his hand paused in mid-air. He let out a long sigh before turning around, leaning his back against the shelves. He scrubbed his hand over his face. "Yeah, I knew Eugene."

Bailey had known Carl Davis for a long time. She'd spent hours and countless dollars in his store. She'd joked around with him, and a few weeks ago he'd spent twenty minutes helping her pick out the right stain to refinish a small end table she'd found in the attic. Even though a few minutes ago, she'd wanted to throat-punch him, she still had a hard time reconciling the Carl she knew with the teenage bully in Harv's story.

"I was a different person back then," Carl finally said, almost as if reading her thoughts. "The biggest regret of my life is the way we tormented that kid."

"You and Gordy?" Bailey asked.

"Yeah."

"Are you still friends with him?" Evie asked.

He shook his head. "No. Not after what happened. For weeks I waited for the knock on the door, for the police to show up and take me away. I lay awake so many nights, terrified of going to juvenile detention, scared of what it would do to my football career, what it would do to my parents when they found out what we'd done." He stared at the floor. "But that knock never came. I guess Eugene and his mom packed up and moved away and never filed any charges. Which you would think would have been a good thing, but it didn't change the way I felt. I was so ashamed of myself.

"I stopped hanging out with Gordy that summer. And I couldn't bring myself to look Mr. Jenkins in the eye when I saw him at school. I tried to make up for what I did—I went to church, I volunteered, I did community service. Then I went away to college and just tried to forget about it, to pretend it never happened."

He let out another long breath. "Then three or four days ago, Eugene walked into my store. I didn't even recognize him. Heck, my wife watches his show. I've seen it a handful of times, and I never would have guessed it was the same guy. He'd grown taller and lost the weight. His skin had cleared up, and his hair was a different color and cut a new way. But it was more than that. He had a kind of confidence he'd never had before."

"What did he want?" Bailey asked.

Carl let out a dry laugh. "Money."

"Money?" She hadn't expected that.

"He told me his news station was going to do a show on bullying, and he was going to tell his story. Talk about what Gordon and I had done to him. I told him how sorry I was. I told him I'd changed and that I had a wife and two sons. And that I just couldn't imagine the contempt I would see in their eyes if they learned about what I'd done. I begged him not to do the show. And he said he'd can the idea . . . if I paid him fifty thousand dollars."

"Fifty thousand dollars?" Evie held up the small box she was holding. "That's a lot of decking screws."

"Did you agree?" Bailey asked, her mind already whirling with thoughts about what happened to the cash and who might have it now. "Did you give him the money?"

Carl shook his head. "No way. I don't have that kind of money. Look around . . ." He gestured to the empty store. "It's not exactly Home Depot in here. This was my father's store. I work here because it was important to him. And because I want to leave that legacy to my sons. It doesn't make me rich, but it pays us enough to get by. I just don't have *that* kind of cash. And trying to come up with it would ruin me."

"That was probably the idea," Bailey said.

"What did he say when you told him no?" Evie asked as she placed the last of the boxes on the shelf.

"He told me I should think more about it. Think about my family. Think about what a story like that—presented on national television—would do to my reputation as a good upstanding citizen of Humble Hills. Then he said he'd be back in a couple of days to see if I'd changed my mind."

"But he didn't come back, did he?" Bailey asked. "He was murdered before he had a chance to make good on his threat."

Carl pushed away from the shelf and stood to face Bailey. "I didn't have *anything* to do with that. I've spent my whole adult life regretting what I did to that kid, wishing I could apologize, feeling sorry for him. Then one day he just walks into my shop and threatens to burn my life to the ground. But that doesn't mean I *killed* him."

The bell above the front door jangled as a customer entered the shop. "Hey, Carl," a voice rang out. "My dang toilet just broke. Can you help me find a fill valve and a two-inch flapper?"

Evie and Bailey left the store as Carl greeted the customer. They turned to each other when they reached the sidewalk outside.

"Well, what do you think of that story?" Evie asked.

"I think it sounds like a fifty-thousand-dollar motive to me."

"Agreed," Evie said as they walked toward the car. "And as much as the man makes my skin crawl, I think we need to talk to Gordy again. See if Rex tried to blackmail him too."

Bailey tried to call Sawyer on the way out to the fairgrounds, to fill him in on everything they'd learned, but he didn't pick up his phone. She left him a message that she needed to talk to him.

Evie had better luck getting through to Griffin. After he answered, she put the call on speaker so she and Bailey could tell him everything they'd learned.

"Dang," he said. "I'm impressed. So where are you off to now?"

"We just pulled into the fairgrounds. We're going to try to talk to Gordy again," Evie told him.

"Be careful. And call me if you need me," he said before disconnecting the call.

They crossed the fairgrounds but stopped at Edwards Hall when they saw the television crew sitting outside. The motor home was still there, and the crew was scattered around the seating area. Gregory and Imani were at the picnic table, sharing a basket of ribbon fries. Toby and Sibia were seated in neighboring chairs. She was working on her laptop, and he was reading a book, but Bailey's heart melted at the way their knees touched and the way Toby kept brushing his fingers over Sibia's arm.

"Hi, guys," Bailey said, walking up to the group. "Any news on Rex or when they're going to let you go home?"

Gregory shook his head. "No news on either. And if I keep eating corn dogs and ribbon fries, I'm going to gain ten pounds. Not to mention, the horror it will do to my complexion."

"I love it here," Toby said, grinning as he snuck a glance at Sibia, who was still focused on her laptop. "The weather's amazing, there's no bugs, and the company is great. I could stay here another month."

"Don't even talk like that," Imani said. "I left my dog with a neighbor. And he'll never forgive me if I don't come home for a month."

"Who?" Bailey asked. "The neighbor or the dog?"

Imani nodded. "Yes. Both."

Bailey laughed.

Gregory pointed his finger at her and Evie. "So, Daphne and Velma, tell us, what are you two up to today?"

Evie shrugged. "We're just kickin' butt and takin' names."

Bailey frowned. They *had* heard a lot of new information in the case, but she wasn't sure they'd done any real butt kicking. "We've just been talking to people, asking questions."

"Learn anything new?" Imani asked.

"Yeah. We know someone laced Rex's protein shake with Ex-Lax," Evie told them.

"How'd you know—" Gregory started to say, then blanched as he looked at Imani. "I mean . . . how do you know that someone spiked his water bottle with Ex-Lax?"

"I didn't say they spiked his *water bottle*," Bailey said. "I said they spiked his protein shake."

"Well . . . I mean . . . everyone knows that he drinks his protein shakes in a water bottle. That's just an honest mistake."

"Really?" Bailey used the mom tactic on Gregory that she'd learned from Granny Bee—keep silent and just hold them in a death stare until they eventually break.

Gregory stared back at her. Ten seconds . . . then twenty went by. He let out a frustrated breath. "Okay, fine. I spiked Rex's water bottle with Ex-Lax."

"Oh, for fridge sakes, Gregory. You broke like a dry twig getting stepped on in the forest," Imani said. "You sang faster than a canary."

Gregory hung his head. "I was trying to stay strong. But she was giving me the mom death stare."

Ha. Score one for moms and grannies everywhere.

Imani sighed. "He didn't do it alone. I helped."

Chapter
Twenty-Seven

B ailey gasped. "You *both* did it? *Together?* Why?"
  Gregory cocked an eyebrow and planted his fist on his
hip. "You *know* why. Rex was an A-hole. I told you what he did to
my Anders. Well, he wasn't the only one who suffered from Rex's
evil deeds. That man loved humiliating people. Didn't matter if it
was the receptionist, his coanchor, or even people who were trying to help him, like his assistant." He glanced over at Sibia, who
had closed her laptop and was leaning forward in her chair. "Rex
took any chance he could to try to make the people around him
feel *less* than him. He was a total bully."

"We just wanted to give him a taste of his own medicine,"
Imani said. "We wanted him to know what it felt like to be
embarrassed in front of everyone."

"Oh, he knew," Bailey said. "He used to get bullied terribly as
a kid. I guess he was overweight and kind of nerdy and he got
picked on. *A lot.*" She didn't think it was her place to tell Rex's
whole story, but it seemed okay to share those details.

"So . . . what? He grew up to become a bully himself?" Gregory asked.

"It happens," Bailey said.

"Look, it was a harmless prank," Imani said. "We just wanted to embarrass him. We snuck into Edwards Hall the night of the Bear Run. It was late, and we'd crushed up a bunch of Ex-Lax and were going to put it in something of his. We couldn't agree where but decided to just mix it in with his protein shake powder. But it wasn't enough to kill him." She frowned at Bailey. "Right? We didn't really kill him with that stunt, did we?"

Bailey shook her head. "No. You didn't. It was the twenty-pound mixer whacking him on the head that did him in."

"Whew." She winced. "You know what I mean."

"Yeah, I do," Bailey told her. "And thanks for telling us you guys were the Ex-Lax culprits. At least that solves one mystery." Actually two, since it sounded like Gregory and Imani were probably the man and woman Charlotte had heard arguing while she was hiding in the supply closet.

Gregory lifted his chin and peered down his nose at them. "Do you really think you two are going to solve Rex's murder?"

"We could," Bailey said. "We've done it before."

"And you certainly know your way around a good mystery," Toby said, lifting the book he was reading from his lap.

Bailey was surprised to see it was one of hers. She offered Toby a grateful smile. "Thank you. That's nice. But sometimes all it takes is figuring out the right person, or people, to talk to and asking the right questions." *And sometimes an occasional breaking and entering with a bestie who has recently acquired some lock-picking skills.* "So, if you all think of something that might help us, something you saw that didn't seem right, or maybe something you overheard, even if it seems small, please let us know."

Toby, Sibia, and Imani all nodded and assured her they would.

"Don't wait around for a call from me," Gregory said. "Other than that laxative business, which was just a silly prank, I didn't see or hear anything related to Rex's murder. Especially anything that might keep me in this town a day longer than I need to be. I miss the ocean, and there's no oxygen this high up. I don't know how you people breathe. And the air is so dry, I've gone through two tubes of lip balm." He pointed to Bailey. "And just because you know how to solve fictional crimes, doesn't mean you know how to solve *real* ones. An actual person was killed, so that means someone out there is dangerous and might not want you snooping around."

Bailey narrowed her eyes at the stage manager. *Was that a threat?* Surely not. Gregory always seemed so sweet. *But they always say it's the sweet ones that you never suspect.*

Gregory picked up another fry and dipped it in ketchup before pointing it at her. "I just think you'd be better off focusing on the rest of the Bee Festival and leaving this murder business up to the professionals. Like that handsome sheriff of yours."

Now he sounded just like that handsome sheriff of hers.

And speaking of Sawyer.

Her eye caught a familiar gray uniform and cowboy hat, and she was surprised to see Sawyer walking toward Vendor Row. She nudged Evie and pointed out the sheriff. "Let's go see what he's doing here."

They said quick goodbyes to the production crew, promising to touch base with them later, and then hurried after Sawyer.

"Fancy meeting you here," Bailey said, casually strolling up beside him and trying not to sound out of breath from the power walk they'd just done to catch up to him.

He smiled down at her as he wrapped an arm around her shoulder. "I am always glad to see you, Bails, but somehow I don't imagine you're back at the fairgrounds because you were craving another corn dog."

"Hey, Sawyer," Evie said, falling into step with them. She wasn't even breathing hard. *Must be all the running around she does at the restaurant.*

The sheriff looked from one to the other. "You two are like a couple of bad pennies."

Evie laughed. "Yeah, we've been told."

"So, what *are* you doing out here?" he asked.

"We came out to try to talk to Gordy again," Bailey told him. She might as well be honest. He would figure it out anyway. "And since you're heading toward his booth, I assume that's what you're doing here too."

Sawyer groaned.

"Actually, I left you a message," she said before he could start grumbling about her staying out of *his* case. "We have a ton of stuff to tell you."

"A *crap* ton," Evie said.

Sawyer stopped in front of the hot tub display and peered around. No Gordy. He walked through the center aisle of the hot tubs and stopped at the last one. It was the only one of the six that had the cover on it, and Sawyer turned and leaned his hip against it. "All right. I'm listening."

Together, Bailey and Evie told him everything they'd learned, talking over each other at times and filling in gaps the other one missed. But they finally got the whole story out, and from the several shocked looks that Sawyer had given them, Bailey guessed a lot of it was a surprise to him.

"That's awful," Sawyer said when they'd finished. "I can't imagine what that would have done to a kid."

"Or what a jagoff Gordy Russell really is," Evie said.

"I've known the guy a long time," Sawyer said. "That's much easier to imagine."

"We thought since Rex had threatened to blackmail Carl, he probably threatened Gordy too," Bailey said. "They were both on the list in Rex's pocket."

"So were Harvey and P. J.," Evie pointed out. "But Harv said he hadn't seen Rex yet, or if he had, he's a darn good actor, because he seemed genuinely surprised to hear that Rex was really Eugene. And we haven't talked to P. J. yet to figure out why he was on the list."

"Wait. You said 'he.' Have you figured out who P. J. is?" Sawyer asked.

Bailey grinned, loving that they'd found out something else before Sawyer. "Yep. P. J. stands for Paul Jenkins, the school custodian."

"Huh" was Sawyer's only response to their revelation. Which, Bailey had to admit, was a little disappointing. The sheriff scrubbed a hand across the back of his neck. "But you haven't talked to him yet? Mr. Jenkins?"

Evie shook her head. "We were going to check in with Gordy first."

Sawyer glanced from one woman to the other. "I don't suppose either of you have any idea where Gordy is?"

Both Bailey and Evie shook their heads this time.

Sawyer blew out a frustrated breath. "Neither do I. He wasn't home when I stopped by his place last night, and he hasn't been answering his phone." He pulled his phone from his breast pocket and tapped the screen. "I haven't tried him in an hour or so. Maybe we'll get lucky, and he'll pick up."

Bailey and Evie stopped talking as they waited, mostly because they both wanted to hear what the sheriff had to say to Gordy.

The muted lyrics of LMFAO's "Sexy and I Know It" sounded from somewhere behind Sawyer. Bailey twisted her head, leaning her ear closer. Was that sound coming from his phone?

Sawyer must have heard it too, because he pushed away from the hot tub and turned to face it. The sound stopped. He frowned at Bailey. "Did you hear that?"

She nodded. "I think so."

"I heard something too," Evie said, scanning the ground as she walked around to the other side of the hot tub.

"Call him again," Bailey said.

Sawyer tapped his phone, and they all three leaned toward the hot tub as the lyrics, "I'm sexy and I know it" rang out again.

Bailey pointed to the hot tub. "I think it's coming from inside there."

"Me too," Evie said. "That's gotta be his phone. Maybe he dropped it in the hot tub as he was putting the cover on."

Sawyer pointed to the cover's handle closest to Bailey, then he grabbed the one on the other side. "Help me lift this up."

Together, they heaved up one side of the cover. It was the type that folded over on itself and then tilted off the back of the hot tub.

"There it is," Evie said as they started to lift the cover. She pointed to a black cell phone floating on the water next to the side of the tub.

Then she screamed as a hand floated out next to it.

Chapter
Twenty-Eight

B ailey covered her mouth to keep from screaming too as Sawyer heaved the cover the rest of the way off to reveal the swollen body of Gordy Russell floating in the water.

Even though Gordy was face down, she still recognized the shape of his body and the black polo shirt he'd been wearing the last time they'd seen him. His hands had already started to bloat, the skin bulging around the fake designer watch on his wrist.

She gagged at the overpowering stench of death.

Evie's face wore an expression that was a mix of horror and disgust as she took a few steps back, then bent forward and tossed her cookies.

Sawyer raced around the hot tub and wrapped Bailey in a tight hug. "Just breathe, darlin'."

He must have seen that she was teetering on the edge of shock. She fought to stay calm, to keep her breathing steady so her anxiety didn't kick in and she didn't hyperventilate.

There was a display of water bottles next to one of the hot tubs, and Evie grabbed one for herself and tossed one to Sawyer. He twisted the lid off and passed it to Bailey. "Here. Take a drink. You're okay."

She had a tendency to hyperventilate when her anxiety really ramped up. She'd had her first episode when she and Sawyer were in high school. After that, he'd studied up on what to do and was good at getting her to calm down and breathe through it, or finding her a paper bag to breathe into.

The water was lukewarm from being outside all day, but it was wet and felt good on her suddenly parched throat. She took a few deep breaths and took another sip. "You okay?" she asked Evie.

Her friend nodded to Gordy. "I'm a heck of a lot better off than he is." She swallowed and leaned slightly forward. Her mouth stretched in disgust as she peered into the tub again. "What happened? Did he fall in?"

Sawyer narrowed his eyes as he surveyed the scene. "Not unless he fell in and then pulled the cover over on himself."

Evie winced. "Good point."

He pointed to the swollen lump on the back of his head. "And I doubt he hit himself on the back of the noggin. Looks like he took a good whack."

Bailey peered into the tub and pointed at a large pipe wrench that lay on the bottom. "And that looks like the murder weapon."

"Dang," Sawyer swore as he pulled his phone back out of his pocket. "I guess I'd better call this in."

*　*　*

Within twenty minutes, the medical examiner and half of the sheriff's department had arrived on the scene. Which sounds like more people than it actually was, since the department only had about ten employees total, and that included the dispatcher and the cleaning lady.

"We have to stop meeting like this, lass," Leon told Bailey as he passed her on the way to the hot tub.

"Still not giving him a Scottish accent," she called after him.

"Can't stop me from trying," he called back with a grin.

Thankfully, Daisy wasn't at the fairgrounds. She'd gotten a ride back to the ranch earlier with Lyle, the farm manager. But Granny Bee was still there and had hurried over as soon as she heard the sirens. Evie had texted Griffin, and the guy must have sprouted wings and flown over, because Bailey swore he'd showed up within three minutes of her sending the message.

"I'm gonna take her home," Griffin told Bailey, keeping one arm securely around Evie's shoulders.

"I want to get out of these clothes." Evie wrinkled her nose. "And take a shower. I feel like I can smell Gordy on me. And I think I got vomit on my shoes."

"I'll call you later. Thanks for everything today." Bailey gave her a quick hug.

"You want to get out of here too?" Granny Bee asked her. "I have my truck. I can run you home."

Bailey shook her head. "No. I'm okay. As long as I'm standing over here and can't see into the hot tub, I'm good." Although she was pretty sure she was going to be seeing the replay of Gordy's body floating out from under the cover in her nightmares.

"Do you want me to stay with you then? Or go find you a Diet Coke? Or a fried Twinkie?"

"No. Really," she told her grandmother, the idea of a fried Twinkie making her stomach roil. "I promise, I'm fine. And this is great material for my writing. I'm learning a ton about how to actually process a crime scene. I already have several ideas of how to incorporate this into my next book." She rested a hand on

Granny Bee's shoulder. "But you look dead on your feet. You should go home and get in a nap before you have to come back tonight."

News of the murder had already swept through town like a wildfire on a dry day, and the festival committee had called an emergency meeting for later that evening to discuss the effects of the latest body found at the fairgrounds.

"I think I'll do that," Granny Bee said, giving Bailey's arm a squeeze. "But I'm just a phone call away if you need me."

After her grandmother left, Bailey perched on the edge of a picnic table not far from the hot tub and watched as Leon, Sawyer, and his deputies processed the scene. A couple of the deputies had set up barricades to keep the lookie-loos out, but there was still quite a crowd of people watching from behind the blockades.

She studied the crowd, running her gaze over people she'd known most of her life. Could one of them have killed Gordy? And Rex? The two murders had to be connected, but she had no idea how. If this linked back to the incident in the woods when they were kids, it didn't make sense that someone would kill *both* the bully *and* his intended target.

She sat there for at least an hour, waving to Jin when she arrived with the stretcher, and watching as they wheeled Gordy's body away. The deputies had probably used three rolls of caution tape to block off the scene, wrapping several rows of tape around the booth, as if creating slats of a fence.

Since no one was paying attention to her anyway, she opened a Word document on her phone and typed in a bunch of notes about the scene and some ideas of what she could use in the book she was currently working on.

Sawyer came over to stand next to Bailey after the body had been taken away. "You okay?"

"I'm good. It may sound morbid, but this whole thing is like mystery writer catnip to me."

"That does sound morbid. But I get it."

"Any clues to who might have done this?"

Sawyer sighed. "Not a one."

"How long do you have to stick around here?"

He quirked an eyebrow. "Why do you ask?"

She lifted one shoulder in a shrug. "No reason."

"I know you. You're just dying to go talk to Paul Jenkins, aren't you?"

"He's the last person on the list. He might have the clue that makes this all fit together."

Sawyer looked around the scene. "Come on. They can finish this up without me."

Bailey hopped off her picnic table perch. "You mean I get to come with you? To question Mr. Jenkins?"

"Might as well. I know you're going to find a way to talk to him anyway, and I'd rather hear his story directly from him instead of after the fact from you. As it is, I'm going to have to visit Harv and Carl tonight too. I'll need to get their official statements."

She hurried along next to him, trying to keep up with his long strides as well as contain the giddiness at getting to accompany him. "And I *really* get to come with you? You're not just teasing me and then you're going to leave me standing in the parking lot when we get to your truck?"

"Hmm. Tempting. But no. I'm letting you come along, but you have to let *me* do the talking."

"Yes, of course."

"I mean it, Bailey. I'm the sheriff."

"Yes, I know. Yes, sir." She gave him a mock salute.

They reached his department SUV, and he opened the passenger door for her. "Don't touch anything," he warned.

She buckled in, then held her hands in the air until Sawyer made it around the truck and settled in the driver's seat next to her. "Can I run the siren?" she asked as he started the engine and pulled out of the parking lot.

"No."

"Can I look something up on that computer thingie?"

"No."

"Can I touch your gun?"

He'd pulled up to a stop sign and turned his head to offer her a sly grin. "Maybe later."

Oh. My.

* * *

Ten minutes later, they pulled up in front of Paul Jenkins's house. Sawyer had called in to dispatch to get the address. The house was a small rancher on the west side of town, close enough to the school that the custodian could have walked to and from work.

Mr. Jenkins had retired a few years earlier and must have taken up gardening, because the flower beds around his porch and lining his sidewalk were lush with red rose bushes, bright pink peonies, soft yellow columbines, and tall periwinkle-blue delphiniums. His grass was cut, the edges of his lawn had been neatly trimmed, and there wasn't a weed in sight.

He answered the door wearing tan chinos, a white undershirt, and a pair of sheepskin slippers. He had to be in his

mid-seventies by now, but he still had a thick head of silvery hair that was neatly combed. A pair of glasses hung from a cord around his neck.

If he was surprised to see the sheriff or Bailey at his door, he didn't show it. Instead, he stood back and welcomed them in. "Sawyer Dunn. Bailey Briggs. Good to see you both. Come on in."

"Mr. Jenkins," Sawyer said, taking off his cowboy hat as he stepped inside, "hope we're not interrupting you." A small brown terrier mutt jumped off the sofa and came running to greet them. Sawyer bent down to give the dog's chin a scratch.

"Not a bit. Stella and I were just watching a little *Jeopardy* and discussing the idea of sneaking a cookie before supper." He waved a dismissive hand toward the television. "But I miss half the clues anyway. I'd much rather have the company." He winked at Bailey. "And an excuse to get out the cookies."

They followed him into the kitchen, which, like his front yard, was tidy and neat. Bailey wondered if Mr. Jenkins had ever been in the military and was sad to realize she didn't know if there had ever been a *Mrs.* Jenkins. He'd been the custodian at the high school when she and Sawyer had been there as well, so of course, she knew him, but she wasn't sure she'd ever really had much more than a passing conversation with him.

"Have a seat," he said, grabbing a jar that had puppy paw prints printed around it and set it on the table. He pulled off the lid, and she half expected to see dog treats inside but was glad to see peanut butter cookies instead.

Still, she waited for Sawyer to take a bite of one before she took a cookie from the jar.

Mr. Jenkins grabbed a cookie before sinking into a chair across from them. Stella jumped into his lap, and he broke the cookie in half and held one piece out for her. She gently took the offered cookie and settled across his legs to eat it. "Now, what can I do for you?"

Sawyer set his hat on the table, his expression grim. "I'm afraid it's not a very pleasant topic we've come to discuss."

"Oh?"

"It's about an incident that happened with a few former students."

"You're going to have to be more specific. I've had plenty of incidents with any number of students."

"This one happened about fifteen years ago and involved Carl Davis, Gordy Russell, Harv McCormack, and a kid named Eugene Dix."

Mr. Jenkins sighed, and a look of sadness crossed his face. "Oh."

"You remember that day?" Sawyer asked.

"Son, I will never forget that day." He lifted the dog off his lap and set her in the chair next to him, then stood and crossed to the electric tea kettle sitting on the counter. "I'm gonna need a cup of tea to tell that story, though. It's a tough one."

Bailey's phone buzzed in her purse, but this felt too important to interrupt with a phone call. And if whoever was calling really needed her, they would send her a text.

Mr. Jenkins turned the kettle on and set three hearty stoneware mugs and a metal tin of assorted tea bags in the center of the table. Bailey and Sawyer each took an Earl Grey. They unwrapped the bags and dangled them in their cups as Mr. Jenkins passed them each a saucer. It only took a few minutes for the kettle to boil. He poured water into their cups before returning the kettle to its stand and taking his seat at the table.

Kill or Bee Killed

The dog jumped back into his lap as he picked out a tea bag, taking his time before finally settling on a honey-lemon. He cleared his throat. "I was a custodian at that school for twenty-eight years, and I saw a lot of things in my time. But I've never seen anything like that. I know kids can be mean and they can tease one another, and I've seen plenty of bullies in my time, but what Gordy Russell did to that kid was just pure evil."

Chapter
Twenty-Nine

Bailey had eaten two cookies and drunk half her tea, but Mr. Jenkins had drained his cup by the time he finished telling them the story.

It was similar to the one Harv had told, but he filled in a few more details from after Harvey had left with his mother. Eugene had ended up with a sprained wrist, a split lip, and bruised ribs, and one of his eyes was completely swollen shut. When they'd washed the mud away, they'd found his torso was covered with bruises and scrapes.

Mr. Jenkins had convinced Eugene's mother to let him drive them to the emergency room. She'd had meager insurance with her employer, and he admitted that he'd covered the copay and then come back the next day with a few hundred dollars to help cover the hospital bill. They'd put Eugene's wrist in a splint and were able to use steri-strips on the cut above his eye.

He said that Eugene kept insisting that he fell and wouldn't let his mom call the police or tell the doctors what really happened.

"I don't know that any charges were ever filed," he told them. "No one ever came to talk to me. I made a chicken noodle casserole and took it out to their house the next night, but Eugene's mom—I think her name was Janet—had already packed their things in her car. She told me they were going to stay with a cousin in Iowa."

"That makes sense," Sawyer said. "Iowa was where Eugene changed his name."

Bailey felt her phone buzz again. She snuck a glance at her smart watch but didn't recognize the number displayed there, so she ignored it again.

"It seems like Eugene and his mom only lived here about a year, but I don't know if his time here was all bad. He did have the one friend, and I always think that helps—for a kid to have at least one friend. And the two of them were thick as thieves. She was a year ahead of him in school, but they were both book-worms, and I saw them laughing a lot when they were together. She got a car in the middle of the year, some kind of fancy con-vertible, so she usually drove Eugene to and from school, but she must have had something else going on that day, and that's why he was walking home through the woods on his own."

Mr. Jenkins seemed lost in his memories as he recounted the events from all those years ago. "Ya know, I never heard from them again. I always hoped to get a letter, or even a postcard, just to hear how they were getting along, but nothing ever came. But I tell ya, I kept my eye on that snake Gordy Russell for the next few years, though. I still chastise myself for not paying better attention, and I wonder if I could have done something to stop it from happening."

Bailey's heart broke for him. "No, don't do that. You can't blame yourself." The blame lay on Gordy, but Bailey kept that part to herself, hesitant to speak too ill of the recently dead.

Mr. Jenkins shrugged. "I don't know. I still wish I'd paid closer attention. I'd noticed a few times how awful Gordy was to the two of them, but I didn't know how bad it had gotten. But after Eugene left, I kept my eye on the girl. There was no way I was letting Gordy do anything to her."

"It's recently come to our attention that Eugene Dix legally changed his name to John Stone," Sawyer told him before Bailey had a chance to ask about the identity of the girl. "From what we can piece together, he graduated college in Iowa and then moved to Los Angeles to pursue a career in broadcasting."

"He must have grown out of his chubbiness, and his skin obviously cleared up," Bailey said. "With a great hairstylist, a trainer, and new clothes, he changed his appearance enough that he looked like a completely different person."

"He registered a stage name with the Screen Actors Guild," Sawyer said, picking up the thread of conversation. "And for the last several years, the public has known him as Rex Rafferty." He let the name sit in the air of the tidy kitchen, the only sound, Mr. Jenkins' small gasp.

"Rex Rafferty?" Mr. Jenkins asked, his eyes wide. "The same fella who does that morning show with Rachel Ward?"

Sawyer nodded. "The very same."

"You're telling me Rex Rafferty used to be Eugene Dix?" Mr. Jenkins shook his head as if he still couldn't fathom the information.

"Did you know he was in town for the Bee Festival?" Sawyer asked.

"Sure. Everyone knew. A big celebrity like that in our little town. I even went down and watched a couple days of that

Bake-Off. But it never even crossed my mind that Rex might be . . ." His sentence tapered off, his expression still bewildered.

"We thought he might have come to visit you," Bailey said, earning a raised eyebrow from Sawyer.

Mr. Jenkins shook his head again. "No. I never even spoke to him. I was just there to watch the cooking. I'm a big fan of that *Great British Bake Off* show. I've seen every season. And obviously I've eaten at all three of our local contestants' restaurants. To tell you the truth, I didn't really pay that much attention to the host. I was too engrossed in watching Evie, Charlotte, and Spike make those fancy dishes."

"And you don't think he saw you either?"

"I don't think so. My knee gets stiff if I sit too long, so I sat in the back of the audience both days. But the show was so much fun, I didn't even notice my stiff knee. It would have been nice to see him, though," Mr. Jenkins mused. "I'd like to think he might have been planning to visit me before leaving town."

Bailey offered him an encouraging smile. "I'm sure he was." Although because Rex had turned into such a pompous jerk, she wasn't sure. "He did visit Carl Davis, though." *To threaten him with blackmail.* "He's the only one we know he talked to for sure."

Mr. Jenkins frowned. "That surprises me. I would have thought he might have visited Harv; he and his mom were real good to them right after it happened." He rubbed a hand over the fine stubble on his chin. "I can't imagine he would have wanted to see Gordy. Although, Eugene *had* turned into something of a big deal, so maybe he would have wanted to rub his success in Gordy's face. Have you talked to him yet? Gordy?"

"We tried," Bailey said. "But someone killed him too."

"What?" Mr. Jenkins' face blanched. "What happened?"

"Someone whacked him with a wrench and pushed him into a hot tub," Bailey said before realizing she probably shouldn't have. She tried to save herself by adding, "Allegedly."

Sawyer cleared his throat as he offered Bailey a steely stare. "I'd appreciate it if you'd keep that under your hat, Mr. Jenkins. For the time being, at least. Since we haven't had a chance to notify the next of kin."

Bailey shrank back. "Sorry. I didn't think about that being confidential. I figured since there were at least fifty people at the fairgrounds watching them cart his body away, half the town would have heard by now."

Mr. Jenkins waved a dismissive hand in her direction. "Don't worry about it. I won't say anything. Who do I have to tell?" He smiled down at the dog asleep in his lap. "Besides Stella?"

Sawyer pushed up from his chair and held out his hand. "We've taken up enough of your time, Mr. Jenkins. But we appreciate the hospitality and the tea, and you taking the time to talk to us."

"Anytime," Mr. Jenkins said, shaking Sawyer's hand. He nudged the dog, who woke up and jumped off his lap before he stood. "Like I said, I appreciate the company." He walked them to the door. "Stop by anytime."

Bailey paused at the door. "Mr. Jenkins. Earlier, you said that Eugene's friend drove a fancy convertible. Do you happen to remember what kind of car it was?"

He scratched his head. "Can't say that I do. Something foreign, I think. But I sure remember the color. It was a custom paint job. A really pretty blue. I still see her driving it around sometimes. I think she called it 'electric blue.'"

Bailey's Spidey-senses were tingling like crazy. *An electric-blue convertible? Like the one Gordy had recently acquired?*

"Do you remember Eugene's friend's name?" Bailey held her breath, somehow feeling like his next words *had* to be important.

He grinned. "Course I do. I still see her all the time. She lives here in town and stops by for tea a few times a year. I'm sure you know her too. Her name's Jane Johnson. She's a reporter over at the *Humble Hills Herald*. She lives in that little cottage behind the paper. I'm real proud of her." He frowned. "She's always been such a nice girl. Never understood why the kids teased her so much. They called her 'Plain Jane,' poor thing. I think the nickname started in elementary school, but I still heard kids calling her that in high school."

Plain Jane?

They'd been looking in the wrong place. The initials on the list didn't stand for Paul Jenkins.

Bailey looked at Sawyer as she mouthed, "P. J."

Chapter Thirty

Bailey climbed into Sawyer's SUV and buckled her seat belt. Her brain was a whir of thoughts, and she started talking the minute he slid into the driver's seat. "P. J. didn't stand for Paul Jenkins. I mean, I know he was an integral part of what happened to Eugene that day, but I'm just sure that those initials are for Plain Jane."

"I'm tempted to agree with you," Sawyer said.

"But that seems weird, because she was at the taping of the show, and neither she nor Rex acted like they knew each other, although we saw her heading to his motor home after the first day of taping. If I remember, she said she was looking to interview him or get a quote from the contestants."

"Do you think she recognized him?

Bailey shrugged. "I don't know. I mean, Mr. Jenkins didn't, but he must be in his seventies, and he wears glasses. And Carl, Gordy, and Harv are men, so we know how observant they are." She put her hand on his shoulder. "Present company excluded, of course. But Jane is a woman *and* a journalist. And it sounds like they'd been good friends, so it stands to reason that she *would* recognize him."

"But if they were such good friends, she wouldn't have any reason to kill him."

"Agreed. But maybe she knows who did." Bailey jumped up and down in her seat. "And you heard Mr. Jenkins tell us she drove an electric-blue convertible, right?"

"Yeah."

"When Evie and I went to talk to Gordy yesterday, he pulled up in an electric-blue Toyota Solara convertible. Which they don't even manufacture anymore."

Sawyer's eyes widened. "I'm impressed you know that."

She shrugged. "I didn't. But Evie mentioned it to him. *And* he told us that it was a custom paint job and that he'd *recently acquired* it. Which now that I think about it, seems a weird thing to say. Why wouldn't he say he'd just bought it?"

"And why would Jane sell a car she'd had for years to the guy who had bullied and tormented her in high school?"

"Good point." Bailey tapped her chin. "Maybe she was desperate for money."

"I can't imagine anyone being *that* desperate."

"Maybe the transmission was getting ready to go out, and she was sticking him with a costly lemon."

Sawyer frowned. "I think that's reaching a bit."

"Probably," she agreed. "Only one way to find out." She steepled her hands like she was praying and offered him her best puppy-dog eyes. "Can I please, please go with you to talk to her next?"

"I don't know. You blabbed to Mr. Jenkins that Gordy had been murdered, and we haven't even made that official yet."

She winced. "I know. That was totally my bad. I'm sorry. I promise that it won't happen again." Her eyes went wide as her stomach let out a loud growl.

Sawyer chuckled and glanced over at the clock on his dashboard. "Tell you what. It's almost six. Why don't you let me take you out to dinner, and then we'll go talk to her together."

Her starving stomach and her inquisitive brain warred with wanting to eat and wanting to interview a potential suspect. "Fine. But I need to let Daisy know." She pulled her phone out of her purse and frowned at the black screen. "Shoot. My battery died." The last few days had been so busy, she couldn't even remember the last time she'd charged it. And then she'd taken all those notes on it earlier that day. No wonder it was dead.

Sawyer pulled up one of the cords that dangled in the center console. "Here. You can use my cord to charge it."

"Thanks."

She was reaching for the cord as the mic on Sawyer's shoulder squawked. "Sheriff Dunn, this is dispatch."

Sawyer depressed the button on the side of the mic. "This is the sheriff. Go ahead."

"Yeah, Sheriff. We've been trying to locate Bailey Briggs."

Bailey plugged her phone in at the same time the dispatcher said her name. She looked up, and her mouth went dry at the dispatcher's next words.

"A nurse over at the hospital called in and said you might know where she is."

A nurse?

Bailey reached for Sawyer's hand as panic began to build in her chest.

"She's here with me," Sawyer said. "What's going on?"

Enough time must have elapsed for a charge to take hold because Bailey's phone lit up and started buzzing as message after message and missed call notifications filled up the screen.

"It's about her daughter, sir," the dispatcher continued. "Can you tell her she needs to head over to the hospital?"

The hospital?

Bailey's breath left her lungs, and the familiar tingling sensation when she hyperventilated started up her cheeks. "Daisy," she whispered before the pressure in her chest grew so that she couldn't seem to find another breath.

Sawyer's grip tightened on her hand. "What happened?" he asked his dispatch.

Bailey shook her head, her eyes wide as her heart pounded hard against her chest. She didn't want to hear the next words. Didn't want to hear that something had happened to her baby girl.

"I'm not sure," the dispatcher said. "They wouldn't give me all the details, but it sounds like her daughter was involved in an accident with a motorcycle."

Chapter
Thirty-One

S awyer popped open the glove compartment and dug out a small paper sack. He shook it open, then wrapped his fist around the top, crumpling it closed except for a small opening. He passed it to Bailey. "Here. Breathe."

She pressed the paper bag to her face, making it pop when she exhaled a long breath. The only sounds in the car were the crinkle of the paper sack as she drew a breath in, then the pop as she filled it back up with air. Breathe in. *Crinkle.* Breathe out. *Pop.*

Sawyer took her phone and quickly scanned the messages before he dropped it back into her lap and started the engine. "There's no new information in your texts," he said as he turned the truck around and sped toward the hospital. "Just that Daisy was in an accident and that Granny and Evie would meet you at the hospital."

She started to pull the bag away to respond, but he held up his hand. "You focus on breathing. I'll get us there as fast as I can." He was already flying down the highway. "We'll be there in two minutes. But you need to be okay so you can take care of our girl when we get there."

Bailey blinked as she took another long, deep breath in.

Our girl?

Had he just meant that in a general term because everyone loved Daisy? Or did he suspect he might be her father? He had to have wondered. But he'd never asked.

Still. He was a detective—he could do math. But guessing months and weeks was never exact. And especially not if he'd heard that Evie's brother had stepped in to take care of her after he'd left, like she'd been a wounded bird with a broken wing. And she'd been so desperately hurt that she'd let him.

But it didn't last. They'd stayed friends, thankfully. Because she'd needed Mateo in her life, but they both knew he wasn't Sawyer.

The tingling sensation in her cheeks abated as she continued to take slow, deep breaths, and she had it under control by the time they reached the hospital. Sawyer pulled into a spot at the front, and she grabbed her phone and her purse, and they ran toward the entrance.

A familiar bark sounded, and Bailey gasped as she saw Cooper sitting by the front door. The golden came sprinting toward her, and she squatted down to hug him to her. "You're such a good boy," she told the dog. "Thank you for keeping watch."

The automatic doors whooshed open, and she and Sawyer rushed in, Cooper at their heels. There was no way she was leaving him outside any longer. How had he even gotten here? Had he been with Daisy when she'd been in the accident? Or had Granny Bee brought him with her?

Maybe it was the determined look on her face, maybe it was because she was with the sheriff, but no one told her the dog couldn't come with them as they raced toward the admission desk.

"Daisy Briggs," Sawyer demanded.

The woman at the desk pointed down the hall. "The family's in the next waiting room."

They'd both been here before, so they knew where they were going as they flew down the hall and burst into the next waiting room.

Everyone stood at their arrival. Marigold and Aster were sitting together on one side of the room, and Evie, Rosa, and Mateo sat on the other. Griffin was already standing next to Evie's chair, as if he were holding guard over the space.

Her family stepped toward her, calling her name, but it was the sight of Spike Larsen that had her attention. That had her stopping in her tracks and stole the breath from her lungs.

When they'd burst in, he had his elbows propped on his knees, his head cradled in his hands. He glanced up as they came in and had such a look of torment on his face that it ripped Bailey's heart in half.

But it was his shirt that she couldn't take her eyes off of.

Instead of his normal black garb, he had on a white T-shirt with a small "Hog Wild" logo on the breast pocket. Except it wasn't white. It was smeared with brown dirt and covered in bright red blood.

Daisy's blood.

Her knees buckled. Mateo had crossed the room in two long strides and was there to grab her before she sank to the ground.

Not Sawyer.

Sawyer was charging forward, grabbing Spike by his blood-soaked collar and yanking him up and out of his chair. "What the hell did you do?"

"I didn't—" he tried to say, but Sawyer was already pulling back his fist.

Griffin grabbed his raised fist and put an arm around Sawyer's waist. Pulling him back, his tone was deep and commanding. "Sawyer. Stop. He didn't do this."

Sawyer's eyes were wide, his voice hoarse as he shouted, "He's covered in her blood!" He leaned toward Spike, fighting against Griffin's hold as he continued to shout. "Did you hit her with your motorcycle?"

The blood drained from Spike's face as he furiously shook his head. "No. She wrecked her bike. I saw it happen."

Griffin tightened his hold around Sawyer's shoulders as he kept his voice strong and steady. "Spike is the one who brought her in. He's covered in her blood because he was carrying her."

"What happened?" Bailey cried, finally finding her voice. "Is she okay?"

Evie pulled her into a tight hug. "We're waiting to hear."

Cooper sat next to her and pressed his body into the side of her leg. She tried to keep the panic out of her voice, but it came out too shrill anyway. "Will someone please tell me what happened?"

"She was riding her bike," Spike said. "I saw her pedaling on the road up ahead of me. But she must have been going too fast down that hill by the fairgrounds. I was a ways behind her, but I saw her lose control and go off the side of the road. She laid the bike down, then wrecked into the ditch. She must have cut her head on something when she went down because it was bleeding pretty bad when I got to her. She was scraped up, bleeding in a couple of places, and might have broken her arm. I didn't know what else to do. I just picked her up and put her on my bike and brought her here." He pointed to Cooper. "He was racing after us the whole way."

"Sorry man." Griffin had let him go, and Sawyer dipped his head and held out his hand.

"No worries," Spike said, gripping his hand and giving it a firm shake. "We're all scared."

"Granny Bee is in there with her," Evie said. "We're waiting for the doctor."

"What can we do?" Sawyer asked, sounding as helpless as Bailey felt.

"We've been prayin'," Aster said, rubbing her hand over Bailey's arm.

Marigold pointed to Spike's shirt. "It looks like she lost so much blood. Maybe we need to donate blood. Just in case she needs some."

"What blood type is she?" Griffin asked.

"I don't remember," Marigold said, wringing her hands. "But Bailey's blood type is pretty rare. She's a B-negative."

"So, only a negative could match Daisy's," Griffin said. "And that's going to be hard to find because only twenty-five percent of people are a negative blood type."

"I'm an O negative," Sawyer said.

Mateo stepped forward. "So am I."

Chapter
Thirty-Two

The room had gone quiet as Bailey looked from Sawyer to Mateo, then back to Sawyer again.

Both men turned to stare at her.

The door of the waiting room opened before she had a chance to say anything, and Dr. MacFarlane walked in.

Bailey had known Tom McFarlane for years. He was their primary doctor and had served as Daisy's pediatrician when she was little. He gave a cursory glance at the dog, then looked back to Bailey. "She's okay" were the first words out of his mouth, and Bailey wanted to throw her arms around him. Either that or collapse to the floor.

"But the blood . . ." was all she could say. Somehow Sawyer was next to her again, and her hand was clasped tightly in his.

Dr. MacFarlane nodded. "She cut her head on something, not sure what, but we stitched her up and gave her a tetanus shot just in case. Head wounds tend to bleed a lot." He smiled at Bailey. "You know that. You used it in your last book. But don't worry. Like I said, she's okay. She has some road rash, a few scrapes, and a couple of bruises. She really bit it on her bike. But it could have been worse."

"Her arm?" Sawyer asked. "Is it broken?"

"It looks like it might be a small buckle fracture, but we'll know for sure in a bit. We're going to get her in for an X-ray. If it is, we'll put it in a splint. We won't be able to cast it until the swelling goes down."

"Can I see her?" Bailey asked. She needed to hold her daughter, to touch her, to look at her face and to see for herself that her baby was really okay.

"Of course." The doctor pushed the door open, then held up a hand as every person in the room surged forward. "But the exam room is small, so only a couple of people at a time."

Bailey didn't let go of Sawyer's hand, and he didn't even hesitate, falling into step next to her as they followed the doctor down the hall and into the emergency room exam area. He stopped and pointed to a closed curtain.

Bailey let go of Sawyer to push the curtain aside and rush in.

"Mom" was the only word Daisy managed to say before Bailey was next to her and gently pulling her into her arms. "I'm sorry, Mom," she whispered into Bailey's shoulder.

"It's okay—*you're* okay." Bailey repeated the words a second time, then pulled back to examine her daughter's face.

A raw scrape cut across Daisy's cheekbone. Six stitches formed a diagonal line across her eyebrow. The skin around them was shiny with what Bailey assumed was antibiotic ointment. Daisy's T-shirt was torn at the sleeve and covered in dirt and blood. One patch of road rash went from her shoulder to her elbow, and another one went along her knee. Thankfully, she'd been wearing one of her longer pairs of jean shorts, or it could have been worse.

A white-gauze bandage covered her knee, and another was taped to her ankle. A large bruise blossomed across her shin. Her sneakers and dusty socks were on the floor.

Cooper jumped up onto the bed and lay down gingerly next to Daisy's legs. He gave one tender lick to her knee next to the bandage, then sighed as he rested his head next to her hip.

Tears welled in Daisy's eyes as she reached out to rub the dog's head. "You're a good boy. I'm so glad you're okay." Tears leaked down her face as she looked at her mom. "I didn't know what happened to him. I kept praying he would run home. Or someone would recognize him and pick him up. Spike said he was following us, but I didn't know what happened to him after they brought me in."

Bailey touched her daughter's cheek, gently wiping away the tears. "He was waiting outside the doors of the hospital when we got here." She reached out a hand to clasp her grandmother's. "Thank God you were here. I'm so sorry. My phone died. I didn't get your messages until after the dispatcher contacted Sawyer."

"The dispatcher?" Granny Bee glanced at Sawyer.

"One of the nurses here called into the sheriff's station to see if they could get a hold of me and track down Bailey," he explained. "But she was with me when I received the call, so we came right over."

Thank goodness for small towns.

Bailey brushed her fingers across Daisy's forehead. "I would have been here sooner if I had known."

"It's okay, Mom." Daisy's face took on a tortured expression. "I'm sorry I wrecked my bike and caused all this trouble. I didn't mean to worry you and Gran. And I know the hospital bill will probably cost a ton. But I'll help. You don't have to pay me allowance for the rest of the summer."

"Oh, honey, don't worry about that." Leave it to her daughter to be more concerned about everyone else than herself. Wait until she found out there was a whole waiting room of people worried about her.

Daisy looked beyond Bailey's shoulder and offered a sheepish grin to the sheriff. "Hi, Sawyer. Thanks for bringing my mom."

He stepped forward and pressed a gentle kiss to the side of her head that wasn't cut. "Hey, kid." His voice was husky with emotion, and he swallowed and took a deep breath before trying to talk again. "I'm just glad you're okay."

"Thank goodness Spike was there and saw me crash," Daisy said. "I don't know what I would have done. And I don't know how bad my bike is wrecked."

"Don't worry about that now," Bailey said. "But later we're going to have a talk about why you weren't wearing your helmet."

Daisy cast her eyes down. "I know. It was stupid. I took it into the barn earlier, and I was in a hurry, and I just forgot it."

"Lyle already picked up your bike and took it back to the ranch. I told him to grab you a fresh change of clothes from that basket of clean laundry on the kitchen table and bring them down here." Granny checked her phone. "He just texted a few minutes ago. He's on his way. And he said your bike's okay. Couple of dings, but he can fix it up, no problem."

Daisy leaned back against her pillow, a look of relief on her face.

Bailey brushed a lock of hair from her cheek. "Honey, what were you doing? Why were you riding your bike out on the highway?"

Daisy dropped her chin to her chest. "I was going back to the fairgrounds."

Bailey didn't get why that would cause her distress. They'd spent the last several days at the fairgrounds. "Why? And why didn't you just ask someone for a ride?"

"Granny Bee was still over there, and Lyle was doing chores. I didn't want to bug anyone. And I really needed to talk to Gordy Russell."

Bailey drew her head back. She hadn't expected that. "Gordy? Why in the world would you need to talk to Gordy Russell?"

Daisy couldn't meet her eye, and her voice was quiet as she spoke. "Because I needed to apologize to him."

"To *Gordy*? For what?"

More tears filled Daisy's eyes. "Because I was the one who vandalized his hot tub. Well, it was me and Josie. We're the ones who poured the soap in it. I didn't want to do it—I promise. It was Josie's idea." She dipped her chin lower to her chest. "But I didn't stop her. She said it would be funny. No big deal. It was just supposed to be a prank. She didn't like Gordy. She said he'd gone out with her mom, and he was a real jerk."

Bailey could believe that. But she had a hard time believing Daisy would be involved in vandalism.

"I'm sorry, Mom," Daisy continued. "I swear, I didn't know that it would really harm the hot tub or cost him money. I feel terrible."

Bailey snuck a glance at her grandmother. Granny Bee gave a quick stern shake of her head. So, that meant she hadn't told Daisy yet about Gordy being dead. That was probably for the best.

"I appreciate you telling me now. And I think Gordy said it *could* have caused him trouble, but I don't think it really did."

And it's not like it was going to matter to him now. "Still, I have to say I'm disappointed in you that you'd purposely damage someone's property." It was taking everything in her to stand firm. All Bailey wanted to do was hug her daughter close and tell her none of that mattered. But it did matter. Daisy had done something wrong, and Bailey couldn't just excuse it because she'd gotten hurt. "I don't think I want you hanging out with that Josie for a while."

"No, I was already kind of thinking that," Daisy said. "She doesn't even like to read."

Bailey tried to contain her smile. She took Daisy's unhurt hand and clasped it in hers. "Are you really okay?"

Daisy squeezed Bailey's hand back as she nodded. "I am. I was really scared at first. But I'm okay now. We have to find a way to tell Spike thank you."

"You can tell him yourself," Bailey said. "He's still in the waiting room."

"No way."

"And he's not the only one," Bailey said.

"Speaking of which," Sawyer said, "we should probably let a few of them in to see you. Now that I know you're okay, I can step out and let one of the great-aunts come in."

"I'll come with you," Granny Bee said. "I want to find Lyle. And then Marigold and Aster don't have to have a leg-wrestling match to see who gets to come in first."

Daisy giggled, and the sound was music to Bailey's ears.

Sawyer reached down and gripped her hand before slipping out of the curtain.

Bailey took Granny's empty chair and kept an eye on her daughter as first Marigold and Aster came in to hug her, and then

Griffin and Evie took their turn. Spike seemed even taller in the small exam room, but Daisy's face lit up with a big smile at seeing the huge biker.

"Thanks for finding me," Daisy told him. "And for bringing me to the hospital."

"No problem, kid," he told her as he reached out to scratch the dog's ears. Cooper was still on the bed; he hadn't left her side. "But promise me you'll be more careful on those turns. And next time, wear your helmet."

Bailey nodded. "We've already had a serious discussion about that."

"I almost always wear it," Daisy said. She must have thought better of using an eye roll at that moment and instead offered her mother and Spike a chastened expression.

Bailey went out to the waiting room for a few minutes to stretch her legs and let Rosa, Evie, and Mateo have a chance to go in to see Daisy. She smiled as Sawyer walked back in, then her heart melted as she saw what he was carrying: two bottles of water and a fluffy stuffed unicorn that he must have found in the gift shop.

He shrugged when she saw it. "I just wanted to do something. I know she's twelve, but I thought she might still like it."

Bailey wrapped her arms around Sawyer's waist and pressed into him in a tight hug. "She'll love it. Why don't you run it into her now."

He passed her a bottle of water. "This is for you."

"You're a pretty great guy, Sawyer Dunn."

"I can be," he said, his expression turning serious as he raised his free hand to run the back of his knuckles tenderly across her cheek. "Especially when it comes to the people I care about."

She stared up at him, trying to convey in one look everything she was feeling.

The sound of a throat clearing had them pulling apart, and Bailey looked over to see Griffin sitting on one of the sofas, his laptop balanced on his lap.

He offered them a small wave. "Just wasn't sure if either of you realized I was in the room with you."

Bailey laughed and couldn't help the grin that creased her face. She pointed to the door. "You go give that to Daisy," she told Sawyer. "I'll see you in a few."

She took a seat next to Griffin. "Sorry."

He shrugged and nudged her side. "No biggie. But it looked like the sheriff was about to throw you over his shoulder and drag you off to his man cave, so I thought I'd better let you know I was in the room."

"Where is everyone?" she asked, avoiding Griff's comment about her and Sawyer. Especially since the idea of being alone with him in his man cave, or anywhere for that matter, was making Bailey's skin heat.

"Lyle took Granny Bee and the great-aunts down to the cafeteria."

Bailey's stomach growled in response. She looked up at the clock, surprised to see it was already past five. "I'm glad they're eating. I know Gran still has stuff to do down at the fairgrounds tonight."

"I'm in town for a couple more days, so let me know if there's something I can do to help."

"Thanks." She offered him a grin as she nudged his leg. "It's kind of funny how much time you've been spending in town since you met Evie."

"Maybe I just like the fresh mountain air," he answered, but a smile tugged at the corners of his lips.

"I think it's cute." She looked toward the door, surprised to see Sawyer striding back into the room.

"Hey, I'm sorry," he said. "Dispatch just called me, and I have to go into the station for a bit. But I hate to leave you here without a car."

"I'll be fine," she told him, pushing off the sofa to stand next to him. "I'm not going anywhere. Daisy still has to get her X-ray, and if I did need to leave, there are ten people here that I'm sure would be willing to give me a ride." She quirked an eyebrow. "Is it about the case?"

Sawyer smiled as he shook his head. "You're like a dog with a bone. And no, it's not about the case. You do remember that I'm the sheriff for the *entire* county, and sometimes that county needs me for *other* things. But keep me posted with what's going on. I'll be done in a few hours, and I'll either come back here to bring you both home, or I'll stop by the ranch to check on how Daisy's doing." He wrapped an arm around her waist and pulled her to him in a hug, then pressed a quick kiss against her temple. "I'll see you later."

"See ya." She breathed the words out on a small sigh.

"Speaking of cute," Griff muttered, keeping his eyes trained on his laptop.

Bailey wanted to hug herself. They were kind of cute. "I'm going back in. Let Gran know when they come back, would ya?"

She made it through the door but paused as her phone buzzed in her pocket. She pulled it out and was surprised to see Sibia Kumar's name on the screen. Granny had made her program the phone numbers of the entire production crew into her own phone when they'd first arrived, just in case they needed anything. But she couldn't imagine why Sibia would be calling her now.

"Hi, Bailey," Sibia said after she'd answered. "I hope I'm not bothering you. Do you have a few minutes to talk?"

"Sure. What's up?"

"I was thinking about what you said, about if we remembered or thought of anything that seemed unusual or that we'd seen at the fairgrounds that felt off."

"Yeah?"

"Yeah, well, it's probably nothing, but I did just remember something."

"Sometimes a nothing turns out to be something. What did you remember?"

"It's about that reporter. The one who was at Rex's trailer when that thing happened with Evie?" That thing where Sibia's boss got handsy with her best friend and Evie slapped him, threw his coffee at him, and threatened to kill him if he ever touched her again. "I think her name was Jane something," Sibia continued.

"Yes, I remember," Bailey said, trying to contain her excitement at what Sibia was going to tell her. Somehow, she knew it just *had* to be another clue to the murder. "Jane Johnson."

"Yes, that's it. I thought she looked familiar when I first met her, but I couldn't place where I'd seen her. Then I remembered that I *had* met her before."

"How? I thought you'd never been to Colorado."

"I haven't. I didn't see her here. I met her in California. She came to the studio. To see Rex."

Chapter
Thirty-Three

Jane had been to California to see Rex?

Okay, Bailey hadn't been expecting that. The reporter must have seen him on television and figured out he was her old friend, Eugene. "When was this?"

"I don't remember exactly. Probably six months ago or so. But she looked different. Maybe that's why I didn't recognize her at first when I saw her again here."

"Different how?"

"Um . . . like she was more made up, I guess. She had her hair all styled and was wearing makeup and this pretty pink top with a skirt and heels."

That *was* different. Not that she'd met her that many times, but Bailey had only ever seen the reporter in drab black or tan clothes and wearing sneakers.

"Do you know what she was doing there? Did she get to see Rex?"

"Yeah, she saw him. She didn't have an appointment, and I remember he seemed surprised to see her, but he said it was okay. And she was in his office with him for a while. Then when she came out, it looked like she'd been crying. And she practically ran out of the studio."

"Did you ask Rex about her?"

Sibia sighed. "No. I'm sorry. And I'm sorry to say she wasn't the first—or the last—person to leave Rex's office looking like she'd been crying. You just experienced a small taste of how he was. You have no idea what a douchewad he could be. He was either sweet and charming when he was trying to get in your pants, or overbearing and condescending if you told him *no*. That is, *if* you were still able to keep your job."

"That Rex was a piece of work."

"You're not kidding."

"This helps," Bailey told her. "Are you okay if I share this with the sheriff?"

"Yeah, sure."

"Okay. Thanks for calling," Bailey told her. "I'll check in with you later. And Sibia?"

"Yeah."

"I'm really happy for you and Toby."

Sibia let out a small rush of air, and Bailey could hear the smile in her voice as she said, "Yeah, I'm happy for us too. He's a great guy. I wish he'd told me sooner how he felt. Or that Gregory or Imani had told me. According to them, he's had a crush on me for a while now."

"Yeah, it was kind of obvious."

"Not to me. It makes me feel bad that I didn't notice and that we wasted all this time that we could have been together."

"You're together now," Bailey told her. "That's all that matters. Thanks again for the call."

She couldn't help but think the same thing about Sawyer and herself. If they had only known how to find each other, they wouldn't have wasted so much time apart.

She was surprised to see Daisy's bed empty when she pushed through the curtain to her exam room. Well, not exactly empty. The golden retriever was sprawled out on his back with his legs and front paws wide open. But Daisy was gone.

"It's okay, mi nina. They just took her down to get her arm X-rayed," Rosa told her. "They'll bring her right back."

Mateo slipped an arm around her waist and pulled her to him. It was comforting, but like a brother—nothing like the thrills that ran through her when Sawyer had done almost the same thing moments before. "You doing okay, Bails?" he asked.

She smiled up at him. "I am now that I know she's going to be okay. Thanks for being here."

"Of course. We're family. That's what we do."

Rosa stood and gave her a hug too. "But I think we're going to go for now. I've got carne asada in the slow cooker at home, and we need to eat before we head back to the fairgrounds."

"Will you take Griff home with you and feed him too, Abeulita?" Evie asked. "I want to stay here with Bailey for a bit longer."

"Of course," her grandmother said. "Do you need me to send him back to pick you up?"

"No. I have my car. Just tell him I'll meet him there in about an hour. And I'll text him too."

Someone must have brought in an extra chair, and Bailey sank into it, next to Evie, after her grandmother and brother left. "Thanks for staying with me," she said, leaning her head on Evie's shoulder.

"Yeah, yeah, I'm so nice. But you know I'm really just dying to hear what happened when you and Sawyer went to talk to Mr. Jenkins."

Bailey sat up. It had been less than an hour since they'd left the custodian's house, but it felt like so long ago. She'd forgotten that she'd texted Evie to tell her they were headed over to talk to him. She filled Evie in on their conversation and about the discovery of Jane Johnson's nickname.

"So, you think the 'P. J.' on Rex's list stands for 'Plain Jane'?" Evie asked.

"I do. Don't you?"

Evie frowned. "I'm not so sure. It makes more sense that it would be Paul Jenkins, since every other person on that list was there that day when the 'incident' happened with Eugene."

"True. But I just took a call from Sibia, and she told me that she remembers seeing Jane *in California*. She went to the studio to see Rex. So, Jane's known his identity for months now." Bailey told her everything Sibia had said on the phone.

"That's nuts. But then, it doesn't make any sense to think that Jane had anything to do with Rex's murder. We already know that he's a blackmailing, lying, conceited pervert. It makes more sense that *he* would threaten *her* to keep her mouth shut about him."

"Maybe he did. And that's why she whacked him with the mixer," Bailey suggested.

"Isn't she like five foot nothing? How could she have reached it? There wasn't a ladder or a stepstool in the closet, was there?"

Bailey shook her head. "Not that I remember. But it wasn't on the top shelf. I think it was one or two down."

"Orrrr . . . maybe Jane is a lying blackmailer too, and she was threatening to expose Rex's secret if he didn't pay her a bunch of money."

"Then it still doesn't make sense for her to have killed him. Why would she murder her cash cow?" Bailey kept her next thoughts to herself as a nurse wheeled Daisy back into the exam room in a wheelchair.

"Don't worry, Mom," Daisy said, pushing up out of the wheelchair and scootching the dog over to get back into the bed with him. "They made me ride in this thing, but I can walk." She waited for the nurse to leave, then pointed at Bailey and Evie. "I heard you guys talking about Rex's murder as she was bringing me back in. I feel like I missed out on so much today. So tell me everything."

"Honey, you should really rest," Bailey said.

Daisy narrowed her eyes at her mother. "Haven't we already established today that we shouldn't keep secrets from each other."

"I think we established that *you* shouldn't keep secrets from *me*," Bailey said.

"*Mo-om.*"

"We might as well tell her," Evie said. "She might have some different insight."

"Yeah," Daisy repeated. "I might have some different insight. I *am* pretty insightful. And remember, I did help with the mayor's murder."

Bailey relented, and she and Evie filled Daisy in on everything they'd learned so far.

"There is one more thing we need to tell you," Bailey said. "You're not going to be able to give Gordy that apology."

Daisy brow wrinkled. "Why not? I feel bad for what I did, and I want to tell him I'm sorry."

Bailey took a deep breath before letting it out slowly. "You can't tell him you're sorry, because someone killed him."

Daisy gasped.

"We found him floating face down in one of his hot tubs this afternoon," Evie said.

Daisy wrinkled her nose as if she'd smelled something bad. "Do you know who killed him?"

"Not yet," Bailey told her.

"All we know so far," Evie said holding up her fingers and ticking off the details, "is that *Mr. Russell* was killed *at* the fairgrounds *with* the pipe wrench."

Bailey just wished there was an envelope they could open to reveal the killer.

"Mom, something else happened the night with Josie. I didn't think it mattered until now," Daisy said, absently running her hand over the dog's back.

"What happened?" Bailey asked, praying her daughter wasn't going to divulge another act of vandalism.

"Gordy showed up while we were there—he and another woman. Gordy must have been walking back from getting something to eat, because he had a big carton of ribbon fries in his hand. We didn't know what to do—he would have seen us if we'd run, so we crouched down behind one of the hot tubs and hid. We were sure he was going to come in and find us, but a car pulled up, and we saw this woman get out and, like, march toward him like she was super angry."

"How do you know she was mad?" Evie asked.

"You could just tell by the way she was walking and the look on her face. Then when she got up to him, she shook her finger at him and poked him in the chest."

270

"What did he do?"

"At first, he just laughed. Which I think just made her even more angry," Daisy said. "But then he got mad too. And they started yelling at each other."

"Could you hear what they were yelling about?" Bailey asked.

"Some of it. Josie wanted to sneak out of there while they were yelling at each other, and I did too, but I was too scared Gordy would see us. So we just stayed there and listened to them arguing."

"What did they say?" Evie asked.

"The woman was trying to convince him of something, but Gordy just kept being a butt to her. I heard her say, *I'm telling you, it's him.*'"

"Was she talking about Rex?"

Daisy shrugged. "I didn't know who they were talking about at the time, but now that we know all this other stuff, I think she had to have meant Rex. And Gordy was just acting like she was . . . I don't know . . . overreacting or something. I remember him telling her that she was just trying to stir things up. And then he really hurt her feelings because he told her that whoever the guy was that they were talking about had already ditched her and left her behind once, so why did she think this time was going to be any different. I thought that was pretty low. I felt sorry for the woman."

"Did you recognize her?" Bailey asked. "The woman he was arguing with?"

"Yeah, I think so. I'm pretty sure she was that reporter who did that not-so-great piece about Evie being a suspect in Rex's murder. I think her name's Jane Johnson."

Chapter
Thirty-Four

*A*ll roads seemed to be leading to Jane.

Bailey still had a hard time imagining the petite, mousy woman killing a man, let alone *two* men. "I know it's too late now, but I wish you had told us all this the night Rex was killed. We . . . um . . . I mean, Sawyer could have started looking into Jane right away."

Daisy lowered her chin to her chest. "I'm really sorry, Mom."

"It's water under the bridge now," Bailey said.

"Or, in this case," Evie said, "water splashed out of the dead guy's hot tub."

Bailey swatted her friend's leg and then shuddered. "Ew."

Evie just grinned and turned back to Daisy. "Did anything else happen? Or did Jane just leave?"

"Yeah, one other thing did happen," Daisy said. "And it was super gross. Gordy started coming on to her. We peeked around and could see him pulling on her and trying to kiss her neck. I don't understand what he meant, but he told her if she was just looking for a good time with an old classmate, he'd be willing to drink a little more so his beer goggles would start working, or something like that."

Evie made a gagging noise. "He is . . . was . . . so disgusting."

Daisy nodded her head. "You think *that's* disgusting? He also told her something about him working in a sandwich shop and wanting to give her a footlong." She glanced at her mom. "I knew what that meant. And that was so gross too. Josie and I were trying not to barf and laugh at the same time."

Bailey grimaced. "I hate to ask, but what did Jane do?"

"Oh, she thought it was super gross too," Daisy said. "She told him he was disgusting and a creep and that he could take his footlong and shove it. She told him she wouldn't hook up with him if he were the last man on earth."

"Good for her."

"Yeah, but he was not getting the 'no means no' part," Daisy said. "Or the 'I think you're a perv and that also means no' part. He was still being super handsy and, like, still trying to kiss her. He told her he thought she was underestimating him, and she said it was impossible to *under*estimate him, which I thought was a pretty good insult, but it totally went over his head. Then she told him she thought he was a total loser and that she didn't have the crayons to explain to him why he was a total failure as a human."

"I can't believe you remember all that," Evie said.

"They were pretty good insults," Daisy said. "But Gordy was just too dumb to get them. But then he grabbed her bottom and pulled her right against him, and he said something else disgusting that I'm not going to say in front of my mom, and then Jane slapped him across the face. And it was *loud*, so it must have been really hard. She pushed him away, and then he shoved her down and started calling her names."

Bailey pressed her lips together, trying not to scold her daughter again for sneaking out and putting herself in such a terrifying predicament. Especially now that they knew Gordy's tendencies toward violence. If he had caught the girls, who knows what he would have done. "Daisy. That sounds really scary."

"It was. He got super mad. And Josie and I kept looking at each other, like trying to decide if we should do something to try to help. But then Jane just fell backward and scrambled back up on her feet and ran for her car. She opened her door and yelled back at him, 'You're not the dumbest person in the world, Gordy Russell, but you better hope they don't die.' Which, I also thought was pretty funny. But apparently Gordy didn't. Because he picked up his carton of fries and threw them at her car. But the ketchup from the carton splattered across his arm, so he started swearing some more and then stomped off toward the bathrooms. We figured that was our chance to get out of there, so we ran in the other direction."

Bailey let out the breath she didn't realize she had been holding.

"I'm really sorry, Mom," Daisy told her again. "I know now that it was a really dumb thing to do. And it was a stupid prank. All we did was pour some dish soap into one of the hot tubs. We don't even know when he turned it on or what happened."

"I just wish you had told me," Bailey said.

"I know. I feel really bad. Especially now that I know that what I heard could have had something to do with Rex. I don't know what any of that could mean as far as his murder goes, but I still feel like it's important."

"It could be," Bailey said. "Sawyer's coming back to check on you tonight, so I'd like you to tell him everything you told us when you see him. Will you do that?"

Daisy nodded. "Yeah, sure. But don't you guys want to go talk to Jane? She's gotta know something more about Rex that might help you figure out who actually killed him."

"Yes, I'm dying to go talk to her," Bailey said, her brain already swimming with theories. "Especially, now that we know Gordy knew Rex was Eugene and that he was in town and had done well for himself. That totally makes Gordy a suspect."

Evie tilted her head. "But if Gordy killed Rex, then who killed Gordy? And why?"

"That's a great question," Bailey said. "I don't know."

"That's why you and Aunt Evie need to go talk to Jane," Daisy said. "Like, right now."

Bailey shook her head. "No way. I'm not leaving you. You may have broken your arm."

"So? It's not like you sitting in this room can change the outcome of that. The doctor already said that even if it is broken, they're still just going to wrap it in a splint," Daisy said. "Come on, Mom. I'm not a baby. And there's nothing else for you to do here anyway except wait. And you know emergency rooms: we could be here for another half an hour before they let me go, or another *three* and a half hours. And Granny Bee is here. She and Lyle can take me and Coop home." She rubbed the dog's back and was rewarded with a lick to her hand in return.

"Did I hear my name being taken in vain?" Granny Bee said as she pushed through the curtain.

"I'm trying to convince my mom and Aunt Evie that I don't need them to wait around here for me when they have other important things to do. And that you and Lyle can take me home," Daisy said.

"Of course we can," Granny Bee said. "But what are these other important things you need to do?"

They filled her in on the latest information they'd found out.

"See?" Daisy said to her great-grandmother when they'd finished. "Tell them it's more important that they go talk to that reporter than to wait around here."

The doctor came in before Granny had time to offer her opinion.

"I have good news and bad news," Doctor MacFarlane told Daisy. "The bad news is that you did break your wrist, kid."

Daisy pushed her bottom lip out into a pout. "Oh."

"But the good news is that it's just a small buckle fracture, so you'll probably only have to wear the cast for three or four weeks. I'm going to have the nurse come in and wrap your wrist and rig you up with a splint. You'll need to come back in a few days, when the orthopedic doc is here—we have one that comes up on Fridays. He'll take a look at it, and they'll put you in a cast if they deem it necessary. Other than that, your mom has a little paperwork to fill out, and you'll be ready to go home."

He turned to Bailey. "There'll be detailed instructions in the take-home packet, and the nurse will go over any at-home care like staying ahead of the pain with ibuprofen, and maybe some ice if she's really hurting. She'll probably be sore for a few days, but as far as the wrist is concerned, the splint will keep it immobile for the next few days, so she shouldn't have too much trouble with it. And I'll see you all in my office in about a week to get those stitches removed. My receptionist will call you to set up an appointment. Any other questions for me?"

"No—thanks, Doctor," Bailey said. "You've been really great."

He left as a nurse came in carrying a handful of supplies to make a splint. Another nurse came in a few minutes later and went over the paperwork with Bailey. The nurse had Bailey sign a few forms and left her with a packet to take home. The first nurse finished and told Daisy she'd be back in a few minutes with a wheelchair to get her out of there.

"See, Mom?" Daisy said when the nurse exited. "All that's left is for them to wheel me out to Lyle's truck. You guys should go. I'm dying to know what you find out."

"Me too," Granny said. "I've got this covered. Now, give your girl a hug and get out of here."

* * *

They took Evie's car because Bailey's was still at the fairgrounds. Mr. Jenkins had told Bailey and Sawyer that Jane lived in the cottage behind the paper, which was located in an old warehouse on the edge of town.

Bailey had tried to call Sawyer, just to tell him Daisy was okay and that she'd meet him out at the house later. She debated telling him what they were doing, but she had a feeling he would just tell them not to go, so she was almost glad when his phone clicked over to the recording telling her his voice mailbox was full. She figured she'd just ask for his forgiveness later. *After* she'd cleared her best friend's name.

The offices were at the front of the building, and the printing was done in the back of the warehouse. Evie pulled up in front and cut the lights. She'd been out to the paper to purchase some advertising for the restaurant, so she knew there was a footpath that led around the building to the cottage. The actual driveway came in from a different direction somewhere at the back of the property, but neither one of them could remember how to get to it.

Bailey slipped her crossbody bag over her shoulder as she climbed out of the car. She checked her phone one more time—no messages from Daisy or Gran—then slid it into the front pocket of her shorts. Evie had a spare charger cord in her purse, so she'd been able to charge it in Daisy's room while they were waiting. Evie activated the flashlight on her phone as they started around the building.

They both jumped as the strains of "I'm Bringing Sexy Back" blasted out into the air.

"What the heck is that?" Bailey asked as Evie scrambled to turn off the volume on her phone.

"That's Griff. I forgot to call him. He's probably still stuck at my abuela's."

Bailey raised both eyebrows. "*That's* your ringtone for Griffin? Does *he* know?"

"Ha. No. He'd kill me." She chewed her bottom lip as she stared down at the phone. "I'm afraid if I don't answer, he'll start to worry and come try to find me."

"Then answer it," Bailey said. She pointed toward the car. "Just talk over there. And hurry up. I'm going to scope out the cottage, but I'll wait for you to go up to the door."

Evie tapped the phone and held it to her ear as she hurried back toward the car. "Hey Griff," she said in a quiet voice. Hopefully he thought she was just trying to sound sexy instead of talking softly because she and her bestie were on a stakeout and ready to go interrogate another murder suspect.

Bailey just hoped that Jane would be able to provide another clue into who killed Rex. And Gordy.

Her eyes had adjusted to the dark by now, so she crept forward along the path, staying close to the side of the building. When she reached the end, she peeked around the corner, hoping to see lights on in Jane's house. They'd already agreed that if she wasn't home, they would only look through the windows and wouldn't break into her house to dig around for clues. But if the door happened to be open . . .

An electric-blue convertible sat in the driveway.

There's no way that there were two custom-painted, electric-blue Toyota Solara convertibles in a town so small that it didn't even have a car dealership. This had to be the same one Gordy had been driving. But how had Jane gotten the car back?

The top was down, and the trunk was open, and Bailey could see a large suitcase and several smaller tote bags stuffed inside it. She took a few steps closer but couldn't see any better. So, she took a few steps closer still. Then somehow, she was standing next to the car, peering into the trunk, when the front door of the cottage burst open, and Jane came barreling out.

Her arms were full of dog accessories: food and water dishes, a small bag of dog chow, a leash, and a tote full of toys. She wore khaki chinos rolled up at the ankles, low-top black Converses, a black T-shirt, and a cropped jean jacket. Her hair was half falling out of a loose ponytail, and her bangs stuck to her damp forehead. A small scruffy white dog was racing along at Jane's heels. It looked like a cross between a terrier and a chihuahua, with thin legs and eyes that bugged out just a little. Bailey couldn't tell if it was kind of adorable or one of the most pathetic-looking dogs she'd ever seen.

Jane stopped in her tracks, eyeing Bailey with suspicion, but the little dog came running over to sniff her legs. It could probably smell Cooper on her. The dog sat down and peered up at her with an inquisitive expression. *Aww.* Now Bailey was leaning more toward it being on the adorable side.

"What are you doing here?" Jane asked, her voice wary.

"I just came out to ask you a few questions." Bailey kept her voice light, trying to sound casual, like she'd just stopped by at eight o'clock in the evening for some fun girl chat.

Jane dumped the dog paraphernalia into the back seat of the car. "What kind of questions?"

Bailey shifted from one foot to the other. Where was Evie? She was so much better at this than her. "I love your car. This blue is so cool."

"Thanks." Jane's answer was curt. Apparently, she wasn't big on small talk at the moment.

"I thought I saw Gordy Russell driving this car yesterday. I think he said he'd just bought it. Did you sell it to him?"

Jane huffed. "I wouldn't sell water to that guy if he were dying of thirst in the desert."

"Oh? Then how did you get it back?"

Jane planted a fist on her hip and studied Bailey. "What do you *really* want?"

"I told you, I just wanted to ask you some questions."

"Well, I'm in a bit of hurry, so maybe you can come back another day." She turned to go back toward the house.

"I won't take up much of your time," Bailey said, stepping toward her. "But I'd really like to talk to you. It's about Rex."

Jane froze, then turned back to face Bailey. "What about Rex?"

"Well, not so much about Rex, but about Eugene Dix." Bailey dropped the name, hoping for some kind of reaction.

Jane kept her expression neutral. "Who?"

"Come on, Jane. I already know that Rex used to be Eugene and that you and he were friends."

Jane marched toward her and tilted her face up to glare at Bailey. "What are you playing at? Do you think just because you write murder mystery novels that you're qualified to try to solve them?"

Now she sounded like Sawyer too.

"No." *Well, actually, yes.* "It's just that my best friend is a suspect in Rex's murder, so I'm just trying to get to the bottom of what happened to him."

"And you think *I* had something to do with his murder?"

Bailey held her gaze, trying the mom stare again. "Did you?"

Jane held her stare. Maybe she'd seen this method before.

Thirty seconds passed, at least. Maybe a minute. Maybe ten.

Finally, Bailey broke. She gestured to the packed car. "Where are you going in such a hurry? You're not leavin' town, are you?" She tried to make that last question sound flip, like she was joking around, but the question came out flat and sounded too aggressive.

Jane squeezed her eyes shut, tightening her hands into fists and pressing them against her eyebrows. She let out a long breath.

"I really wish you hadn't come out here. Why couldn't you have just left this alone?"

Ha. Bailey knew Jane was involved in this somehow.

She tried to shift her tone to one of innocence. "Left *what* alone?"

But instead of answering her question, Jane reached behind her and pulled a small pistol from behind her back and pointed it at Bailey. "Get in the trunk. We're going for a ride."

Chapter Thirty-Five

Bailey blinked at Jane, still trying to comprehend the situation of the other woman pulling out a gun and pointing it at her face.

She held her hands up. "Listen, Jane, I think there's been some kind of a misunderstanding. It seems like you're busy. Why don't I just let you get on with your packing, and we'll pretend this never happened."

"The trunk!" Jane shouted. "Get in the trunk!"

"Okay, fine, no need to get upset," Bailey said. "Let's all just stay calm, and I'll get in the trunk." She slowly moved to the back of the vehicle and peered down into the trunk. "Um . . . I'm not sure . . ." She lifted one foot over the tailgate and squeezed it in between the suitcase and one of the totes. She twisted the bag one direction, then the other. "I'm not sure I'll fit in here with this suitcase. Could we maybe move it up front?"

Jane made a growling sound in the back of her throat.

"No? Okay, I'll try to make it work." She shifted the suitcase to one side and then pushed the tote bags to the other, leaving approximately a two-by-two-foot square of space for her to squeeze her honey-fattened body into. "Remember, I'm taller than you, and that convertible mechanism thingy that holds the roof takes up some of the space too."

Planting one hand on the bumper and the other on the lip of the trunk, she hauled herself in then sort of squatted down in the small space between the luggage. She picked up a tote bag full of toiletries and a long round bag that she thought might be a tent and held them on her lap.

She was still sitting up way too tall to even try to close the trunk, so she tried to squirm sideways while leaning her body to the side. "I got it," she told Jane, sucking in a breath as if she were trying to fit into a too-tight pair of jeans.

Flashbacks of being stuck in the biker bar's bathroom window flew through her mind. Then she couldn't think at all as a searing pain shot through the arch of her foot.

"Ouch! Ouch! Ouch! I have a cramp in my foot!" She leaned back against the suitcase and tried to stick her foot out of the trunk, flexing her toes to alleviate the cramp.

The dog must have thought she was playing a fun game because it jumped up into the trunk and tried to scramble onto her lap and lick her chin.

"Scoop. Get out of there!" Jane said, waving the gun wildly in her direction.

"Careful with that thing," Bailey said, ducking her head, which made the cramp worse and made the dog more excited. She huffed out a frustrated groan. "I'm doing my best here. Curvy girls are not meant to Tetris their bodies into tiny trunks with fifteen tote bags, a pup tent, and a super-sized Samsonite."

"Oh, for cripes sake." Jane let out another growl and waved the gun some more. "Fine. Get out. You can ride in the front. Just don't hurt my dog."

"I wouldn't dream of it. I love dogs," Bailey said, gently lifting the pup off her lap and leaning out of the trunk to set it on the ground. Unfortunately, between the cramp still pulsing in her outstretched leg and the awkward position she was sitting in, her center of gravity shifted, and she tumbled forward, falling out of the trunk and onto the dirt driveway.

Small bits of gravel dug into her palms and the knee she landed on first. But thankfully, she didn't smoosh the dog. And she could finally stretch out her leg to ease the cramp. The dog must have been really thankful she didn't smoosh it too, because it ran back over to her and proceeded to start humping her leg.

At least she was out of the trunk, so that was an improvement.

"Get up," Jane told her. "Shut the trunk."

Ignoring the aches in her body from the fall, Bailey pushed off the ground and rearranged the items in the trunk enough that she could slam it shut.

Jane waved the gun toward the passenger door. "Get in the car. And don't try anything funny."

Try anything funny? Like what? Her latest ideas for a standup routine?

Even with falling out of the trunk and the dog humping her leg, having a gun in her face made the situation anything but funny to Bailey.

Jane kept the gun trained on her as Bailey slid in and fastened her seat belt. *Safety first, right?* Then the other woman slowly walked around the front of the car, keeping the gun pointed in her direction as she opened the driver's door, whistled for the dog to get in, then slid into the seat after it. The dog jumped across the console and into Bailey's lap.

285

Jane switched the gun to her left hand to start the car and put it into drive, then switched it back to her right and pointed it at Bailey. "Where's your phone?"

"My phone?" Bailey acted confused, but she'd already been trying to think of how she could get to her cell.

"Your phone! Where is it?" Jane's eyes were wild as they raked over Bailey's body.

She patted her crossbody bag. "It's here. In my purse." *It wasn't.* It was in her pocket. But Jane didn't know that.

"Hand it over." She held out her free hand and beckoned with her fingers. Then shouted again when Bailey didn't immediately comply. "Give me your purse!"

"Okay. Okay." She passed Jane the purse, who threw it into the backseat.

It didn't matter. There was nothing of any use to her in it right now anyway. Just her wallet, keys, a pack of gum, a used Kleenex, and approximately fourteen lip glosses. Not like Evie, who carried a monstrous tote for a purse that held everything a person might need in the unlikely event of a zombie apocalypse.

The last time they'd gone to the movies, the cashier had already handed Evie her Diet Coke and bucket of popcorn, so she asked Bailey to grab her wallet out of her bag for her. In the depths of her friend's purse, Bailey had spotted an unopened package of superglue, a Phillips screwdriver, a headlamp, three hair clips, a pocketknife, a can of pepper spray, a stapler, a full-sized bag of peanut M&M's, and a small jar of crunchy peanut butter. See? Wasn't Evie Delgado someone you'd want to be stuck with when the zombies arrived?

Speaking of her friend—where *was* Evie?

Part of her was praying her friend would come running out with a war cry and blast Jane in the face with that can of pepper spray she hopefully still had in her purse. The other part of her was praying Jane would drive away before Evie was put into danger too.

One of her prayers was answered as Jane lifted her foot off the brake and pulled the car out onto the dirt road that led to the highway.

Oh, so this is how to get into the driveway.

Bailey's hair flew around her face as the car picked up speed. "So, now that you're holding a gun on me, I'm feeling like maybe you *did* have something to do with Rex's murder."

Jane swallowed, and her breath hitched in her chest. "I didn't *mean* to kill him."

Oh.

She'd been tossing that comment out like a shot in the dark. She hadn't expected Jane to just *confess.* And the side of her brain that watched one million crime shows started freaking out because it knew that once the killer confessed to someone, they had to get rid of that person. Like make sure they never revealed what the killer had just told them. Like shoot them with a small revolver and dump their body out of their electric-blue convertible.

Bailey couldn't breathe. She didn't want to die. She had too much to live for. She wanted to see Daisy graduate from high school, dance at her daughter's wedding, and hold her first grandchild. She wanted to make things right with Sawyer. And kiss him again, and this time not in the town square where half of Humble Hills could be watching.

Do not hyperventilate.

She forced herself to draw long, even breaths. *Breathe in. Slowly breathe out.* She needed a plan. And she needed to keep Jane talking. As long as she was talking, she wasn't pulling the trigger.

Chapter
Thirty-Six

Jane pulled the convertible out onto the highway. Bailey noticed she didn't use her turn signal. But now probably wasn't the best time to call her on that.

A pair of headlights bobbed in her sideview mirror, and Bailey prayed it was Evie following them. But even if it was, she still had to help herself. She tried to think rationally, to imagine the scenario from a different perspective. What would she have the heroine in her latest book do in this instance? Not let the killer's dog slobber all over her chin while she waited patiently to be shot and tossed out of the car.

Her phone. She still had her phone. Bailey shifted in her seat, trying to casually slide her cell from her pocket without letting Jane see it or guess her intention.

She bounced her legs, jostling the dog so it couldn't settle as it scrambled over the console toward Jane, then came back into Bailey's lap as Jane pushed it away. She used the distraction of the dog to pull her phone the rest of the way out of her pocket and wedge it between the door and the seat. Trying not to look down, she tapped the screen in the area of the call button and then pressed and held the bottom of the volume button on the side.

Sneaking a glance at the phone, she saw Sawyer's name on the screen. He was the last person she'd called, so whatever she'd tapped must have automatically redialed him. She hit the "Speaker" button, then spoke loudly to the dog in an effort to mask the sound of the phone ringing or of Sawyer answering. "You're a good girl, aren't you? Or are you a good boy?" she asked, as if Jane had not just confessed to her that she hadn't meant to kill Rex.

"Boy," Jane confirmed.

"And his name is Scoop? Like a scoop of vanilla ice cream because of his white fur?"

Jane huffed out a dry laugh. "No. Idiot. I'm a reporter. Do you think I'd name my dog after a scoop of ice cream? His name is Scoop—like getting the *scoop* on a good story."

"Aw. Yeah, that makes more sense." Another quick glance down showed the phone screen had changed, so Sawyer must have picked up. Either that, or the recording was playing again, telling her that his voice mailbox was full. She prayed it was Sawyer and that he could hear her over the windy road noise of the convertible.

"Listen, Jane," she said, as if they were old friends instead of captor and hostage, "you really don't need that gun that you're holding on me. I'm in the front seat of the car with you. I'm not going anywhere." Okay, that might've been a little too obvious, but Jane didn't seem to have noticed. "Where are you taking me anyway?"

"I don't know yet." She slammed her fist onto the top of the steering wheel, making the dog jump. Scoop whined and tried to crawl toward Jane, but Bailey held him in her lap. She needed him to camouflage the sound of the phone and any lights that the screen might shine. "I wasn't planning this," Jane said. "You just couldn't leave well enough alone."

"I know. I'm sorry. I've been told I have a bad habit of that." She tried to think of the best way to get Jane to go back to talking about the murder. "Mr. Jenkins was the one who told me you and Eugene used to be besties."

Jane huffed. "*Used to be* is right. Or at least *I* thought he was my best friend. We used to do everything together. And we made plans to both go to college at Colorado State and then move to New York together, where we'd both get jobs as investigative reporters."

"Must have been hard when he left. Harv told me what happened."

"You have no idea. Gene and his mom left without a word, and I never heard from him again. He knew how to get a hold of me. He could have called or texted or written me a letter or an email. Anything. But instead, he just left me behind. Acted like I'd never even mattered to him."

"I'm sure that wasn't true."

"Oh, it was true. He told me so himself."

"When you went to see him in California?"

Jane gave her a sideways glance. "How do you know I went to California?"

"Sibia recognized you. Not at first. But then she figured it out. She said you looked . . ." She was about to say "really different" but decided against insulting the woman who was currently plotting how to get rid of her. "That you looked really pretty when you came to the studio."

Jane huffed out a laugh. "Fat lot of good it did me. I spent almost five hundred bucks buying a new outfit and going to the salon and having them do my hair and makeup. I recognized Gene . . . or Rex . . . or whatever the heck he was calling himself . . . on television. He looked different, really different, but when he laughed, I *knew* it was him. It's no wonder no one in town recognized him. I don't think anyone else ever even heard him laugh. Except for me. I made him laugh all the time."

Bailey's emotions warred with feeling sorry for the teenaged Eugene, who had spent his days getting bullied, and angry with the adult Rex who had become popular then turned into a bully himself.

"Were you guys a couple?"

Jane shook her head.

"Did you want to be? Was that why you got all gussied up?"

Jane shrugged. "I don't know. Maybe. I'm sure they told you that Gene had been overweight and had braces, but there was still something kind of charming about him. And maybe I did have a crush on him. And then when I saw him on television, and he looked so different, so good-looking, I don't know . . . I guess I started thinking about him more and sometimes imagined that if we saw each other now, maybe . . ." Her voice drifted off. "But the main reason I went out there was to try to get a job."

"A job?"

"Yes. I never planned to get stuck in this town writing stupid articles for *The Herald*. And no matter what my *other* feelings were for Gene, we'd always been good friends. Which is why I thought he would be willing to use his connections to help me get a job. He knew everyone in LA. He was famous. And I wasn't asking for a handout—just a foot in the door. And I was willing to do whatever. I just wanted out of Humble Hills and to have a chance to do some real reporting."

"I take it Rex wasn't that helpful."

"No. Rex was not helpful *at all*. He barely even acted like he recognized me. Although I know he did. I saw it on his face when he walked out of his office. For just a second, it seemed like he was happy to see me, before a flash of fear sparked in his eyes. Like maybe I was going to reveal his past. But I wasn't there to cause trouble. I just wanted a job. And to see him."

"What happened?"

"Rex turned into a total douche is what happened. He was walking around his office, acting like a total big shot. He offered me a drink and sat down next to me on this little sofa he had by the window. Then he put his arm around me and tried to kiss me. He said sure he could find me a job, but what was I willing to do for him?"

"What a pig," Bailey said, and meant it. True, Jane was holding her hostage, but she still felt bad for her.

"That's not the word I would use. He'd turned into a totally different person from the sweet Eugene I used to know. At first, I thought he was kidding, but then he grabbed my breast with one hand while he shoved his other hand up my skirt. It happened so fast. I was trying to push him off me, but he was so strong. He held his hand over my mouth, and then he was on top of me. I'd done a story on self-defense for women, never imagining that I'd ever have to use those techniques myself, but I managed to get my forearm between us and shoved it against his throat, then kneed him in the crotch. I scrambled out from under him as he fell back."

"Good for you."

"Gene didn't think so. He was so mad. Started yelling about how dare I show up there and come on to him, then push him away. Which, for the record, I did *not* come on to him, I swear."

"I believe you."

"Then he said that I just showed up to humiliate him and that he'd never cared about me and just wanted to leave the past in the past. He told me to leave him the hell alone and never to try to contact him again."

"Oh, Jane. I'm sorry. It sounds like he was just lashing out. What did you do?"

"What could I do? I left. I went back to the hotel, packed up my stuff, and came scurrying back to Humble Hills with my tail between my legs. I'll admit that I might have harbored a few fantasies of him seeing me and sweeping me into his arms and telling me we'd always belonged together. But I didn't want it to happen that way—with him trying to take advantage of me on the sofa in his office. I never wanted anything like *that*."

"I'm sorry," Bailey said again, not knowing what else to say and not wanting to stop her flow of conversation. "What happened then?"

"Nothing. I figured I'd never see him again. I couldn't believe it when I heard he was coming to Humble Hills to host the Bake-Off."

"I remember the paper did a story on how exciting it was to have him as the celebrity host."

"Yeah, they did. But I didn't do the story. I couldn't. Honestly, I didn't even want to see him. But I couldn't help myself. I guess in the months since I'd seen him, I'd convinced myself that maybe I was remembering it wrong. That maybe he hadn't meant to be so rough, or that maybe I'd given him mixed signals. I don't know. I guess I just wanted to see him again. So, I went to his motor home after the first day of the Bake-Off, to try to talk to him. That's when I saw you and everyone sitting out in front of it."

"You said you were there to get a quote for the paper."

"I lied. But then I saw what happened with Evie, how he'd obviously made the same kind of advances on her, and I knew that my memory was correct. I didn't know what to do. A few nights later, he caught me after the taping and told me that he needed to talk to me and to meet him backstage at eleven that night. I tried to get him to just meet the next day, but he said that was the only time he could get free and that he really needed to see me.

"I'd been covering the Bear Run and was still in costume when I went to meet him. But once I got inside the building, I felt stupid, so I took it off and left it on the side of the stage. Plus, it was hot. I'd had on a hoodie over a tank top and running shorts, and I took that off too. I think when Rex saw my clothes lying on the stage, he must have gotten the wrong idea, because when he came backstage, he was smiling and gave me a hug and acted like that day in California never happened. He said he was so glad to see me, and then he took my hand and led me into the supply closet."

Bailey was afraid to move, afraid to say anything for fear that Jane would stop her story. Her heart was already pounding. Yes, Jane had just tried to stuff her into a small trunk at gunpoint, but dang it, everyone wants to be loved. And Bailey could already tell where this story was heading.

"He was being super sweet and charming." Jane seemed almost lost in her own thoughts. "Just like he used to be. And I really started to believe that he cared about me. He was drinking this chocolate protein shake and acting all casual. He told me he'd seen Carl and Gordy and that he was going to make them pay for what they'd done to him. What they'd done to *us*. He kissed me again, but this time it was gentle and tender—just like I'd imagined. And I just sank into him, like a lovesick little puppy." She whacked the steering wheel again with the butt of the gun, startling Bailey and the dog again. "I'm so stupid."

"You're not stupid" was all Bailey could think to say. She didn't know if she was stupid or not, but it sounded like she was about to admit to being a murderer, and that seemed worse.

"Oh, I am," Jane assured her. "I let myself get caught in the middle of the night, in a closet, in the back of a building where no one would hear me if I screamed, and no one was around to help. And Rex knew it too. The man who started out kissing me felt like Gene, but the man who wouldn't stop when I told him no was definitely Rex.

"He had me pinned against the shelves, and he started pulling at my clothes, and I was telling him no, but he wasn't listening. And I was feeling along the shelves behind me, trying to find something to hit him with—I just wanted to get him off me—and my fingers touched the metal of the mixer. I don't know that I really even thought about how heavy it was, I certainly didn't think it would kill him. I guess I wasn't thinking at all, I just yanked on the base, and it fell forward. I ducked to the side, and it hit Eugene on the head and then he wasn't grabbing at me anymore. He was just lying on the ground, and there was all this blood . . ." Her voice trailed off as if she were lost in the memory.

Bailey swallowed. This was it. Jane had just confessed to the murder of Rex Rafferty aka Eugene Dix.

Bailey had been so caught up in the story that she'd almost forgotten about the phone wedged in between the seat and the door.

Jane slowed the car, peering into the darkness ahead.

Bailey glanced in the side mirror. The headlights were still there—she prayed it was Evie behind them. If she trusted anyone to get her out of a jam—even a "pistol-waving murderer who'd taken her hostage" jam—it was Evie Delgado. Bailey knew her friend would figure something out. She just prayed it wouldn't be too late.

"This will have to do," Jane said, more to herself than to Bailey, as she turned onto a dirt road.

"Wait. What will have to do? Why are you turning onto the road that leads to the reservoir?"

"Come on, Bailey. You're not stupid. You know how this goes. I just told you I was responsible for killing Rex. You know I can't just let you go."

"Sure you can." Bailey's heart pounded so hard against her chest, it felt like it was trying to break out. "I won't tell anyone. I promise. And it sounds like Rex deserved it anyway. From what I heard, you weren't the only woman he didn't listen to when she told him no. And it sounds like it was just an accident. You said it yourself, you didn't mean to kill him."

"No, and it turned out I wasn't the one who actually *did* kill him. But I think I *did* mean to kill Gordy. And now that I'm responsible for killing two people, how much harder can it be to kill one more?"

Chapter
Thirty-Seven

B ailey was in real trouble here. Jane really *was* going to kill
her.

As Jane turned the car deeper into the trees leading toward
the reservoir, Bailey's heart sank as she saw the headlights of the
car following them speed past on the highway.

If that *had* been Evie, she must not have seen them turn.

Bailey was all alone now. With a woman who had just admitted to being responsible for killing *two* men.

She'd had one chance with the phone, but she had no idea if
she'd gotten through to Sawyer or if she'd gotten his voicemail
again. And if she *had* gotten through, could he even hear her—or
Jane—with the wind and road noise of the convertible?

Jane turned again. Bailey recognized the road that led to a
picnic area by the lake. It was in a small clearing with a lot of trees
and right by the water.

Her palms were sweating, but she had to keep her wits about
her. "Seriously, Jane, you can just drop me off at this picnic area.
It will take me hours to walk out of here. And you'll be long gone
by then. There's no reason to kill me. Please, Jane, I have a
daughter. And I'm all she has."

Daisy had the love and support of her grandmother and the great-aunts and Evie too, but Bailey was her only mother. And she knew what it was like to grow up without a mother and a father. Her father had chosen to walk away from them when she was five years old, and then her mother had made the same choice five years later. She'd never heard another word from either of them—no birthday cards, no calls at Christmas, nothing. She could never imagine doing that to Daisy.

But this was different. *She* wouldn't be making a choice to leave her daughter behind. The choice was being made for her.

Bailey pulled back her shoulders. She wasn't dead yet. And by golly, she was going to fight to live with every last breath in her body. Whatever it took to save herself.

She had to let Sawyer know where she was.

"Well, I guess if I have to die somewhere," she said, raising her voice and praying Sawyer was listening on the other end of the phone, "at least this place has good memories. When we were in high school, Sawyer—he was my boyfriend—and I used to bring sack lunches out here in the summer and sit at these very picnic tables. They have a great view of the south dock, and we liked to watch the tourists try to figure out how to get their giant boats into a mountain lake."

Thinking about Sawyer had emotion clogging her throat. They had so many memories. And there were so many things she still wanted to say to him. She fought back tears as she realized this might be her last chance.

"Did you know that Sheriff Dunn and I dated in high school? He was my first kiss, my first love, my first *everything*. It's really been amazing having him back in my life. I wish I had one more chance to talk to him—just to tell him that I still love him and how important he is to me *and* to my daughter."

Please be listening, Sawyer.

"Yeah, well I'll be happy to put everything and everyone in this town in my rearview mirror," Jane practically spat. "And I'm swearing off men for the time being. They only cause trouble."

"Is that what happened with Gordy? Did he cause trouble?"

Might as well find out what happened. She was still trying to figure out how to make it out of her current predicament alive, but if she didn't, at least Sawyer would hear the other woman's confession.

Jane chuckled, but her laugh didn't hold much humor. "*Trouble* was Gordy Russell's middle name. I'm pretty sure he might've been the devil himself. I swear when he fell in that hot tub, I half expected the water to start boiling."

"How did he fall in?" Bailey asked, although she already knew there was a large pipe wrench involved.

"Oh, he fell forward into the water after I whacked him on the back of the head with a giant wrench." Jane lifted her chin. "I might not be as tall as you, but I work out. And I'm strong. Especially when I'm mad."

Bailey winced. She believed her. That KitchenAid mixer had to have weighed a good twenty pounds, and that pipe wrench would have been at least the same, if not more. "Why did you hit him? Did it have something to do with him trying to buy your car?"

"He wasn't trying to *buy* my car. He was trying to *steal* it. He was trying to blackmail me for fifty thousand dollars. And he took my car as collateral. Said if I didn't pay him the money by this weekend, he was keeping the car."

"Funny. That's the same amount Rex was trying to blackmail Carl for. I wonder if he was shaking down Gordy too, and then

Gordy was trying to get the cash from you." She snuck a sideways glance at Jane. "Do you *have* that kind of money?"

"Heck no, I don't have that kind of money. I work for a local newspaper that barely survives on the advertising dollars of, like, five businesses."

"So basically everyone was trying to blackmail each other for the same nonexistent cash?"

"Yeah, and Rex started it. And he was the famous one, so he probably had a zillion more dollars than all of us combined."

"What were you going to do?"

Jane shrugged. "I don't know. I made myself sick worrying about it. I think I went through a dozen rolls of antacids and half a bottle of Pepto."

Bailey tilted her head. "I guess I don't get what Gordy thought he had on you. What was he blackmailing you *for*?"

"Because he knew what I'd done to Rex."

"What? How?"

"He was out at the fairgrounds—working on one of his hot tubs. Some kids had put some dish soap in it, and apparently that's bad for hot tubs. It was late, and he didn't think anyone else was around. He was trying to steal a beer and some chips from the concession stand, and I guess he saw me coming out of Edwards Hall. I'd put the bear suit back on, but he recognized my face. He actually waved and said, 'Hi, Jane' when he walked by me. Like we were ordinary neighbors instead of him being the guy who'd tormented me all through junior and senior high school.

"Then I guess he got curious about why I'd been in there. I didn't know this until yesterday, but he went into the building after me. He said he'd found Rex in the closet. He told me he was still alive."

Bailey gasped.

"Yeah. I was surprised too. I'd spent the last several days thinking I'd murdered a man. I never felt for a pulse or anything, but there was so much blood, and he was lying so still. I was sure he was dead. I was terrified. I knew enough to wipe my fingerprints off the mixer, but I just wanted to get out of there, so I grabbed my stuff and ran."

Bailey wrinkled her brow. "But what about all the contestants' stuff that was around the body?" All the stuff that had cemented Evie as a person of interest.

"That was all Gordy's idea. He told me that Rex wasn't dead when he got there, but he'd taken care of that problem. He said Rex must have done something to me to make me hit him so hard with the mixer, but now neither one of us ever needed to worry about Rex Rafferty again. And he told me he'd seen the Bake-Off contestants' tote bags sitting there, so he stole something from each of them and placed them around the body to lay the blame on *them* instead of us. Which kind of surprised me, because I thought that was kind of brilliant, and I didn't think Gordy had ever had a smart idea in his life."

Bailey was surprised too. Gordy Russell hadn't ever struck her as any kind of mastermind. "But if Gordy was the one who actually killed Rex . . ." Bailey was still having a hard time wrapping her head around this. Apparently, however, that's why Jane kept saying she'd been *responsible* for Rex's death, not that she'd actually killed him. "Then it seems like he lost his leverage that he was using to blackmail you."

"That's what I thought too. I asked him how he was going to try to keep blackmailing me if I knew he was the one who had actually killed Rex. But he had all that figured out and said he knew how to pin all the blame on me. He was standing by the hot tub, looking into the bubbles, his face all smug and smirky. There was a box of tools next to him, and I saw that big old wrench sticking out, and I thought . . . no actually, I didn't think at all . . . I was just so tired of men running rough-shod over me. And treating me like I was nothing—like I didn't even matter. So, I just picked up that wrench and whacked him in the head with it as hard as I could.

"He fell forward into the hot tub. I wasn't taking any chances that time, so I held his head under until the bubbles stopped coming out of his nose. Then I rubbed my fingerprints off the wrench, tossed it in the tub with him, and closed the cover. And then I climbed back into *my* car, drove home, guzzled a bottle of wine, and passed out on my bed. I hid out at my house today, waiting to hear that he'd been discovered, but it wasn't until after supper that I decided maybe I'd better leave town."

Jane pulled up to the picnic area and cut the engine. "Here we are. Time to get out."

The night air was cool, and goose bumps rippled across Bailey's arms. There was no one else around, no boats on the lake, no orange flickers of light from a camper's fire. The only sounds were crickets chirping and the soft lap of water against the rocky shore.

"Yep, here we are," Bailey said, trying to keep the tremble out of her voice. "Here at the picnic area at the reservoir, where Sawyer and I used to bring sack lunches."

Jane exited the car but told the dog to *stay*. She started around the front of the hood, still holding the gun on Bailey. "Get out."

Oh no. If she opened Bailey's door, she'd see the phone wedged between it and the seat.

"Okay, I'm coming." She coughed as she opened her door, hoping to mask the sound of the phone falling to the ground. She put her foot out and kicked it under the car as she stood. Then it would still be there for her to call for help if Jane happened to leave her alive.

People survived gunshots all the time.

At least on television they did. Although Jane seemed to have learned her lesson with leaving people alive after Rex.

"Walk toward the water," Jane directed.

Bailey stumbled as she took a step forward. Her hands weren't tied. Jane was relying solely on the threat of the gun to get her to comply. She had a few inches on Jane, even if the other woman *had* bragged about how strong she was. Jane wasn't a single mother fighting for her life. Bailey was sure she could take her.

"What's your plan here, Jane?" *Forewarned is forearmed.* If Bailey knew what she was planning, she might be able to figure out a chance to escape.

"The plan is to shoot you while you're already in the water, so I don't have to try to carry you. Then I'll just load up your body with some rocks and watch you sink. I'll be in Canada before they ever even find your body."

"Solid plan," she had to admit. And now at least Sawyer would know to look for her murderer in Canada. *If* he could still hear them talking.

Except Bailey did not want to get shot or have her body loaded down with rocks to sink to the bottom of the reservoir.

She slowed her steps so Jane would be closer to her.

She had one chance.

She pretended to stumble again, then whirled around, planning to slam her body into Jane's and try to take the other woman down in a tackle.

But when she whirled around, her feet slipped on the rocky beach, and she lost her balance. Lurching forward, she still tackled Jane, but it was more like she landed on her as she fell as opposed to any kind of actual tackling maneuver.

Her chin smacked into the top of Jane's forehead, banging her teeth together in a jaw-cracking collision. She blinked at the stars swirling in the air around her.

But she didn't have time to see stars or to lose consciousness. This was her one chance to fight. And she tore into Jane with all she had, letting out a primal yell as she punched and kicked, trying to knock the gun from the other woman's hand.

But Jane was right, she *was* strong, and she was like a tiger backed into a corner. She bucked her body, trying to get out from under Bailey, screaming and swearing as she swung the gun wildly.

Then a shot rang out, and Bailey rolled away as pain seared through her.

Chapter
Thirty-Eight

"You shot me," Bailey yelled.

"I told you I was going to," Jane yelled back.

Bailey stared down the barrel of the gun, the weapon even closer now that she was on her back next to Jane.

She pressed her hand to the wound, then pulled it back to see it covered in blood. She fought the urge to throw up at the bright red sight of it—*so much blood*—then fought for breath as panic seeped into the edges of her control.

But she couldn't lose it now. She had to stay focused. Had to stay alive.

She pressed her hand back against the wound, applying pressure to staunch the flow of blood.

"Dammit," Jane shouted, scrubbing her hand through her hair. "You were supposed to be *in* the water when I shot you."

"Sorry!" Bailey shouted back. "I didn't want you to shoot me at all." She peered down at her arm, not knowing if the bullet had grazed it, gone all the way through, or was still lodged somewhere in her shoulder.

It could be worse, she told herself. A few inches in another direction and that bullet would have been in her heart.

Focus. Stay alive.

"Please, Jane. It's not too late. Just drive away. I swear I won't tell anyone about this. About *any* of this."

"It *is* too late, Bailey," Jane told her. The tears running down her face contrasted with the steely reserve in her voice. "Now get in the water."

Bailey pushed to her feet, her mind fighting against the pain in her shoulder as she tried to come up with a new plan. Another way to save herself.

Maybe she could get in the water then dive under the surface and swim away. She staggered across the rocky beach, then stepped into the reservoir. The icy water of the mountain lake seeped through the fabric of her sneakers. She shivered as she took another step and the freezing water splashed against her legs.

She turned back around to plead with Jane one more time.

The woman had taken a few steps back, but still held the gun straight out. The pistol wobbled in her shaky hands, but it was aimed right at Bailey's chest.

"Please Jane," Bailey said, not even bothering to fight the tears streaming down her cheeks. "Please don't do this."

The water was freezing, but trying to swim was the only option Bailey saw, and she prepared herself to dive into the icy water.

Then a voice called out from the trees to their right.

"Hey, what's going on over there?" a man's voice asked.

A voice that Bailey recognized.

Griff?

Jane turned toward the woods on the right. Then another man came barreling out of the trees on the left.

Bailey couldn't believe her eyes. She thought she must be imagining the sight of Sawyer sprinting out of the darkness. Then he slammed into Jane, and the gun went off again as they hit the ground.

Bailey ducked. Not sure how she thought she could duck from a bullet—it must have been instinct.

Like another flash, Griffin came tearing out of the woods too, racing straight toward the sheriff and Jane.

"Sawyer!" Bailey screamed as Jane tried to turn the gun toward him. "Watch out!"

But he had already grabbed Jane's wrist and was knocking her hand against the rocks to get her to release the gun. Then Griffin was there, wrestling it away from her hand as Sawyer flipped Jane to her stomach and yanked her hands behind her back. She might have been working out, but she was no match for the lawman as he cuffed her hands together.

The sound of Jane's dog barking came from the direction of the car, but it didn't come running. But Sawyer did. He ran toward her, splashing into the water as she was trying to make her way out of the lake.

He swept her into his arms and held her against him, pressing his lips hard against the top of her head. "I got you, Bailey. It's okay. You're safe now." He leaned back to look at her, then his eyes widened as he saw the blood covering her shirt. "You're bleeding. Did that bullet hit you?"

She shook her head as she leaned into him, not wanting to take her hand off the wound. "Not that one. She shot me before you got here." She peered up at him, still not believing he was real. And that he'd saved her. "How are you here?"

"I got your call," he said, letting go of her to examine the wound. He had a flannel shirt on over his uniform one, and he took it off and held it firmly against her shoulder. He dipped his chin and spoke into the mic clipped to his own shoulder. "Suspect secured. Backup requested." He gave their location, then slid his arm behind Bailey's legs and lifted her out of the water. He cradled her to his chest as he carried her up the shore.

"You got my call?" she asked as sirens sounded in the distance. "You heard me talking through the phone? I can't believe that worked."

"I couldn't always hear everything," he said. "But I heard enough. Evie had already called me. She said she saw Jane force you into her car at gunpoint, and she was following you."

"I prayed that was her," Bailey said.

"I was already in my truck and headed her way when you called. I hung up with her and called her back from my work phone. She'd already called Griff, and he was on his way too. I kept your call on mute so Jane wouldn't hear me and kept Evie on speaker. You gave us great directions. I knew just where to find you."

"I have her secured," Griffin called out as he hauled Jane to her feet. "You can come out now."

With a muffled cry, Evie came running from the direction of Jane's car and threw her arms around Bailey. "Oh my gosh, I was so scared. Are you okay? Why are you bleeding?" She looked up at Sawyer as panic rose in her voice. "Why is she bleeding?"

"Jane shot me," Bailey told her. "But just in the arm."

"I've got backup on the way," Sawyer told Griffin. He nodded at Jane. "Can you keep an eye on her while I take Bailey to the hospital?"

"Of course," Griffin answered. He'd been a police officer for years before he'd gotten shot himself and retired to become a private investigator. "She's not going anywhere."

"I'm coming with you," Evie said, her hands fluttering in the air as she tried to figure out how to help Bailey.

Sawyer raised his chin toward the woods. "I'm parked just on the other side of those trees. Stay here with Evie. I'll be right back to take you to the hospital."

They stopped at Jane's car, and he set Bailey down. She leaned against the door. A yip drew her attention downward, and then Scoop was trying to climb up her legs. He was tied to the door handle, and a scattering of dog toys were on the ground next to him.

"I didn't want him to get hurt," Evie said, leaning down to pet him and keep him from scratching Bailey's legs. "I saw his leash and all those toys in the backseat."

"He's a good dog," Bailey said. "Make sure Griff takes care of him." Her voice was hoarse from yelling, and she suddenly felt so tired.

Tires sprayed gravel as Sawyer's truck flew out of the woods and then screeched to a halt next to the convertible.

Bailey gripped her arm tighter, feeling the sticky blood under her palm. Her knees threatened to buckle again.

Then Sawyer was there, picking her up again and carrying her to his truck. "I got you, darlin'," he whispered against her ear.

That was the last thing she heard before everything went black.

Chapter
Thirty-Nine

O ne week later, Bailey was standing in her bedroom, swearing as she tried to pull a sling over her head.

"Let me help," Sawyer said as his head came into view at the top of the stairs. He was holding two bouquets of flowers, one of red roses and one of white roses mixed with daisies. He held them up. "Brought these for you and Daisy. The red ones are the closest thing I could find to the color of the Bailey Red rose." He set the flowers on her dresser and crossed the room to help adjust the splint around her shoulder. "How are you feeling?"

"Like I'm tired of this dang splint already." Her voice was grumpy, but her insides were twirling and twisting with excitement at seeing him, and nerves at having him in her bedroom. "I'm doing fine," she said, changing her tone at his look of concern.

The bullet, it turned out, had just grazed her upper arm. Dr. MacFarlane was still on duty when they'd arrived at the emergency room, so he'd washed it out—which hurt like a bear—then administered some fluids while he stitched her up before sending her home. She'd had no idea someone could get shot and not even spend *one* night in the hospital. The splint was to keep her arm immobile so she didn't tear the stitches, but they were scheduled to come out in a few days, so she was almost free of the blessed thing.

Sawyer, who had called, texted, and come by every day since she'd been shot, tucked the end of the tie inside the splint. "Thought you'd want to know they're transferring Jane to a women's prison facility tomorrow. She'll await her trial there."

Jane had been arrested and charged with one count of murder for Gordy, and one count of attempted murder for Bailey and another for Rex, since it was still unclear if it was she or Gordy who had actually killed him. Seeing as Jane had already attempted to flee the country once, she'd been denied bail.

"At least she'll get her wish of getting out of Humble Hills and swearing off men for a while."

He huffed out a small laugh.

"The members of The Hive have been taking turns pet-sitting for Scoop, but I think the great-aunts have fallen in love with him and are calling dibs on keeping him," Bailey said.

"That's good. He seemed like a sweet dog." He let his gaze wander around the room. "It still looks the same in here. It's almost like stepping back in time."

After Bailey's mother had abandoned her, Granny Bee had wanted to do something special for her granddaughter, so she'd had the entire attic renovated into a living space for Bailey, complete with a walk-in closet; an en suite bathroom with a soaking tub; a desk area; and a reading nook with a window seat flanked by floor-to-ceiling bookshelves.

She'd always loved the soft pink walls with the crisp white trim and wainscoting, so, when she'd moved back in as an adult, the only things she'd changed were putting a new quilt on the bed and some nicer artwork and photos of Daisy on the walls to replace the posters of Justin Timberlake and the Backstreet Boys.

"A lot has happened since you used to sneak up here when we were teenagers," she told him.

Sawyer sighed and rubbed his hand across the back of his neck. "Heck, a lot has happened just in the last week." He shook his head. "Thankfully, the news stations and reporters have all finally left town."

Rex's mom had been located, and she was flying out to collect her son's ashes. And a memorial service for Gordy had been planned for the following week. Bailey still wasn't sure if she was going to go or not.

"The production crew stopped by the ranch to say goodbye on their way back to the airport in Denver," she told him. "Toby said he really loved my book and asked me to sign his copy before they left." Bailey liked how he'd held the door open for Sibia and the sweet, caring way Rex's former personal assistant had looked up at Toby when he took her hand as they walked back to the rental car. "They promised to stay in touch."

"I'll just be happy to get our boring little sleepy town back. Speaking of which, I was out there this morning, and it looks like the Bee Festival committee and their happy band of volunteers have restored the fairgrounds to their former glory."

"I'm not sure how I feel about the Town Council's decision to leave the Bake-Off kitchens set up. I know they spent a lot of money on them, and it sounds great to use them to teach the 4-H kids how to cook, but still . . . a murder happened in there."

"Maybe they'll use that to get more kids to sign up," Sawyer said. "By the way, did they ever announce the winner of that thing? The Bake-Off?"

"No. The festival committee decided, under the circumstances, to declare a three-way tie, and told everyone to visit Charlotte, Spike, and Evie's restaurants to judge for themselves." She leaned a little closer and lowered her voice. "But Leon told me secretly that he thought Evie was going to win. Although he might've just been being nice. You know, he sent me flowers with a card that said how sorry he was that I'd been shot and that in this instance he was glad I hadn't ended up back in the morgue, visiting him again."

"That guy is too funny," Sawyer said with a smirk. Then his expression sobered. "I still can't believe you were shot. I'm sorry I didn't get to you sooner."

"It's okay." She nudged his shoulder playfully. "Now I have a cool scar and a great story to tell. And I'm totally using this in a book."

"You should. And you should have your heroine use that phone trick too."

"I still can't believe it worked. Or that you could even hear me." Bailey thought back to all the things she'd said in hopes that Sawyer was listening in.

He slid an arm around her waist and gently pulled her to him. Lifting his hand, he tucked a stray lock of hair behind her ear. He peered down at her face, locking her gaze with the sincerity in his gorgeous blue eyes. "I heard you," he said softly. "I heard everything."

"Everything?"

"Everything I needed to. And I want you to know that the time that I've spent with you and Daisy has been amazing, and important to me too." He leaned down and pressed a tender kiss to her lips. Then he pulled back and captured her gaze again. But this time his expression was more serious. "Are you ever going to tell me who Daisy's father is?"

She swallowed, not expecting *that* question. "You've never asked."

Speaking of her daughter, Daisy's voice yelled up the stairs. "Mom."

"I guess I'm asking now," Sawyer said.

She nodded. "I've been thinking more and more about how it might be time for Daisy to need her dad. For so long now, it's just been the two of us, and we've been okay. You and I both know what it's like to have an awful dad, one who didn't give a crap about us." Bailey's dad had walked out on her when she was young. Sawyer's mom had done the same, and his father had taken the desertion of his wife out on his son, with his belt and his fists. "But despite all that, I still want my daughter to have a dad. I think a father is an important part of a girl's life."

"I do too." His voice was barely a whisper.

She looked up at him, the words she wanted to say caught in her throat. "Do you think you'd be a good dad?" she whispered back.

"I hope so. I think I'd try my best. I certainly know what *not* to do."

"Mo-om!" Daisy yelled up the stairs again.

"Just a second," Bailey called back. She needed to stay in this moment. It mattered too much. She reached up to touch Sawyer's cheek. His face was older, but it still held so many of the same features of the face of the boy she'd given her heart to all those years ago. "We've only been back here a few months, but I think Daisy has already fallen in love with you."

"How about you?" His voice was so soft, she had to lean closer to hear him. "Have you fallen in love with me?"

She smiled. "Oh Sawyer. I never *stopped* loving you."

He leaned in to kiss her again, but then the sound of Daisy clomping up the stairs drew them apart.

Her daughter waved her pink cast-clad arm. "Mom. I've been calling you. There's a man at the door downstairs. He says he wants to see you."

A man? She prayed it wasn't another reporter. She'd been dodging them all week.

"Who is it?"

Daisy shrugged. "I don't know. I've never seen him before. But he says he's your dad."

The end . . .

. . . and just the *bee*-ginning . . .

Recipes

Bee Festival Bake-Off Recipes
Honey-Ricotta-Stuffed French Toast

From the kitchen of Evie Delgado Espinoza

Ingredients

¼ c. honey
⅔ cup ricotta cheese
zest from a medium lemon
2 eggs
¾ c. milk
1 tsp. vanilla
1 loaf of French bread
3 T. butter

For topping

fresh berries
honey for drizzling
powdered sugar

Instructions

In a small bowl, stir together the honey, ricotta cheese, and lemon zest. Then, in a wide shallow dish, stir together the eggs, milk, and vanilla.

From the center of the French bread, use a serrated knife to cut four large slices (about an inch and a half thick). Use the widest part of the loaf. With a serrated knife, carefully make a deep cut in each slice to form a pocket. Then carefully spoon a fourth of the ricotta cheese mixture into each pocket.

Heat griddle or large skillet to medium and melt the butter. When the pan is hot, dip each piece of stuffed toast in the egg mixture, then cook for 3–4 minutes per side until nicely browned and the egg mixture is cooked through.

Transfer to plate, then drizzle with honey and sprinkle with powdered sugar. Serve with your favorite berries—blueberries, raspberries, and strawberries all are delicious with this rich and creamy breakfast treat.

Honey-Baked Vanilla Pears

From the kitchen of Evie Delgado Espinoza

Ingredients

4 ripe, firm pears
2 T. honey
1 T. melted butter (unsalted)
¼ tsp. vanilla
½ c. apple juice

Instructions

Preheat oven to 350°.

Cut the pears in half, and scoop out the seeds. Slice a bit off the bottom of the pear so it will sit flat and not tip to the side, then place pears cut side up in a 9 x 13-inch pan.

In a small bowl, stir honey, vanilla, and melted butter, then spoon mixture over the pears.

Pour apple juice into the bottom of the pan, cover with foil, and bake for 20 minutes.

Spoon some of the juice from the bottom of the pan over the pears, then continue to bake, uncovered, for another 10 minutes (until pears are tender).

Serve warm. Can be topped with vanilla ice cream, whipped cream, or yogurt and granola. Drizzle with extra juice from pan.

Iced Honey Lattes

From the kitchen of Evie Delgado Espinoza

These iced honey lattes are so delicious and so easy to whip together.

Ingredients

¾ c. of your favorite cold brew coffee
3–4 T. honey
1 c. of ice
4 T. table cream or half and half

Instructions

Find a cup with a lid, and pour in the cold brew, the honey, and the ice. Secure the lid and shake it like crazy. Then add the cream, stir, and enjoy!

Pecan Praline Honey Butter
From the kitchen of Charlotte Shine

A delicious twist on traditional honey butter!

Ingredients

1 c. (2 sticks) unsalted butter, softened
¼ cup pecans
⅓ cup honey
1 tsp. vanilla
½ tsp. cinnamon
Small pinch of salt

Instructions

Preheat oven to 350°.

Finely chop pecans, spread in a thin layer on a cookie sheet, and bake for 5–7 minutes, or just until light golden brown. Watch carefully so they don't burn. Then allow pecans to cool completely.

Stir together softened butter, honey, vanilla, cinnamon, and salt until smooth. Then stir in pecans. Spread on warm biscuits, toast, pancakes, waffles, or biscuits. Or try a spoonful on your sweet potatoes. So delicious!

Honey Butter Smashed Potatoes
From the kitchen of Charlotte Shine

Ingredients

1 lb. baby Yukon gold potatoes
4 T. unsalted butter
4 T. honey
1 tsp. salt

Instructions

Wash potatoes, then place in a large pot and cover with cold water. Add salt to the water and bring to a boil. Reduce heat to medium-high and continue to boil until potatoes are fork tender (about 15 minutes). Rinse potatoes under cold water, then drain.

Smash potatoes gently with your palm or the back of a spoon. Don't smash potato completely. It should still hold its form, and you should be able to pick up the potato as a whole piece.

Heat a large skillet over medium heat, then add butter, honey, and salt and stir to combine. When honey butter is simmering, gently add smashed potatoes and increase heat to medium-high. Cook 5–7 minutes (until golden brown), then flip and cook another 5–7 minutes.

Sprinkle with pepper and enjoy!

Vanilla Honey Cupcakes with Honey and Cinnamon Cream Cheese Frosting

From the kitchen of Spike Larsen

Ingredients

For the cupcakes

1½ c. all-purpose flour
¾ c. sugar
1 tsp. baking powder
½ tsp. salt
½ c. butter, softened
4 oz. cream cheese, softened
2 eggs
¼ c. buttermilk
1 tsp. vanilla
1 tsp. cinnamon

Ingredients

For the frosting

6 oz. cream cheese, softened
1 stick of salted butter, softened
1 T. honey
1 tsp. vanilla
4 c. powdered sugar
1 T. milk

For cupcakes

Preheat oven to 350°. Spray or line muffin tin.

In a large bowl, stir together flour, sugar, baking powder, and salt.

Using a mixer, cream butter and sugar until light and fluffy. Then mix in cream cheese, vanilla, buttermilk, and eggs on low until combined. Pour in the honey and mix on medium for 1 minute. Then add this mixture into the dry ingredients and carefully stir until combined.

Pour batter into muffin cups (about ⅔ full) then bake for 17–20 minutes (until toothpick comes out clean).

Cool completely before frosting.

For frosting

Using a mixer, cream butter and cream cheese then beat until light and fluffy. Add in vanilla and honey, and mix. Then slowly add in powdered sugar, 1 cup at a time, adding a bit of milk between each cup. Mix for about 1 minute, until smooth and creamy, then add cinnamon and mix until combined.

Frost cupcakes and enjoy!

Acknowledgments

As always, my love and thanks go out to my family—Todd, Nick, Tyler, and Paige! Todd, thanks for your love and support and for sharing your vast knowledge of bees with me. It's no mystery why I love and adore you. I love you. *Always.*

A huge thank-you goes out to my mom, Lee Cumba, for all your help with the plotting of this book. You are always there for me, and we have such fun talking clues and red herrings and plotting fun ways for my characters to get in, and out, of trouble. Thank you for instilling in me a love of mysteries and always believing in my ability to write them.

Big thanks to my sister, Dr. Rebecca Hodges, for spending over an hour helping me to understand and chart out blood types and how they relate to paternity, just so I could correctly write approximately two paragraphs of this book.

I can't thank my editor, Faith Ross Black, enough for believing in me and this book, for loving Bailey, Sawyer, Granny Bee, and the Hive, and for making this story so much better with your amazing editing skills. Big thanks to the whole team at Crooked Lane Books for all your efforts and hard work in making this book happen and for giving me the cutest cover ever.

Acknowledgments

This writing gig is tough, and I wouldn't be able to do it without the support and encouragement of the friends who have been with me from the start. Huge thanks to Melissa Marts, Debbie Clapshaw, Pam Muth, Jennifer Martinez, Roseann Engelage, Linda Kay, and Mona Egger—your lifelong friendships mean everything to me. And thank you to my writer girls, Anne Eliot, Michelle Major, Lana Williams, Ginger Scott, and Sharon Wray—love walking this writer journey with you. Thanks for always listening, encouraging, and for the hours and hours of writing sprints and laughter. XO

Big thanks to my neighbor, Jason Newton, for your advice and guidance with homicide investigations, police procedure, and medical examiner information.

Thank-you to the three random strangers, Charlotte, Sibia, and Toby, that I met on a snorkeling trip in Sayulita, Mexico, who talked plot ideas with me—so fun to meet you, and I told you I would put your names in this book.

I want to acknowledge Bear Creek Nature Center for their wonderful bee exhibit, and thank my favorite beekeeper, my husband, Todd. Thanks for sharing your love of bees and teaching me and so many others about all the fascinating things they do. And in case you're wondering, the Bear Run *is* a real event, and every year brings so much joy and laughter to its participants.

A huge thank-you to my agent, Nicole Resciniti, at The Seymour Agency, for your advice and your guidance. You are the best, and I'm so thankful you are part of my life.

Big thanks go out to my readers. Writing is a labor of love and craziness, but know that I write these stories for you, and I can't thank you enough for reading and loving them. Sending love, laughter, and big Colorado hugs to you all!